PEN

FISH SF

James Delingpole was born in Worcester in 1965. He is a feature
writer and critic for publications including the *Daily Telegraph*,
the *Sunday Telegraph*, *Tatler* and the *Spectator*. He lives in
London.

JAMES DELINGPOLE

FISH SHOW

PENGUIN BOOKS

PENGUIN BOOKS

Published by the Penguin Group
Penguin Books Ltd, 27 Wrights Lane, London w8 5tz, England
Penguin Books USA Inc., 375 Hudson Street, New York, New York 10014, USA
Penguin Books Australia Ltd, Ringwood, Victoria, Australia
Penguin Books Canada Ltd, 10 Alcorn Avenue, Toronto, Ontario, Canada m4v 3b2
Penguin Books (NZ) Ltd, 182–190 Wairau Road, Auckland 10, New Zealand

Penguin Books Ltd, Registered Offices: Harmondsworth, Middlesex, England

First published 1997
1 3 5 7 9 10 8 6 4 2

Typeset in 10/12pt Monotype Bembo
Rowland Phototypesetting Ltd,
Bury St Edmunds, Suffolk
Printed in England by Clays Ltd, St Ives plc

CHAPTER ONE

Stronzo

'Waiter! There's no fly in my soup.'

The waiter, a sullen blond youth in black jeans and fine white cotton shirt monogrammed with the famous 'S' logo, regarded me contemptuously.

'Is sir trying to be funny?' he sneered. 'Because *sir* is only the eighth person to have tried that line this evening.'

Could any of us have been blamed for our quip? The celebrated 'mouche chef' is, after all, one of the main attractions at London's most distinctive new restaurant, an establishment whose very name, mentioned in the right circles, is enough to cause jaws to drop and eyes to widen in admiration, a place so exclusive that it never publishes its address. It has no need. Anyone who is anyone knows where to find Stronzo.

Quite why they should want to is another matter. From the aforementioned 'mouche chef' (a swarthy, dishevelled individual who loiters by the kitchen hatch, decorating each soup serving – when he can be bothered – with its curious garnish) to its icily pulch-ritudinous waiters, from its talentless, egotistical chef to its spectacularly offensive proprietor Guido Stronzo, this is truly the last word in *basse cuisine*.

The misery begins the moment you try booking a table. Sometimes, you will be informed there isn't one free until next year. Sometimes, you will be laughed at and told to try McDonald's. But occasionally, if you are really fortu-nate, you will be grudgingly offered an early sitting. Your credit card details will be taken and you will be warned that if you arrive even a fraction of a second late, you won't get a table but they'll bill you all the same.

Arriving at the restaurant's discreet basement entrance, I discovered that my phone calls had been a waste of time. Outside, I found a long queue of would-be diners, all of whom had been promised a table for the 6.30 slot. It was obvious that we weren't all going to get in. Our fate depended on the whims of the bored flunkey guarding a silk-rope barrier just inside the door. He seemed to derive especial pleasure from turning away anyone who used the phrase 'Don't you know who I am?'

Over expensive drinks at the bar (my Bloody Mary, devoid of celery salt, dry sherry, Tabasco or Worcestershire sauce, cost £7), I asked my neighbour how it was that I could have been allowed in. After all, I said, many of those rejected by the doorman were infinitely more famous, beautiful or exotically clad than me. My neighbour eyed up my tweed suit and explained, 'They love a prat in this place. Gives 'em someone to pick on.'

Roughly an hour later, I was jostled from the bar towards the darkest corner of the restaurant. My table, a tiny wobbling aluminium affair, had not been cleared. My chair, made of tubular steel, was uncomfortable by design, not by accident.

But my luck was definitely in because, barely an hour after I had been seated, my menu was tossed on to the table. And, after no more than another hour a waiter actually deigned to take my order. In the interim, I kept myself amused by counting celebrities (three rock stars, and the casts of two television soap operas), and by watching the antics of Stronzo, as he roundly abused his staff whenever they behaved too politely to the customers.

I opted for the two most interesting items on the otherwise rather dull chop-house menu: 'Calamari Stewed in Their Own Ink: 1990' and the 'Breast of Guinea Fowl: 1980'. ('Aha,' I observed to the waiter. 'Chef is following the modish practice of dating his dishes.' 'Those are the prices, idiot,' he said.)

The waiter snapped that in any case both dishes were 'off' (a patent lie, as I discovered later, when I heard my neighbours successfully order them). 'And the goujons of sole? the calf's liver? the duck?' 'Off, off, off,' snarled the waiter. 'If sir is having trouble making up his mind, perhaps I should come back later . . .' I hastily ordered a clam chowder, a steak (au point) and an uninspiring Bordelais *cru bourgeois* (at £30 a throw).

My soup was watery and tasteless, but perhaps by now I should have known better than to request some seasoning. 'Salt?' the waiter spluttered. 'You'll be asking for sodding ketchup next!' He flounced off, only to return, minutes later, accompanied by the diminutive Signor Stronzo. 'I hear sir is under the impression that chef's soup lacks seasoning,' he hissed. 'Perhaps this will help!' He took a plastic salt cellar from his pocket, removed the lid and emptied its contents in my soup.

The main course consisted of a virtually inedible slab of leathery, overcooked meat, served with a pile of limp, greasy chips. (Too late, I realized that the only way to get your steak rare in Stronzo is to ask for it 'well done'.) Sensing my dissatisfaction, the waiter asked whether I'd enjoyed it. I replied, through gritted teeth, that it had been stupendous – and could he send my compliments to the chef?

Another grave error! My pudding (a thick sliver of alleged Tarte Tatin) was borne proudly to my table by a tall, long-haired fellow dressed in greasy chef's whites. He pulled up a chair, dispatched a waiter to bring me the house's finest champagne, most of which he went on to drink himself. While I struggled through my tarte (tinned apples, half-cooked pastry), he worked his way through a packet of cigarettes and bragged, endlessly, about his culinary talents. 'Mm,' I lied, forcing down the last mouthful. 'That really was the most . . . singular . . . Tarte Tatin I've tasted. There seems to be some special ingredient in it which I can't quite place . . .' The super-chef smiled. 'Trade secret,' he said, scratching at his crotch.

Dinner for one at Stronzo, with a bottle of Bordeaux and one bottle of Krug, came to £252. Disputing the 'optional' 17.5

———————

Whatever the cause – and though I suppose you could trace it to Fish Show, or Belton House, or my christening, or even as far back as The Dreadful Incident in the Sudan – I prefer to date the beginning of my troubles to the clammy Wednesday morning last May when I met the new editor.

I was perspiring heavily by the time I reached the twenty-sixth floor of Canary Wharf Tower. The journey had taken much longer than I expected, partly because the route was unfamiliar, partly because I had been thrown off the Docklands Light Railway two stops short of my destination.

Lurching from the lift, I found a glass door marked 'KNOB'.

Jesus! Couldn't the new management get anything right?

'You'll need one of these,' called a voice behind me.

A woman at a reception desk was waving a plastic-coated card.

'I work here,' I protested.

'And your name is?'

'Giles Fripp.'

She typed the information into the electronic visitors' book.

'Visiting . . . ?'

'I *work* here.'

'I'll need a name.'

'Tamsin May, then.'

As she dialled, she nodded me towards a corner-shaped sofa. One side of it was occupied by a long-haired young man in a black polo-neck and ill-fitting dark suit.

Our eyes met briefly before I turned my attention to the reading matter on the low table in front of us. Nothing but pop magazines, men's glossies and tabloid newspapers.

I sat back, drawing my tweed jacket tight over a belly which, it appeared, had swollen considerably during my fortnight's gastronomic tour of south-western France. The air-conditioning – one of those marvellous new perks we'd all been promised before the move – had started to chill the sweat against my skin. And now my stomach was gurgling. It had been expecting rather more than a hasty breakfast of two dry croissants.

4

The young man was playing nervously with his visitor's card. It was good to see someone even more uncomfortable than me. Barely into his teens by the looks of it.

'Here for an interview?' I asked.

I took his unintelligible reply for a 'Yes'.

'Know how you feel,' I said. 'It wasn't so long ago that I was in your shoes. Brogues rather than trainers, though.'

'Eh?'

'Still, I suppose we must move with the times.'

I looked mournfully round the reception area, decorated in arrestingly unpleasant shades of blue and green. I could scarcely wait to hear what the others had made of it all.

'You should have seen the last place,' I said. 'Wood panelling, high ceilings, antique furniture, a log fire in the library . . . It was more like a gentlemen's club than an office.'

'So I heard.'

'And it was about as difficult to join. With all due respect, you might not have found it all that easy getting in.'

'Oh?'

'It's not just the shoes. It's your hair. Your age. Your accent. Do you know, when I went up for my interview, they even had someone watch me to see whether I put the milk in before or after the Darjeeling!'

'This before the war, was it?' muttered the teenager, removing a packet of Gitanes Maïs from his pocket.

'And if I'm perfectly honest with you,' I said, ignoring his remark, 'I hope the new man carries on the tradition.'

I was about to explain that it was precisely this attention to detail which, for almost 300 years, had sustained *Knobbes Journal*'s pre-eminence over its vulgar rivals. But at this moment, the teenager chose to light his cigarette.

'Do you think that's a good idea?' I asked, drawing his attention to the 'No Smoking' sign on the reception desk.

He took a leisurely drag.

'Mightn't you get into trouble?' I persisted, more firmly.

He smiled.

'If I'm lucky,' he said.

The lift door opened and out stepped a ravishing young girl in tight leather trousers. The teenager waved at her.

'Catch you later,' he said, patting me impudently on the knee. He joined his friend and together they slipped through the door which Tamsin May had just opened.

'How do you like the new editor?' she joked, glancing over her shoulder at Miss Leather Trousers.

I laughed. It was good to see Tamsin had recovered her sense of humour about the appointment. In vain had I tried explaining to her that *Knobbes Journal* would sooner fold than allow a woman to become its editor. 'That may well be its epitaph,' Tamsin had replied.

Much against the wishes of the older hands, she had been brought in as features editor in an attempt to stop circulation from falling even further. Then came news that the magazine was to change ownership. Tamsin had believed that she would be promoted. And so she had been, but only as deputy to a newcomer called Andy Bell.

'So what's he like?' I asked, pecking her on both cheeks.

'If you'd got here earlier, I could have briefed you,' said Tamsin.

'I did try.' I began telling her about my row with the truculent inspector who had thrown me off the train for having an incorrect ticket. But Tamsin wasn't interested.

'Giles,' she said seriously, 'things have changed quite a bit since you've been away.'

Once I'd followed her through the door, I saw what she meant.

For a moment, I stood transfixed by the strip-lit hell of plastic work benches, ringing telephones and clattering computer keyboards. And who were all this people sitting behind them?

Tamsin touched my arm gently. 'I did warn you.'

On the way to the far end of the room, she pointed out a few faces. The chap with the leather jacket draped over his chair was 'Sherman Roach, Rock'. The black girl opposite him was the picture editor, Oriole Styx.

Next came a desk occupied by a couple of inbreds with very short hair and a tall, cadaverous young thing, whose specialities, apparently, were Fast Cars, Bikes and Dangerous Sports.

'That's Fashion,' Tamsin continued.

But I was craning my neck to see whether there were any sections I'd missed. Where was Obits? Heritage? Field Sports?

'You and Rupert are here. Next to the subs.'

I nodded grimly back at Rupert and placed my briefcase next to the vacant chair. Apart from Tamsin, his was the only recognizable face from the old regime.

'And the others?'

Tamsin sighed.

'You were meant to ring me last night,' she said.

'I didn't get the message till after midnight.'

'Yes, I'll tell him,' said Rupert. He put down his phone. 'Andy wants to see you.'

Tamsin, whose own office lay next door, escorted me to the editor's glass-walled lair. The girl in leather trousers was just leaving.

I tapped lightly on the half-open door and entered, blinking against the thick yellow smoke which filled the room. The editor was concealed behind a computer screen. Next to it stood an overflowing ashtray, a stainless steel teapot, a carton of milk and two mugs with *NME* written on them.

'We're all out of Darjeeling,' called a worryingly familiar voice. Its owner pushed away the screen to reveal his grinning, youthful features. 'PG Tips do you?'

The teenager, clearly very pleased with himself, poured out the milk first. Then the tea. He pushed one of the mugs towards me.

'Fripp,' he said. 'No relation of Robert's, I suppose?'

'Not that I know of.'

'Pity. Hoped you might be able to tell me what the fuck prog rock was all about.' He extended a hand. 'Andy Bell, by the way. As in Ride and Erasure.'

His palm felt moist and warm.

'Take a pew,' he said. 'I've got something here I'd like you to read.'

He passed me several sheets of blue writing paper, embossed with the name of a French hotel. I studied him suspiciously, unsure whether this was to be yet another joke at my expense.

'Go on,' he prompted. 'From the top.'

'Motor from Montpellier to Toulouse by the circuitous Route Nationale,' I read, 'and you will meander through narcoleptic medieval hamlets and dappled avenues of *platanes,* past Daliesque melting chequerboards of tutti-frutti *vignobles* until, finally – skirting the industrial town of Castres, whose Roman name promises history and delivers only Fifties *ouvrier* austerity – you will find yourself in the pulsating eighteenth-century aorta . . .'

Andy groaned.

'No, please,' he insisted. 'Do go on.'

'. . . the pulsating eighteenth-century aorta of the world's sausage capital. As I made that journey last month, it struck me how much the typical traveller must miss when he travels by Autoroute. The difference between the two journeys is essential if one is to understand the nuances of French provincial cuisine. Mystical. Elusive. Complex. And yet breathtakingly simple.'

'Enough!' gasped Andy.

I stopped reading.

Andy lit a cigarette. 'Who wrote that?' he asked.

I felt a modest blush warming my cheeks. 'I did.'

Andy agreed. 'You also wrote this . . .'

On his desk, he had gathered together several *Knobbes* back issues, all opened at the culinary section.

'. . . and this . . .' he said, indicating an article entitled 'Whither Port?'.

'. . . and this.' More ominously, he had selected a piece called 'Must Every Dish Be Fumée?', in which I had called for the banning of smoking in restaurants. 'And do you know what I think of it all?' he asked, his voice rising a fraction.

I thought it best not to venture an opinion.

'I think,' he said, sweeping all the articles on to the floor, 'that it's the biggest pile of . . .'

The ensuing expletives were all but drowned by his telephone.

'Who? All right. Put him through.'

Some of the old issues had landed, face up, near my feet. One cover showed the Queen at her birthday parade. Another the Quorn on a Boxing Day meet. At the top of each, in ornate eighteenth-century script, it said '*Knobbes Journal* (Est. 1702)'.

'Watcha got?' Andy was saying. 'Yeah? What does it do? Uh-huh? Bloody well ought to at that price.'

On the wall to my left was a noticeboard on to which had been pinned four photographs of a pneumatic blonde in a skimpy bathing costume. Each had been printed with the word 'Pamela' in a different position.

'Sorted!' announced Andy, replacing the receiver. He followed the direction of my stare. 'If you're going to say what I think you're gonna say, don't bother.'

I was about to ask what he meant when I noticed the bold, lime-green legend at the top of each picture: 'KNOB'.

'Outrageous!' cried Andy, mimicking an irascible old man. 'A disgrace! I must protest in the strongest possible terms, Mr Bell. How dare you fiddle with our *Knobbes*!'

8

Andy found his pun most amusing. Sensing an opportunity to distance myself from my sacked colleagues, I laughed with him.

'And all along it was just a printing error,' I said.

Andy stopped smiling.

'I meant . . . er . . . that the silly fools *thought* it was a printing error,' I explained quickly.

'Right. Yeah.' Frowning, Andy pulled out another cigarette. He surveyed me thoughtfully.

'How old are you, Giles?'

'Thirty.'

'You do get what I'm trying to do with this magazine?'

'I'm beginning to.'

'Only, if I thought you wanted to go on writing stuff like that bollocks you sent in from France, I'd say, "Fine. But piss off and do it at someone else's expense."'

I nodded.

'I've been given six months to get this rag back into the black. And I'm not gonna do it by chasing dead colonels and dowager duchesses. It's the young thrusters we're after now. Kids with money to burn. The type that gets our ads team big in their pants.'

Andy spun on his chair and retrieved a stack of magazines from his shelf.

'Just so's you get a rough idea,' he said, pushing the magazines towards me, 'this is the competition we've got to beat.'

I riffled through the pile of thick glossies. They were illustrated with pictures of starlets, pop groups and sportsmen. 'Masturbation!' screamed the teaser on one of them. 'Top Squash Stars Compare Their Wrist Action.' 'Clitoris: Rock Chicks from Hell?' said the one with a photograph of three leather-clad harlots. I felt little urge to explore within.

'Got a nice little feature lined up for you already,' said Andy. '"Me and My Drug", it's called.'

'Me and My *Drug*?'

'Cannabis. Smack. Charlie. E. Whatever. We're gonna make it a regular slot. You know, grab a celeb. Nice pix. Colourful copy.'

'But drugs are illegal.'

'You don't say.'

'Are you sure it's quite the right job for a restaurant reviewer?'

'Get real, Giles. I'm not paying you fifteen grand a year just to –'

'Seventeen and a half,' I corrected.

Andy shook his head. 'Money's tight. Maybe later we can talk about a rise. But not until you've proved you're worth it. Now, besides "Me and My Drug" I'm gonna need your restaurant piece, *pronto*. Any ideas?'

I bit my lip.

'No?' Andy consulted his notes. '*Thrust*'s resto reviewer has got a piece on dining with the Dayaks. "Heads You Lose", it's called. *Insignia* . . . "best coffee bars in Medellín".' He looked up. 'You like travel?'

'More Rupert's line, isn't it?'

'Mm. Maybe you're right. *Montage* has got a piece right up your street. Virtual Dining. You think you're stuffing your face. But you leave the restaurant even emptier than when you went in. Pity your oppo got there first,' said Andy, looking pointedly at my paunch. 'This is what pulls in the readers. Stuff about the latest trends. What's in. What's out. Who's eating where. Superchefs. Celebs . . . Something the matter?'

'Um, well, I was just thinking. It hasn't got much to do with food, has it?'

Andy looked at me as if I was mad.

'Since when has restaurant reviewing had anything to do with food?'

Tamsin was too busy to listen to my opinion of Andy Bell. So, it appeared, was Rupert.

'You don't care, do you?' I said.

The travel editor looked up distractedly from his screen.

'What?'

'It doesn't bother you one bit what's happened to this magazine?'

Rupert brushed a stray dark curl which had tumbled over his grey-green eyes.

'Can't say I've given it much thought. But it could all be rather diverting, don't you think? Certainly makes an agreeable change from guided tours of the Holy Land.'

'What will?'

'Oh, you know. Activity holidays. War zones.'

'Is Andy sending you off to write about war zones?'

'I *think* that's what he was saying. Half the time I couldn't make head nor tail of what he was on about. This place . . . Kigali?'

'You're not going to Rwanda, surely?'

'Why ever not?'

'Because you'll die!'

'Oh, I don't think so. He's kitting me out with one of those life jackets.'

'You're going to risk your life for fifteen grand a year?'

'There are compensations. Off to sunny California tomorrow.'

'Earthquakes. Drive-by shootings.'

'Scuba diving, actually.'

Seething, I jabbed at the on-button on my computer terminal. I glared at the blank screen, plotting dire vengeance.

'Er, Rupert, how do you work this thing?'

An hour later, I had gained a rough idea of how to create my own file. Rupert's bumbling attempts to explain the rudiments of word-processing had enraged me even more.

My instincts told me to walk out there and then. But this, I suspected, was just what Andy wanted. Perhaps there was another way to make my point.

And that was when it struck me. What better revenge than to do exactly as he asked?

'Waiter!' I typed. 'There's no fly in my soup . . .'

CHAPTER TWO

Bun fight by Giles Fripp, aged 8 years 7 months

There is a café that parents hate taking their children to. It's called Bun Fight. You can't wear your best clothes there and if you go you'll find out why.

When you go there, you pay the lady at the entrance some money and she will give you lots of different bags, with squidgy things in them, like chocolate paste, strawberry jam, peanut butter and blackcurrant jam. You can also buy real Slime, but this is more expensive. If you think they're for eating, though, you're wrong.

Everyone has to arrive at the same time and to start off with it's quite peaceful. But at a certain time the chief waitress shouts 'Bun fight' and quickly she hides underneath a table. If you've been before, though, you will know what she's going to say and will be able to hit her before she's finished.

All the mothers who have brought their children along start screaming at all the mess and how their dresses will be ruined because they are the main targets. But they can't escape.

Also you can bring water pistols for when you run out of things to throw. There are taps near all the tables so you can keep filling up.

At the end, you can't recognize anyone any more because everyone is covered in cream and jam and you are very wet. You have to go home quickly or you'll catch your death, but it's great fun.

My English teacher at Belton House had given it the First Year Fiction Prize. My classmates felt cheated. Their accounts of trips to Mars and battles with aliens were much more interesting than my stupid made-up restaurant. In fact, some of them suspected, perhaps I hadn't even made it up at all.

It came to a head the day my essay appeared in the school magazine. I was sitting with three of my fellow First Years at one end of a long, greasy table in the unheated dining room. There, amid the clatter of cutlery, the stench of cheap polish, stale margarine and rancid boy, they were discussing the contents of the *Beltonian*. The elevated conversational topic had been chosen to impress Mrs Schreck, the headmaster's wife, who was sitting next to us.

'Did you *really* make it up, Fripp?' asked Rampton Minor.

I did not answer. I was staring at the uneaten contents of my plate.

''Course he did. Only Fripp could write something that wet,' chipped in 'Beetroot' Beresford. He eyed Talbot to see whether this was the right reaction.

Talbot was too busy eating to notice.

'Nobody's doubting that Fripp made the thing up,' said Rubric. 'What's at issue is not the question of veracity but of plagiarism.'

'Whatty?' squeaked Rampton Minor.

'All I'm saying is that Fripp's piece is rather derivative. It comes straight out of the pages of the *Magnet*,' enunciated Rubric.

'Gosh. What's he on about, Beresford?' asked Rampton Minor.

'I think he means that Fripp has ripped off Billy Bunter,' said Beresford.

'Oh,' said Rampton Minor. 'That's a pity. If . . . if a place like that really was true, it would be quite fun. Wouldn't it?'

Rubric and Beresford made sneering noises. They both looked for approbation from Talbot, who still wasn't paying attention. His plate was now empty and he was eyeing mine.

Though I had been dying to respond to these attacks on my integrity, I knew that to attract Mrs Schreck's attention would be fatal. She might notice that the ladle's worth of 'Lancashire hot pot' she had dolloped on to my plate ten minutes previously had gone virtually untouched. I had dispatched the easy part – the thin and not wholly unpalatable sliced potatoes that had once floated above the fat and gristle. But the 'meat' still awaited my attention.

'Fripp?' said Rampton Minor, prodding me gently.

'Will you boys stop bothering Fripp until he's eaten his lunch,' intervened Mrs Schreck, the veins in her fat cheeks glowing like bloodworms.

I heaved a deep breath. And, summoning up one of those grave determined looks that schoolboys use to deceive adults, I made an exploratory poke with my knife at the least offensive chunk. It wobbled.

I could feel Mrs Schreck's pale grey eyes boring into me.

I stabbed the lump with my fork, but the blue gristle resisted the thrust and skidded sideways through the thin gravy.

Mrs Schreck was about to pounce. Quickly, as if I were eager to eat the quivering vileness, I moved in again. This time, I plunged my fork into the centre of the lump and, before it could escape, popped it into my mouth.

Trying not to breathe, I let it perch on my tongue for a moment, purchasing a few seconds of freedom from its jellied texture. Mrs Schreck regarded my hamster cheeks disapprovingly.

Unable to escape any longer, I crunched my teeth against the resistant tissue. It fought back, but I chomped again and again, hoping to grind it into oblivion before it touched my tonsils. Then, still holding my breath, I gulped it down, simultaneously seizing a glass of water.

Only seven more to go.

'Come on, Fripp,' said Mrs Schreck. 'You're being far too slow. If you don't finish it all up soon, I'm going to have to feed you like a baby.'

Twice that term already, I had been held back after lunch and, to the titters of the kitchen maids, I had been force-fed, mouthful by mouthful, by Mrs Schreck's varicose claw.

I was getting desperate. Could I get away with the handkerchief option again?

Mrs Schreck was surely wise to the trick. Matron would have told her by now about the suspicious brown stains on my hankies.

It was no good. I was lost. Hyperventilating with apprehension, I slowly steered my fork towards the remaining lumps.

At that moment, fate intervened. One of the kitchen maids tapped Mrs Schreck's arm and asked if she could have a quiet word. The headmaster's wife cocked her head irritably. The maid was trying to keep her voice down but we all caught the gist. Something had been seen scurrying across the kitchen floor. The cooks, who really should have been used to that sort of thing by now, had fled. The rice pudding was in jeopardy.

'Ridiculous,' hissed Mrs Schreck. Before she headed for the kitchen to dispatch the beast, she announced, 'I want you all to make sure that Fripp eats the rest by the time I've returned. Understood?'

As soon as she had gone, I turned to Talbot. Almost imperceptibly, he nodded his assent. He was just leaning over to wolf down the remains of my lunch when a thought struck him. 'If any of you dare –' He didn't need to go on. Who, after all, would be so foolish as to sneak on Talbot, Wielder of the Scorpion (his towel), Brandisher of the Bumnumbers (his slippers), Stripper of Freshly Made Beds, Killer of Squirrels (with his illegal throwing knife), Master of the Chinese Burn, the Half Nelson, the Single Hair Extraction, the Knuckle in That Bit That Really Hurts in the Middle of Your Chest? Satisfied with their terrified expressions, Talbot set efficiently about my gristle.

By the time Mrs Schreck had returned my plate was clean. Too clean.

'Well, Rubric?'

'Miss?'

'Did Fripp eat his lunch?'

'All his food's gone,' said Rubric legalistically.

'I can see that. But was it Fripp who ate it? . . . Beresford?'

Beresford reddened and made a bad job of not looking at Talbot.

Talbot looked unusually angelic. Mrs Schreck knew she was not going to break him and turned to Rampton Minor.

'You'll tell me, won't you, Benjamin?' Mrs Schreck said to the seven-year-old, in that nice, motherly voice she normally reserved for parents.

He went pale.

'Because you wouldn't want me to tell your mummy that you've been lying to me, would you?' cooed Mrs Schreck.

Rampton Minor shook his head.

'Then tell me,' she snapped. 'Did Fripp eat his lunch? Or did Talbot do it for him?'

Rampton Minor's reply was unintelligible.

'Louder, boy. Louder.'

'Talbot,' the boy mumbled tearfully.

Mrs Schreck clasped her hands together. 'Good,' she said. 'Talbot, Fripp, you've been warned about this before. You're to see the head-master after lunch and collect 200 lines which you will write for me on the subject "Waste Not, Want Not" in detention after prep . . . Stop snivelling, Rampton . . . Furthermore, you, Talbot will not be having any rice pudding today.'

Oh well. Could have been worse.

'And before you visit the headmaster, Fripp,' said Mrs Schreck, stirring the remains of the Lancashire hot pot maliciously, 'you will stay behind with me after lunch.'

'I went there once,' said Talbot airily from the other side of the classroom. He had bagged the desk next to the radiator.

I was so taken aback I couldn't answer for a few seconds. Talbot had actually spoken to me. Voluntarily. And at such length.

'Where?' I whispered, praying the duty master prowling somewhere in the building wouldn't hear us. We were in detention, after all.

'That place you wrote about in the magazine,' Talbot said, making no effort to lower his voice.

'Was it . . . any good?' I said.

'Brill! Mum took me there last exeat.'

Talbot was always making up stories. Like the one he'd told near the beginning of term in our dorm. He'd got up early one morning – normally he didn't leave bed until matron virtually had to drag him out, but he had wanted to hide Pelham Minimus's shoes while he was still asleep – and looked out of the window.

'Urrgh,' he said, so loudly that everyone woke up. 'Victor's just gobbed in the milk!' Of course, nobody dared ignore Talbot, so we all padded over to the window, and there, sure enough, was the school caretaker wheezing on his Woodbine at the back of the kitchens. Nearby stood the two churns containing our breakfast milk. One of them had its top suspiciously off.

'Look. There. Can you see it? Floating next to the dead flies,' Talbot crowed.

'Urrgh,' we all said. Apart from Pelham Minimus, who said, 'Where? I can't see it.' Talbot gave him a dead arm.

At breakfast after the Victor incident, I'd stared miserably into my bowl of cornflakes, looking for foreign matter and trying to convince myself that Talbot had been lying.

Then, I tried calculating the odds against my getting the nasty bit. Two churns – so that brought it down to evens. Each churn was divided into five jugs (there were ten dining tables). And even if my table had got the infected jug, only one person out of fifteen would have actually got the nasty bit in his bowl.

So that meant the odds against were . . . what? Even if I had been able to work it out, it wouldn't have made any difference. If there was the remotest possibility that the smallest morsel of the tiniest fleck of the most infinitesimally minute atom of that smelly caretaker's spit had gone into my milk, I wasn't going to touch my cornflakes.

'I'll have 'em,' Talbot had said. And, rather bravely, I thought, he did. Not just that morning but every other day too.

Talbot crept across the classroom and sat on the desk next to mine.

'I was going to ask you,' he said. 'How much did you get for that prize?'

'Just a two-pound book voucher.'

'Two pounds!' exclaimed Talbot.

He fiddled self-consciously with his oversized second-hand blazer. The cloth band around the lapels and sleeves was a threadbare, dirty brown, in contrast to the healthy scarlet on my own brand-new uniform.

'Yeah,' I said. 'But they tell you which book you have to buy. And it's all pathetic stuff like *Treasure Island* and *Babes in the Wood*.'

'Not bad, though,' said Talbot. 'Considering you were meant to have made the place up and everything.'

'Yes,' I said hesitantly. 'I suppose it is.'

Of course I was intrigued. But to show interest would not have been 'cool'. And if there was a chance that this café did exist, I wanted Talbot to think I had written it up in a deliberately cynical attempt to win the imaginative composition prize.

And yet, now that his defences were down . . .

'Talbot,' I began.

'Yeah?'

'How come you've already finished your lines and I've hardly started mine?'

Talbot, who had never been asked by anyone to help them with anything before, was eager to show me where I'd gone wrong.

'First,' he said, 'you're writing much too small. Look at your stuff. You're doing what . . . thirteen words to the line. I try not to do any more than five. And you've got to leave much bigger spaces between each word. And not think at all about what you're writing.'

Oh dear. I had been rather proud of my original, carefully crafted comparison between the predicament of Biafran babies and well-fed English prep-school boys. Secretly, I thought the latter were rather worse off, but I didn't dare say it.

'Because remember,' continued Talbot, 'Mrs Schreck will never read them.'

'You sure?'

'Course I am. She hasn't complained before and if you'd seen the rubbish I've given her.'

Talbot supervised me until, surprisingly quickly, it was over, leaving us time to talk of other things.

Like how unfair it was that he was always being called a bully.

'Rubbish,' I concurred. If I played my cards right, my buttocks might be spared the Scorpion's sting.

And how sick and tired he was of people sucking up to him.

'Yeah,' I said, as if it was something that happened to me all the time too.

And how he hated being the only one in our year who ever seemed to get given detention.

'Not now, you're not,' I said.

'Not now,' he agreed.

From down the corridor, footsteps approached.

'Talbot,' I said. It was now or never. As soon as detention was over, it would be straight to bed. By the time we reached the dormitory, Talbot would have forgotten our temporary intimacy.

But Talbot, whose ears were more finely tuned to danger than mine, was already half-way across the classroom.

When he reached his desk, he motioned me to be quiet. And the moment was gone. We never did talk about the restaurant again. In fact, until the coincidence with Stronzo, it hardly crossed my mind. Shortly afterwards, Mr Norris loomed in the doorway and told us that detention was over, you horrid little boys.

But just before Mr Norris came in, Talbot whispered one more thing which I still find quite moving – even after everything that's happened since. 'Fripp,' he said, 'you don't have to call me Talbot. My name's Eric.'

CHAPTER THREE

'But we've only just got here,' complained Tamsin.

'Don't mind me. You enjoy yourself,' I said, attempting to squeeze through the throng of party-goers towards the exit.

Perhaps it was a drastic measure to go straight back to Fulham having cabbed it all the way to Clerkenwell. But nothing could induce me to stay in this hell hole for another second. Not even the chance to spend just a little longer admiring the ivory flesh so fetchingly exposed by Tamsin's strapless black cocktail dress.

'You could at least stay for one drink.'

'Lager and fudge-flavoured vodka? I think not.'

'Too late,' said Tamsin. 'We've been spotted.'

Hardly surprising, given that I was the only male in the room not sporting a goatee beard and/or sculpted side-burns, a silly haircut, chunky boots and ripped jeans.

At the far end of the gallery, Andy Bell was giving us both a jolly wave. There was something about his smile that made me fear the worst. It was smug, threatening, knowing.

On the table next to him was a stack of *Knob* first issues, each one containing the article which would surely lose me my livelihood. In the preceding weeks, I had somehow convinced myself that I was going to get away with it. Swimming around the computer system, being tinkered with by the sub-editors, the article had seemed vaguely unreal. In print, however, Stronzo had taken on a deadly, job-threatening permanence.

'I'm finished,' I groaned.

'You will be if he sees you leaving so soon.'

'It won't make any difference. He's going to sack me anyway.'

'At a launch party? Don't be ridiculous.'

'Bet you anything you like.'

'Dinner?'

'Whatever.'

'If I win, you'll take me to the restaurant of my choice.'

'*When* you lose, we'll commiserate over foie gras and Château d'Yquem.'

'Done,' said Tamsin. And suddenly the prospect of being sacked didn't seem quite so terrifying.

We pushed through the crowd of hacks, freeloaders and semi-celebrities. Tamsin grabbed a beer. I found an unadulterated vodka.

'Remember the last *Knobbes* bash?' I grumbled. 'Krug all night long.'

'And old farts boring on about cricket.'

Tamsin wanted to see Andy. I suggested we inspect the exhibits.

'Didn't know you were interested in modern art.'

'Beats talking about football with adolescents.'

The show, entitled *Jism*, had attracted almost as much publicity as the *Knob* first issue. Quite why a dozen near-blank paintings and a few ice sculptures should have caused such controversy, I couldn't imagine.

'Looks like an old bedsheet,' I said, trying to make sense of the faint yellow and russet splodges on one of the huge canvases.

'It is an old bedsheet,' said Tamsin.

I read the caption. ' "January. *Blood and semen on cotton*." Who buys this muck?'

'*Knob* readers, I expect,' joked a man standing next to me. Apart from me, he was the only person wearing a proper lounge suit.

'Quite.'

'Are you Giles Fripp?'

I nodded.

'Peter Quinn. Londoner's Diary.'

'Oh, Tamsin, look who it is!' I cried. 'Do excuse us,' I added to the diarist, as I dragged Tamsin into the crowd.

We stopped near a pair of microskirted nubiles. They were tittering at a frozen, milky-white statue of the Madonna. I looked over my shoulder to make sure we hadn't been followed.

'Didn't he write that piece?' asked Tamsin.

I nodded. The *Evening Standard* had run a short item speculating on the whereabouts of London's most fashionable restaurant.

'And you didn't want to tell him the address?'

'Something like that.'

Tamsin studied me thoughtfully.

'You never did tell me how you found Stronzo.'

'Just what I was wondering,' said a dishevelled inebriate, lurching into view. In one hand, he clutched a copy of the *Knob* first issue, in the other a large vodka. In his stained, hand-me-down suit and scuffed shoes, he might easily have been mistaken for a tramp who had just wandered in off the street.

'Rodney. What the hell are you doing here?'

'Bugger off, Giles,' he replied merrily. 'I was invited.'

'That'll be a first.'

I explained to Tamsin that Rodney Holmes was an old friend.

'I'll leave you to it, then,' she said.

'Friendly,' said Rodney, watching her go.

'Discerning, I think, is the word.'

Rodney grabbed two more vodkas from a passing waiter and launched into an account of his fabulous exploits since last he'd sponged dinner off me. After a week at a Bordelais château belonging to an heiress he had met on the tube, he had been lured to the Sinai by an Old Harrovian school chum and imprisoned for a fortnight in a Bedouin encampment.

'Hence the sun tan,' I said, eyeing his pallid, unshaven face.

'Couldn't leave the tent,' explained Rodney. 'Drugged up to the eyeballs on this vicious local weed.'

Then, just two days ago as it happened, Rodney had won £800 at the casino. He had hoped to spend it on a case of '86 Clos de Bèze which, of course, he had planned to share with me. Unfortunately, his mother had confiscated the money to help pay for the damage he'd caused to her car while driving drunk and without a licence.

I could well believe the last bit.

'Funnily enough,' said Rodney, 'it was on the way back from Stronzo. There was I, congratulating myself on having found quite the most exclusive place in town. And then I find my old mucker Giles has beaten me to it. In fact, here's an idea. If you fancy a bite after this, why don't we both –'

'No, Rodney.'

'Suit yourself.'

Having recharged our glasses, Rodney sought new distractions.

'How about leather boy over there? He looks fun.'

We hovered on the edge of a circle comprising Sherman Roach, Oriole Styx and the two girls from the fashion desk, Jessica and Aurora.

They were scrutinizing the other guests.

'How about him?' suggested Aurora.

'Too old,' announced Roach, sucking on a large, hand-rolled ciga-rette. 'The Geezer's only in his thirties, apparently.'

Rodney looked askance at me.

'Our proprietor,' I explained.

'Dark? Fair? Tall?' asked Jessica.

Roach shrugged. 'Recluse. Never been photographed.'

'What makes you think he'll be here?' asked Oriole.

'Just a hunch,' said Roach. 'He's very hands-on, apparently.'

'He can put his hands on me any time,' tittered Jessica.

'Shh!' said Aurora, looking about her. 'He could be listening . . . Oh, hello, er . . .'

'Giles,' I reminded her.

Roach offered me the cigarette. I shook my head.

'Cheers,' said Rodney, accepting the sodden stub.

'Wait!' squealed Aurora. 'I've spotted him.'

'Where? Where?'

'The gorgeous thing in Gaultier?'

'The chap in the red crushed velvet?' asked Rodney.

'Yes! Do you know him?'

'Of course. And Giles does. That's Eric Talbot.'

Aurora and Jessica looked at me with sudden interest.

'You know Eric Talbot?' they chorused.

'If I could just have your attention,' came a loud voice from the far end of the room. Andy had mounted a chair and was finding it difficult to keep his balance. To steady himself, he had planted a lecherous paw on Tamsin's bare shoulder.

'First, I'd like to thank you all for *coming*. Pity you had to make such of mess of the pictures . . .'

I appeared to be the only person in the room who did not find this joke hilarious.

'. . . thought you might like to hear what the critics made of their first taste of *Knob*.' Andy consulted his notes. '"A disgrace", says the *Mail*. "Loathsome", says *The Times*. "Plumbs new depths in the anals . . . sorry, annals . . . of down-market magazine publishing", say our friends at the *Daily Telegraph*.'

There was much celebratory whooping.

'And I think I speak for all us,' said Andy, loosening his belt, 'when I say that this' - he dropped his trousers – 'is what we think of the critics.' Andy whipped down his boxer shorts and mooned at his jubilant audience.

'Now I was going to thank you all individually for the hard work you put into this issue,' continued Andy. 'But then I thought, Why bother? They're all such a bunch of tossers.'

'Geddimoff,' someone shouted amid the laughter.

'Before I piss off, though, I would like to give a special mention to three people. First, to my deputy, Tamsin, who . . . can't read this. Something about giving head . . .'

I shuddered with vicarious embarrassment.

'Sorry . . . who *kept* her head when all about her were losing theirs . . . Second, to the man who has given us such great comedy value over the last month, our drugs correspondent – and occasional restaurant critic – Giles Fripp.'

There was much clapping, jeering and ironic laughter.

'Giles, where are you?' called Andy.

Even people who didn't know me started looking around to see if they could spot this object of derision.

Rodney seized my wrist and waved my arm for me.

The cruel laughter grew louder. My cheeks burned. There were matey slaps on my back. Cries of 'Nice one, Giles.'

'And last but by no means least,' said Andy, 'I'd like you to raise your glasses to the man who made all this possible.' Andy lifted his glass. 'The Geezer. Wherever he may be.'

I had almost made it through the door when I felt a tap on my shoulder.

'You,' said Andy, 'have been a very naughty boy.'

There was nothing wrong with Life's A Beach that a visit from the Noise Pollution Inspectors, the Taste Police and a dose of Agent Orange couldn't have rectified. Or so I planned to write in my corrosive review of the restaurant to which Tamsin led me after the launch party.

In vain had I pleaded that the abundant, Vietnam-style foliage might play havoc with my allergies; that the throbbing rock music would exacerbate my headache; and that my sensitive palate would be traumatized by such monstrosities as 'Turbot with a Zinfandel Reduction'. A bet was a bet, said Tamsin. And I had lost.

'Hi,' said our waiter, smiling perfectly. 'I'm Julian.'

Like his colleagues, Julian was wearing multicoloured surf pants and a pale pink singlet bearing the Life's A Beach legend. And, of course, he had on a pair of rollerblades because that was one of the 'amusing' quirks which dragged punters into the restaurant.

Julian took a deep breath. 'Tonight we have –' he was about to extemporize, as Americans do, about the singular delights of the menu.

'Actually, I think I know what I'm going to have already,' I said.

Julian looked crestfallen.

Tamsin shot me a dirty look.

'Tell us about the oysters,' she said.

Julian perked up instantaneously.

'Okaaay. We got three different kinds of oysters tonight. All of them flown in specially. We have Preston Point, which comes from our own Tomales Bay. It's kinda small but it has a real cute, tiger-striped shell and a wild melony aftertaste. Then we have the Golden Mantle – nice name, huh? – which is from waaay up in British Columbia and has a real delicate flavour of, I guess, watermelon. But I have to say my favourite is the Kumamoto – that's another Califor-nian one, Humboldt Bay in fact, which is just excellent. It's got a real mild flavour, which kinda reminds me of –'

'Melons?' I interrupted.

'Could be, sir. It certainly tastes fruity.'

'Maybe we should have them for pudding,' I said.

Once Julian had slid off, chastened, Tamsin said, 'We're supposed to be celebrating.'

'What exactly? My elevation to Official Laughing Stock?'

'You weren't the only one at the receiving end.'

'The difference is, I didn't enjoy it.'

Tamsin watched me with amusement.

'Do I detect a twinge of jealousy?'

'I just think it sets a pretty poor example, letting him lech over you like that,' I said, hoping my blush didn't show.

'He's young, Giles. It's his big night.'

'I'm surprised you're not still celebrating with him.'

'In his state?'

'Oh. So you would have gone if he hadn't been too drunk to –'

'Giles. Please.'

Julian reappeared bearing two glasses of over-iced water and a bottle of wine.

It was a Californian Gamay. His choice not mine. Julian had described it as 'like Beaujolais on acid, if you know what I mean' (which I didn't). 'OK, OK,' he had continued. 'Imagine a Beaujolais is the Velvet Underground. Well, this one's like the Byrds. Light, easy-drinking. No bass notes. But, like, fruity and, I guess, real harmonious.'

Julian poured me a drop. Colour: mutant fuchsia. Nose: raspberry coulis. Taste: sweetened cranberry juice.

Tamsin caught my sour expression.

'What is wrong with you? An hour ago you were worried sick about being sacked.'

I shrugged, wondering how best to raise my extraordinary conversation with Andy.

'Say you were editor,' I said at last, 'and someone submitted a piece which they'd made up. What would you do?'

'Depends on the circumstances.'

'All right. Imagine if Sherman wrote about a pop group that didn't exist.'

'Doubt I'd know the difference.'

'But say you found out.'

Tamsin frowned.

'Isn't it time you stopped worrying about what your colleagues have or haven't done and started trying to get on with them?'

If I was unhappy at work, she said, I had only myself to blame. I approached every assignment with bad grace; I was aloof and ill-tempered; I had made absolutely no effort to fit in. Surely I could find someone with whom I had something in common. Jessica, maybe. Or Aurora.

'They're not interested.'

'*Make* them interested. Take them out to lunch. *Dazzle* them. You can be quite charming when you put your mind to it.'

'Big of you.'

'There you go again. God knows, you're not going to find yourself a nice girl with that sort of attitude.'

'I already have a girl.'

'You kept that one very quiet.'

I gazed meaningfully into Tamsin's eyes.

She tutted. 'I meant a *proper* girlfriend.'

Julian fussily laid down our starters.

'One oyster platter. One yellowfin carpaccio. Enjoy!'

Tamsin carved herself a sliver of translucent, pale brown flesh and smeared it with sticky port and sweet pepper sauce.

'Mwah!' She smacked her lips. 'How's yours?'

'Call me old-fashioned, but I prefer my oysters to taste of oyster.'

'Try some of this.'

I was certainly not going to turn down the chance of being hand-fed by Tamsin. I helped guide her hand towards my mouth.

'Good?'

I nodded dreamily, thinking of the warmth of her silken skin against my palm.

Tamsin began gushing about Eric Talbot, who had engaged her in long and fascinating conversation about himself. So handsome. So charming.

'So modest,' I added, on learning that it was he who had suggested we visit one of his celebrated 'theme' restaurants.

'If you can cook this well, why hide your light under a bushel?'

'He's never been near a stove in his life.'

'No?'

'Ideas man, that's all he is. Spends his whole life foisting idiotic trends on people too gormless to know any better.'

'Like me, I suppose?' said Tamsin.

My main course was a platter of wild game. It seemed to be the only item on the menu that wasn't smothered in Serrano chillies, lime crème fraîche, cilantro, wok-fried basil with tahini, coconut and mango purée and other Californian ludicrousness.

The deep crimson venison was gamey and tender. The thick slices of marinaded pigeon breast simultaneously crisp and meltingly fatty.

'Fine English game,' I murmured, lest Tamsin imagine I was enjoying it. 'Even an American can't go too far wrong with that.'

But Tamsin had ceased showing any interest in my culinary pronouncements. Indeed, she scarcely looked up from her blackened chicken breast.

I saved the emu till last. It tasted pleasantly redolent of agneau présalé. Nor could I fault the fawn-coloured wild-mushroom syrup. Earthy and feral.

'You know,' I announced to cheer Tamsin up, 'for Mickey Mouse cuisine, that wasn't altogether unbearable.'

Tamsin lit a cigarette and fixed me with a silent, menacing stare.

'What?' I said when it became obvious she wasn't going to stop.

'If this place were French . . .'

'I'm perfectly capable of judging a restaurant on its own merits.'

'Provided it serves boeuf en daube and 600-year-old claret.'

'Fat chance I'll have of tasting anything like that again. From now on it'll be Amazonian Basin, Mongolian Yurt, Radioactive Polynesian –'

'And a bloody good thing too,' snapped Tamsin. 'If you had any idea how boring it is being subjected to your views on *la cuisine* sodding *française* . . .'

'Can I interest you guys in the dessert menu?'

'Just the bill,' said Tamsin.

'Maybe you'll change your mind when you hear about our specials?'

'Go on,' I said. 'It's my treat.'

'Some treat,' said Tamsin bitterly.

We shared a cab as far as her flat in Chelsea. Tamsin rejected my offer of a night cap back at my place.

'You know, Giles,' she said wearily, just before she left, 'maybe it would have been better if you *had* been sacked.'

At home, over a glass of Armagnac, I wondered whether she might have been right. For one thing, she would have been far better disposed towards my advances had she had a reason to feel sorry for me. For another, I was now convinced that the man I was working for was not merely puerile, vulgar and vindictive, but positively certifiable.

What other explanation could there have been for our bizarre exchange at the *Knob* party?

Shortly after ticking me off for avoiding him all evening, he announced, 'I'll tell you, Giles. If I had a quid from everyone who'd asked me where they could find that restaurant of yours, I'd be a very rich man.'

He gave me a conspiratorial nudge.

'But I wasn't going to give the game away, was I?'

I sighed. 'You found out, then?'

'Of course I did.'

'I'm sorry,' I murmured.

'No good apologizing is it?'

I lowered my head.

'I mean,' he continued, 'what kind of prat would want to go to a restaurant where the service was complete shit and the food's so disgusting you need a stomach pump before you're half-way through your soup?'

'It — it was a mistake,' I floundered.

'You're telling me it was. I wouldn't go back there if you paid me.'

I chose not to dignify his cruel joke with an answer.

'OK. So maybe I would. But only if I'd eaten first. Look, matey,

I promise not to tell anyone else where it is. But, you've got to appreciate, I had to check it out. I mean, until I actually saw it with my own eyes' – Andy chuckled – 'I thought you'd made the whole thing up.'

CHAPTER FOUR

Every school holidays, Eric Talbot would invite me to his modern, semi-detached box on the outskirts of Reading. By the fourth year of our friendship, it was painfully noticeable that my parents had yet to return the compliment. My mother was to blame. Each time, she came up with a different excuse: having a stranger staying in the house might frighten the dogs; it was trouble enough looking after one boy, let alone two. But finally she relented, on the strict understanding that I kept my eyes on our guest at all times, especially when he was anywhere near anything valuable.

And so it was, in the summer of our penultimate year at Belton House, that I finally introduced Eric to my home: an eight-bedroomed Georgian manor house set in nine acres of grounds at the edge of Nether Rollright, a biggish village half-way between Stratford and Oxford.

I'd just finished helping Mother stash away the family silver in her bedroom cupboard when a feeble beeping noise from the direction of our gravel drive alerted us to Eric's arrival.

'What a dear little motorcar,' said Mother, as we peeked through the window of the upstairs landing at the Talbots' battered Morris Traveller. 'However did it manage to come all this way?'

I went downstairs to greet them, preceded by Mother's excited labradors, while their mistress preened herself in front of her bathroom mirror.

'Nice place you've got here, Giles,' said Eric's father, gawping at the Cotswold stone, bleached white in the August sunlight.

'Thanks, Mr Talbot,' I said, my voice almost drowned by the dogs' barking. 'Mother'll be along in a minute. Perhaps she'll show you round.' I picked up Eric's case and swung it viciously at the dogs. They fled to Eric, who fussed over them.

'Hello, Errol,' said Mother, congenitally incapable of pronouncing any name she deemed common. 'He's in your room, Giles. Spare towel in the airing cupboard. Daphne and Mortimer's lunch is in the fridge. Yours is on the sideboard.'

She glanced at Mr Talbot. 'Thank you so much for bringing him. If you'll excuse me, I have an urgent luncheon engagement.'

Once the grown-ups had gone I took Eric to the kitchen.

'Hungry?' I said.

'Rather!' said Eric.

'Pity,' I said, looking at the surface near the Aga, where Mother had left a basket containing four curling squares of pre-sliced bread and a tin of oxtail soup. I emptied it into the dogs' water bowls.

'I thought theirs was in the fridge,' said Eric, watching Daphne and Mortimer slobbering over the brown glop.

'*Was,*' I agreed.

In the fridge I found the dogs' fillet steak. It would have made a fine lunch, had Mother not outwitted me. Instead of leaving it on a clean plate, as usual, she had put it straight in the dog bowls.

Eric held his appetite at bay with the stale bread while I inspected the larder. It wasn't exactly teeming with delicacies. Dog biscuits and tonic water, mainly. But after a long search, I found an onion, a tin of tomatoes and a packet of dried spaghetti.

'Do you always make your own lunch?' asked Eric, watching me rough-chop the onions.

'Heavens, no!' I dabbed my streaming eyes with some kitchen towel. 'Normally the daily does it, only she doesn't come in at weekends.'

As the onions turned golden brown in the butter, releasing their sweet caramel scent, Eric made all the right 'oohing' and 'aahing' noises. I sploshed in some tinned tomatoes and seasoned them with the flamboyance I had learned from my favourite television chef, the Galloping Gourmet.

'Don't look,' I said. 'I'm about to add my secret ingredient.'

Eric shut his eyes while I snatched the mixed herbs from the spice rack and sprinkled a good pinch into the sauce.

'Did your mother teach you all this?' asked Eric.

I made a pained face.

'My mother could not cook to save her life.'

'So you just sort of . . . make it up as you go along?' asked Eric, very impressed.

'Sort of,' I said. 'Some of it, I pick up from the TV. But mainly, I think it's just natural talent. Get it from my uncle, I think.'

'What is he? A famous chef or something?'

'Not really sure,' I said. 'I've never actually met him – unless you count my christening. Apparently, he disgraced himself so badly my parents have never spoken to him since.'

'Wow!' said Talbot. 'What did he do?'

'Couldn't tell you exactly,' I said. ''Cos whenever I ask Mr Briggs – that's my father's best friend from when he was in the Midlands – he keeps changing the story. Suppose it's because I only ever see Mr Briggs at Christmas and he's always drunk, then.'

'But what does Mr Briggs say he did?'

'Oh, just performed a magic spell on me. Apparently.'

'Gosh.'

'It happened at my christening. I was just being blessed when my uncle turned up dressed like an African native in this huge red cloak.'

The sauce was now turning from vivid tinned-tomato scarlet to a more professional russet colour. I tasted it for seasoning and then put on the water to boil for the pasta.

'Well, come on, then,' Eric said, impatiently. 'What did he do?'

'Oh, just danced around the font, made a few chanting noises, sprinkled me with some sort of dust.'

'Magic dust, I expect.'

'Probably. And then he ran off.'

'And that was the last you ever saw of him?'

'Yup. Which is jolly unfair, considering he's my godfather and is meant to take me out to tea and give me presents and things. All I've ever got out of him is the odd postcard. And the book he left me at the christening.'

'Not much, is it?' said Eric, gazing distractedly through the kitchen's patio window.

'Well, it is quite a good book, I suppose. In fact it's probably the best one I've got. My uncle wrote it himself. I'll show you if you like.'

Eric was fast losing interest. His attention, as I'd dreaded, had now been drawn to the back garden.

'You've got a lot of sheds,' he observed.

'Fish houses, actually,' I said.

'*Fish* houses?'

'That's what my father does all day. When he's not at his garden centre. He breeds fish.'

'Can we see them after lunch?'

'You'll only have to see them again when Father gets home.'

Eric gazed across the lawn, beyond the fish houses, towards the line of trees at the end of the garden. 'Is that where your river is?'

'More of a stream, really.'

'Didn't you say it had a waterfall in it?'

'Not a waterfall. A weir covered in slimy green stuff.'

'Good for sliding down?'

'Only if you want to cut your leg open. Or get attacked by the rats or the leeches or the pike at the bottom.'

'Got a spare pair of trunks?'

'I thought you wanted to see my uncle's book,' I said, serving up the spaghetti.

'Did I?'

Eric enthused at length about the deliciousness of the sauce.

'I think it's called carbonara,' I said. 'Or maybe pomodoro. No. Can't be. That means apples.'

But after a few strenuous chews, he confessed to finding the spaghetti a little crunchy.

'It's meant to be,' I said. 'I've cooked it *al dente*. It's Italian for "hard as a tooth".'

He soldiered on, gabbling between mouthfuls about the prospects ahead of us. A long, long walk with the dogs. A tree-climbing session. A dip in the stream.

I went to fetch the book before Eric proposed any more exertions. *A Discourse on Divers Cuisines*, it was called. Not a particularly appetizing title, as Eric's yawn confirmed. And the fact that it was a leather-bound edition with no pictures in it didn't do much to encourage his interest either.

I showed Eric the dedication which my uncle had scrawled on the title page.

'To my dear Godson,' it said, 'in the earnest hope that you will succeed where I failed. Your loving uncle G.'

'What does that mean?'

'It stands for Gastronome. His real name is Xerxes Dante. He tells you how he got the nickname, I think, on page . . .' I started flicking through the book.

'I meant the bit about failing.'

'Don't know,' I said. 'But I 'spect it has something to do with The Dreadful Incident in the Sudan.'

'Sounds good. Read me that bit.'

'It's not in here,' I said. 'It must have been later. All I know is that it happened in the Sudan and it was pretty dreadful.'

Eric finished his last strings of spaghetti and made to leave the table. I kept him amused by reading him exciting extracts from the book. First the Gastronome's narrow escape from a crocodile while hunting with the Aborigines (Australia, 1956). Then the grisly account of the banquet in Shanghai (China, 1959) during which the Gastronome's hosts had sliced off the cranium of a living monkey and encouraged him to eat the contents as he would a boiled egg.

'Dis-*gusting*,' enthused Eric.

And the feast held in Bangui (Central Africa, 1960), hosted by someone called Bokassa, during which the Gastronome had complained, 'Waiter! There's a child in my soup.' But on discovering that the punchline of the story meant that my uncle had not, after all, got to taste any of his friend's cannibal dish, Eric decided he had had enough. The book was boring and he wanted to play.

Outside, the grass shrivelled, brown under the sun. The air was thick with noxious pollen. The trees lining the river bank shimmered in the haze. Below them, a pike waited for his prey. And, as he took another hay-fever pill and smeared himself with Factor 30, a reluctant twelve-year-old pondered bitterly on the sacrifices one must make in the name of friendship.

'Elbows!' barked Mother.

Eric, already intimidated by the dining room's grim opulence – dark green walls lined with murky portraits of Mother's ancestors, heavy antique walnut furniture, incomprehensible ranks of silver cutlery – and by the frigid dinner conversation, nervously whipped his arms off the table. From underneath came corpulent stirrings and a half-hearted bark.

My father and I ignored Mother completely. Father was unhappy. He had returned from a major fish show in Staffordshire with two guppy-breeding trophies (one for bottom swords, one for fan-tails) but nobody, save Eric, had expressed any interest. Then Mother had insisted he clean up the runny mess that one of the dogs had left on the drawing-room carpet. And to add insult to injury, she had forced to him to change into a dinner jacket. In protest he was immersing himself in a copy of *Practical Fishkeeping*.

I ignored Mother's remark for similar reasons. It was wantonly cruel to have made me dress up in my horrid velvet jacket when all poor

Eric had to wear for dinner were his jeans and tank top. And I wasn't going to let her get away with playing the stern disciplinarian, just because there were guests to impress.

Mother turned to the blushing Eric. 'At least somebody has some manners,' she said, adjusting her pearl choker. She couldn't possibly have been sincere. All through dinner I'd seen her watching Eric hold his knife like a pen. And now, though he'd emptied his plate, he hadn't put his knife and fork together.

'Would you care for some more salmon?' she asked him, trying to twist her mouth into a smile shape.

'Thanks, Mrs Fripp. That would be lovely,' said Eric treacherously.

With a rustle of raw silk, mother swept towards the hostess trolley and pulled out the platter of half-finished salmon. Even by her low standards, this one had plumbed new depths. The dyed pink flesh was so soggy and overcooked it had collapsed off the bone. When you chewed it, it made a sort of squeaking noise and lodged itself between your teeth. It tasted of wet dish-cloth.

Mother sploshed an extra large lump on Eric's plate.

'What about you, darling?' She was talking to my father. It was not a term of endearment but a euphemism. His real name was Barry.

Father, still engrossed in his fish hobbyist's journal, murmured, 'With you in a minute, love . . . Just reading about this new cure for white spot.'

I examined my salmon's skin for the tell-tale disease specks.

Eric shovelled his food quickly into his mouth. He was trying to avoid my mischievous smirk.

'Pass me some of that Mateus, would you, Giles,' said Father.

I pushed the bottle over. ('You can keep your Châteauneuf-du-Popes and your fancy Liebfraumilchs. You can't beat a good bottle of Mateus,' my father was fond of telling me.)

'Parss, darling,' corrected Mother. Virtually since her wedding day, she had been waging war against her husband's errant Black Country vowels. She and Father were early victims of the Sixties vogue for 'classless' alliances: strapping Midlands lad on the make, handsome in a big-boned, peasanty sort of way, meets plain, well-connected girl with no money and expensive habits to maintain. The mutual attraction had lasted just long enough for them to produce a child (a disappointment to both parties), after which they'd devoted their lives to avoiding each other as much as possible without resorting to divorce.

Father put down his magazine.

'Errol's grown quite a bit, hasn't he, love?' he said.

'I expect it's because he eats properly,' said Mother. 'Giles, you must have some more vegetables.'

In the Coalport dish lurked a mess of carrots boiled to a virtual purée.

'I'm not hungry,' I said.

'I'm not hungry what?' said Mother.

'I'm not hungry and they're overcooked.'

'Darling, did you hear what your son just said? He said those delicious carrots which I spent all day preparing are overcooked.'

'Giles,' growled Father, more out of duty than conviction.

'Well, it's true,' I said. 'They *are* overcooked. Anyway. You didn't spend all day preparing them. Mrs Leighton did it yesterday.'

'How . . . how . . .' blustered Mother. 'You're to apologize at once.'

'For telling the truth?'

'Darling, tell your son to apologize.'

'Giles, apologize to your mother.'

Across the table, Eric glanced at me imploringly.

'I don't see why I should,' I said. 'Eric's mother never cooks him rubbish like this. In fact,' I added, warming to my theme, 'it's so horrible, I'll bet even Daphne and Mortimer wouldn't touch it. Not that you'd give it them anyway. Cause we all know that all you ever feed them is bloody fillet steak.'

Eric reddened. Father drummed his fingers on the table. I froze. We waited for Mother's reaction.

For a moment, I deluded myself that the eerie wailing noise which had filled the room was coming from one of the dogs. But then I saw Mother's mouth was open.

'He swore at me,' she sobbed. 'Did you hear that? He swore at me.'

'That's it, young man,' said my father, rising from the table. 'You're coming with me.'

My buttocks had long ceased stinging and I'd almost fallen asleep by the time Eric joined me in my bedroom. He was looking unusually shifty.

'You all right?' he said.

'I'll live.' I pulled an agonized expression, just to show how bravely I was suffering the pain.

He sat on my bed.

'He hardly ever beats me, you know,' I spat. 'He was only doing it to humiliate me in front of you.'

Eric made soothing noises. I noticed that his sleeves were rolled up. They were wet at the top. Surely he hadn't been so creepy as to help wash the dishes?

'I've been waiting ages,' I said. 'Where have you been?'

'Oh, just downstairs,' he said cautiously. 'Your father said it wasn't a good idea to come and see you till you'd calmed down. And, er, he wanted to show me his fish collection.'

'Great,' I sneered.

'Yes, aren't they?' said Eric, completely missing the point. 'Especially the big one in the lounge . . . er . . . drawing room. The sea thingy . . .'

'The marine tank?'

'Yes. That's the one. It was quite funny, actually, because a wasp fell in while the top was off and this yellow and purple fish swam up and ate it.'

'The Cuban Hog,' I said without enthusiasm.

'And then there were the flat, bright yellow ones which eat all the green stuff; and those brilliant prawns that make shooting noises; and the octopus-type things at the bottom which the orange and white, erm, joker fish like to rub themselves against –'

'Lemon tangs; pistol shrimps, anemones and clowns,' I said.

'Didn't know you were so interested in stuff like that,' Eric said.

'I'm not. Nor would you be if your father had been boring on about it for the last twelve years.'

'Oh,' said Eric. 'Don't you like them at all?'

'Well, there is one good thing about them, I suppose. Mother absolutely hates them. Says they clash with all her antiques.'

Eric laughed nervously. And I realized why his arm was wet.

'You've been helping him clean the fish tanks!'

He reddened. 'Couldn't really say no, could I?'

'Easily,' I said, curling my lips in disgust. 'He's heard it enough times from me. As he probably told you.'

'He did mention something about how, er, he wished you'd take an interest in . . . something . . . instead of lounging around the house all day. But I'm sure he meant it in a nice way,' Eric floundered.

'No, he didn't. He thinks I'm useless. He's always going on about how lazy I am. Even wants me to work in one of his shops during the holidays. Doesn't he realize there are laws against exploiting child labour? And . . . and . . . now I'll bet he wishes that you were his son instead of me.'

'Nooo,' soothed Eric.

'Course he does,' I said. 'He wants someone big and strong to lug sacks of peat and fertilizer around. And someone who likes talking about football and rugger and stuff. I'll bet you did, didn't you? Bet you told him all about the first XV.'

'Only a bit.'

'See. So he does wish you were his son. And Mother probably does too. In fact, I know she does. Because you sucked up to her by being nice about those foul dogs and eating all her horrible cooking.'

'Well, I . . .' Eric stumbled as he thought of something consolatory.

'It's all right,' I went on sulkily. 'Maybe they're right. Maybe I am useless.'

Eric took the bait.

'Course you're not useless. You're good at loads of things.'

'Like what?'

'Er . . . well . . . English and History and Geography and –'

'Not much use if all your father wants you to be good at is Maths so you can be some boring accountant for his Garden Centres . . .'

'And . . . er . . . well, what about cooking? You're brilliant at that.'

'Only omelettes and spaghetti.'

'You could always ask the Gastronaut.'

'The Gastronome? But I don't even know him. I don't know where he lives or anything.'

'You could find out. What's there to lose? You could become a famous food explorer like him . . . or a chef . . . yes, why don't you become a chef? You could open your own restaurant. Or we could open one together, even.'

That night, Eric and I planned our great enterprise together. We couldn't agree on much, other than that it was going to be very, very good. The best in the world probably. So that we were almost certainly going to be very rich and famous.

Eric wanted a place specializing in steak and chips.

'Why?' I asked.

'Because they're my favourite,' he said.

And after thinking it over for a while, I decided I'd quite like a place specializing in fish.

'Is that your favourite, then?' he asked.

'Not really,' I said.

'Why, then?' he asked.

I smiled. In my mind were Technicolor visions of neons, red and blue within a golden soufflé; surgeon-fish dissected by the chef's knife; and prize-winning guppies, fan-tails and bottom swords, browning in a copper sauté-pan.

'Guess,' I said.

CHAPTER FIVE

Two days after the *Knob* launch party, I received a bank statement telling me that I was £1085 overdrawn, a letter warning that my mortgage was over £500 in arrears, another claiming that there was 'no editorial vacancy at present' on *Bon Vivant* magazine, and a summons to the deputy editor's office.

Tamsin had barely spoken to me since our dinner together. Neither of us had wanted to admit being in the wrong. I was so relieved at the prospect of making it up that I managed to assemble a broad grin as I burst through her office door.

But the grin collapsed the moment I met with Tamsin's icy stare.

'Andy doesn't like your piece,' she announced.

She was sitting stiffly behind her desk, puffing in frenetic bursts at one of her low-tar cigarettes. She'd adopted the habit for professional reasons and still smoked rather unconvincingly.

'Hello, Giles,' I said, since she obviously wasn't going to. 'How are you? Pretty awful, actually, Tamsin. How about you?'

Usually it worked. Tamsin would remember that the frosty I-may-look-like-a-pretty-girl-but-you'd-better-take-me-seriously act wasn't necessary with me. She'd smile self-consciously, apologize and make time for a bit of small talk.

Not today. She pursed her thin red lips and said, 'I'm serious, Giles. You're in deep trouble.'

With a sigh, I settled in the chair opposite her.

'I did try explaining to him. No one wants to do "Me and My Drug" after what happened to the first chap.'

My celebrity, the one who'd talked about his marijuana habit to plug his walk-on part in *The Bill*, had been arrested for possession of illicit substances. Released on bail, he had been interviewed by a tabloid journalist and had blamed my article for attracting the police's attention. He claimed he'd been tricked. The *Knob* journalist who had contacted him had sounded so clueless that he had thought it was one of his friends taking the mickey.

It had made my job extremely difficult. All I'd been able to come up with for the latest 'Me and My Drug' was a King's Road antique dealer who'd agreed to chat about how LSD had changed his views on High Victorian painting, provided I made it clear that the last time he'd taken it was in the Sixties. A dull read.

'Andy's not bothered about "Me and My Drug",' Tamsin said. 'He's passing it over to Sherman, anyway. It's your restaurant review he doesn't like.'

'What?' I was desperately proud of my review of Life's A Beach. 'Californian cuisine,' it began, 'the red nose on the clown of joke cooking.'

'He says California's *passé.*'

'But, Tamsin, you saw for yourself. Waiters on rollerblades. Weird food. How much trendier can you get?'

'He says California went out eighteen months ago. About the time *Zed* did a big number on it.'

'Eighteen months? It's bound to have come back into fashion by now.'

I searched Tamsin's eyes for a trace of sympathy. They stared back, dark and remorseless.

'He also says,' she said, pausing for a quick pull on her cigarette, 'that you've completely ignored this month's theme.'

She was referring to Andy's latest stupid idea. From now on every issue was going to have a theme. Future editions would deal with 'Political Correctness', 'Decadence' and – would you believe it – 'Death'. This month's theme was . . .

'Dangerous sports?' I spluttered. 'How the hell was I supposed to find a restaurant which had anything to do with that?'

'You had plenty of notice.'

I clenched my fists in exasperation. Surely Tamsin could see what an impossible task this was? But no. She was more concerned with the tiny fleck of ash which had floated on to the sleeve of her pale silk jacket. She brushed it off and waited for my response.

'Couldn't we just renose the intro?' I suggested. 'Begin with – I don't know – some line about California being a jolly sporty, dangerous sort of place?'

'I don't think it'll wash, Giles.'

'Oh, come on,' I pleaded. 'There's all that surfing they do over there. And then there's the riots and the fires and the drive-by shootings – and there's the sharks. Yes. What about them? Millions and millions of them swimming about in the ocean.'

Tamsin was unimpressed. She claimed that I was exaggerating.

'Hardly,' I said. 'Look at what happened to Rupert on his ludicrous diving holiday. He was almost gobbled up by a bloody great man-eater.'

'No, he wasn't,' said Tamsin softly.

'What?'

For the first time, a faint smile appeared on Tamsin's lips.

'Andy's idea,' she said. 'Sea-lions and kelp didn't sound all that threatening so we got Rupert to spice up his copy with a great white shark encounter.'

It was hard to tell from Tamsin's matter-of-fact tone what she thought of Andy. Though I'd tried, several times, to encourage her to have a good moan about him, she wouldn't take the bait. In my darker moments, I had even wondered whether the malicious rumours about their late-night meetings were true.

Her job, she said, was not to criticize the editor's decisions but to see they were efficiently executed.

'And you approve of this?' I asked. 'You think we should all tell lies just to make our prose more readable?'

Tamsin considered this for a moment.

'I don't like to think of it as lying,' she said. 'More . . . judicious tweaking.'

'But it's so unethical,' I said.

'It sells copies.'

'Sales,' I huffed. 'Is that all anyone thinks about these days? Whatever happened to quality? Or integrity?'

Tamsin smiled thinly.

'I really don't know why I bother,' I said. 'It's perfectly obvious my talents are wasted on this magazine. I've got an imbecile for an editor. Imbeciles for colleagues too' – Tamsin stirred slightly – 'apart from you, obviously . . . I'm on a starvation wage . . .'

'And you think it would be better anywhere else?'

'It certainly couldn't be worse.'

'You reckon?' Tamsin stroked the ornamental spike on her desk. 'Would you rather be back at the *Courier*?'

'That was different. I was young. Desperate. I wanted to get on. I'm hardly in the same position now.'

Tamsin replied with slow emphasis. 'You're in exactly the same position.'

'Oh, come on.'

'You can't have forgotten, surely? Remember that first review you did for Cowan? The one where –'

I cut her short. I hardly needed reminding about that shameful episode.

'I'll do it,' I said.

'Knew you'd see sense.'

Provided I came up with a suitable replacement by lunchtime tomorrow, she said, my job was safe. So I listened as she suggested a few avenues I might explore. Dangerous sports clubs, for example. 'Meals on chutes? Underwater dining?' I suggested. I was joking, but Tamsin seemed to think both of these were valid possibilities.

'Then,' she continued, 'there's the option of risky food. That Japanese fish, for example.'

'The fugu,' I said.

'So,' she said, 'you've got the idea by now. You know what Andy wants.'

'Yes,' I said bitterly. 'Another Stronzo.'

I spent an hour fruitlessly pursuing Tamsin's suggestions. But the secretaries of the parachuting, mountaineering, caving and hanggliding associations I rang all assured me that their hobbies were dangerous enough for their members not to seek further hazards when dining out.

Exhausted, I put off my pursuit of the deadly fugu while I took a coffee break. With no time to pop downstairs for something drinkable, I had to make do with the caffeinated dish water from the machine near Andy's office.

I went through my post. Press releases mostly, all of which I binned. I saved the two handwritten letters and the cardboard-wrapped package till last. The former, which I hoped might be fan mail or job offers, turned out to be letters demanding to know Stronzo's address. Like the previous ones I'd received, these went in the bin. The package too was disappointing. Another stupendously dull review copy – *Memoirs of a Boar-Hunting Man*. I was about to toss it on to a growing pile which included *Green Cuisine*, *Cooking with Flowers*, *Salads for Fun and Profit* and *Rock of Ages: A History of Salt* – when it struck me that here was a way of killing at least half an hour.

On page 127 there was a good picture of the author, a frightening-looking bearded fellow, displaying a gaping wound he had sustained on an ill-fated hunt in the Cévennes. Below it was another juicy image from the same expedition. It showed an enormous black boar, fur stiff, jaws flecked with foam and blood, surrounded by the bodies of dogs which it had gored in its death throes.

Pity the author lived in France, because he might have been able to give me a few useful leads.

At the back of my head, the voice of conscience whined, *No, Giles. Remember all the trouble you got yourself into last time.*

I reminded the voice that, far from getting me into trouble, it had earned me the editor's praise.

Only because he thought Stronzo existed. He won't make the same mistake twice.

It's a risk I'll have to take. Where else am I going to find him a restaurant he likes?

The fugu. Try the fugu.

It's bound to have been written up in *Zed*, *Montage*, *Insignia* or *Thrust*.

But your integrity! How can you prostitute your talents in this way?

Watch me.

I turned on my computer. Created a file. And wrote.

Hunters

There are many candidates for the coveted title Most Hazardous Restaurant in Britain. One could, no doubt, make a good case for the Stornaway Sub-Forties, the select, underwater dining society which meets, once a month, on a Scottish wreck site 40 feet below the surface to sup on (soggy) 'neaps and tatties'. Or for Flying Tonight, the airborne restaurant which circles above Grimsby every Friday, serving fish and chips to skydivers who, according to custom, must consume their supper before they pull the rip-cord. And yes, before I get any angry letters complaining about its omission, I should give an honourable mention to Haute Cuisine, the picturesque Lake District establishment which requires its clientele to climb for their dinner: starters are lodged on a shelf 50 feet up a crag; main courses at 100 feet; and puddings at the top.

Not being the outdoors type myself, I am unable to vouch for any of these restaurants. What I can do, however, is nominate as strong a contender for the title as any of the above. Located deep in a forest, just north of Abergavenny, it combines the thrill of the chase with the pleasure of pick-your-own. Its name is Hunters and its house rules are simple: you are only allowed to eat what you have first killed.

Rob Hunter, the hairy, bearded giant of a proprietor/cook/gamewarden is a stickler in this respect. He maintains a dim view of the weedy would-be outdoorsmen who flock to his remote wooden lodge each weekend.

Woe betide the slacker tempted to snatch a few more minutes' sleep after the 4 a.m. wake-up call. With one powerful arm, Hunter will upturn your bed and boot you out into the forest. There, you must scavenge for your breakfast, praying the while that you don't run into any of the boars which Hunter keeps on his estate (surrounded, for safety's sake, by a 20-foot-high electric fence).

'The second most dangerous beasts on my land', as Hunter describes them. He points to a chart illustrating wild boar, ranging from the young *marcassin*, with its stripy light and dark brown fur, to the *solitaire*, a hefty, swarthy tusker.

'And anyone know what the most dangerous animal of all is?' Hunter continues. 'You?' suggested one wag, whom we nicknamed the Jester. He would come to regret his flippancy. Hunter waited for the nervous laughter to die down. 'You,' he said, stabbing the Jester's chest with his trigger finger.

It was not until midnight that Hunter finally completed our induction course. His scrupulousness owed less, I suspected, to concern for our welfare than for his personal liability. Sure enough, he closed his lecture on safety and hunting procedure by handing us a form to sign. It indemnified Hunter against any responsibility for death or accident, whether by tusk or bullet, negligence or incompetence.

At 6 a.m. we were out on the forest trail, trying to

keep up with a pair of yapping dogs as they sniffed the boars' scents. How we had envied these hounds their biscuit breakfast. All we'd eaten since our arrival was a couple of mushrooms somebody had scavenged. They didn't go very far, divided six ways. The Jester had brought some Kendal Mint Cake, which he was just about to share round when Hunter confiscated it.

What we ate in the next twenty-four hours would depend on our hunting skills. Were we to bag a boar early enough, Hunter promised, there would be sufficient time to prepare a ragout. Any later than midday and, by the time we'd finished gutting it, all we'd end up with would be a boar steak. None of us dared quibble at the prospect of eating game which had not been properly hung.

'A hungry hunter,' we had been told, 'is an accurate hunter.' If only I had been given the chance to prove it. By lunchtime, our party of six must have walked at least ten miles on steep, slippery tracks, without the merest glimpse of a *sanglier*. I wondered whether these alleged wild boars had been invented by the proprietor as part of an elaborate hoax.

Suddenly, as we were moving forward in line formation, I heard an excited whisper from my left. The Jester had spotted something 'large and bristly' in the undergrowth. 'Wait!' hissed Hunter. But the Jester wasn't going to starve any longer. He fired wildly at his target. There was an agonized animal cry. And at once, we all began to cheer. All of us save Hunter, who sharply reminded us that there were few things more deadly than a wounded boar.

We cowered behind the nearest available trees, while Hunter advanced, rifle at the ready, to finish off our supper. There was another shot! He'd done it! The cheering resumed, louder than before. It reached a fortissimo as Hunter reappeared, dragging something – a 150-pounder at least – behind him. And then the cheering stopped. We had killed one of Hunter's cherished hounds.

There was to be no more boar hunting today. With

the butt of his rifle, Hunter drove us back to the lodge. We took it in turns to carry the dead dog, which was to be given a proper burial.

Dinner that night was a bleak affair. Hunter tucked into pâté and roast boar. We ate nothing. But we were too scared to drive home, lest Hunter did something truly dreadful.

At last he finished his dinner and turned to my group. 'Gentlemen,' he said, 'you may think me a harsh man, but I am also a fair one. You have, I hope, learned your lesson by now. And it pains me to see you all starve, when you have paid £150 for the privilege of dining here.'

With that, he disappeared into his kitchen and emerged with a steaming casserole. No sooner had he ladled it into our plates than we had eaten it.

'Not such a bad chap, after all,' muttered the Jester. 'No,' someone agreed. 'It's not as if we didn't know the rules. You know, about only being allowed to eat what you've killed.'

Hunter must have overheard, for he stood over us, beaming, and said, 'But I *never* break my own rules.'

———————

CHAPTER SIX

I had no difficulty guessing who, out of the handful of people waiting on the platform of Exeter St Davids to meet the mid-morning express from Oxford, was my uncle. Only one of them stood six foot five in his scuffed brown brogues, weighed in at around 18 stone, and wore a red-and-white Arab *keffiyeh* on his head. As he squinted at the newly disgorged passengers, my first instinct was to pretend to be part of the family of three who had sat in my compartment. Surely it wasn't too late to change my mind?

But as I shuffled closer to the ticket barrier, I couldn't resist risking a sidelong glance at those faded, shapeless cords, the belly which forced at the buttons of a faded Viyella shirt, and the grizzled chins scarred with fresh shaving wounds, wobbling beneath fat, sensuous lips, full cheeks and a bulbous nose. Our eyes met.

'Giles,' he boomed, walking towards me and squeezing my shoulder. He shook me like a bear trying to decide whether its prey is still alive. 'You are Giles, aren't you? Course you are,' he said. 'See you ended up with Bella's looks. Poor bugger!'

He grabbed my overnight bag and led me briskly to his old Daimler.

We drove, alarmingly quickly, through the Exeter traffic, out past the ring road and on to the winding, narrow, high-hedged lanes leading to his village.

'Hungry?' he asked. 'I'll say! You're all skin and bones. Bella's cooking, I'll warrant. Here. Have an apple.'

He reached under his seat and passed me a wasp-gnawed specimen. It looked as if something might still be living in it.

'Want something more substantial?' he barked. 'Try the glove pocket.'

Fortunately, the catch was stuck.

The car veered from side to side as he tried to open it.

Inside, on a side-plate sticky with congealed dripping, sat a hunk of crimson meat.

'That should keep you alive till we get to Jebel Mara.'

The meat was almost raw.

'Hell's bells!' said the Gastronome, aghast. 'You're not one of those bloody vegetarians?'

I shook my head weakly.

'Then grab a chunk before I force it down you!'

I ripped off the smallest bit I could and gnawed. Despite the off-puttingly salty taste and sanguineous texture, it was more tender and succulent a piece of beef than ever I had experienced. A revelation, in fact.

'Pass me some while you're at it. Don't fiddle about. Just give me the rest.'

We chomped noisily, the blood trickling down our chins.

'I've never eaten beef quite this pink before,' I confessed.

The Gastronome frowned. 'Perhaps you're right. I think I left it just a smidgen too long in the oven.'

I appeared to have passed my first test.

The Gastronome waxed lyrical about the home he had bought two years before. Remote from prying busybodies; mature orchard – apples, pears, even the odd peach in a good summer; a copse nearby teeming with blewits, ceps and puffballs; a pond on which he was hoping to establish a colony of ducks and geese – '*à la gavade*, of course,' he observed.

'Of course.'

'Not a patch on France. But given that one has to live in this benighted land – which my publisher insists I do if m'book's going to come to anything –'

'The sequel to *A Discourse on Divers Cuisines*?'

'A sequel? To that pile of tosh?'

'I thought it was rather good. In fact –' I was going to say it was one of the main reasons I'd responded to his invitation. It had arrived on a postcard which, luckily, I'd found before my parents.

'How old are you?'

'Thirteen,' I said.

'And you have the gall to tell me whether my writing's any good or not?'

The Gastronome snorted and shook his head.

'If I tell you that I've spent the last thirteen years trying to forget about that damned book, will you have the decency not to mention it ever again?'

The rest of the journey passed in silence.

The Gastronome's house, half a mile from a hamlet called Tor Cross, sat squat and mouldy like a block of Stilton. The whitewashed walls were turning green; there were holes in the slate roof; several of the windows had been cracked and crudely repaired with brown masking tape. I could see no sign of the fabled orchard or pond because the garden was overgrown with brambles, nettles and giant rhubarb.

Outside the heavy front door, as he fumbled in his pockets for his keys, the Gastronome noticed a hole in one of his windows.

'Wretches!' he said. 'Their parents' fault, of course. Filling their heads with stories about what the fat man will do to 'em if they misbehave.'

We entered a gloomy corridor lined with maps and watercolours of foreign scenes and, having dumped my suitcase at the foot of the stairs – 'We'll sort out your bedding later' – he pushed open a door at the end.

From inside came simultaneously a rush of heat and a complex range of scents – the pungent whiff of high game and ripe cheese, a warm beany aroma, the smell of exotic herbs and spices – which intensified as we entered the kitchen.

It was a vast room. It would probably have looked even bigger had every crevice and corner not been jam-packed with culinary equipment. At its centre stood an oak table crawling with unwashed pots, pans and cutlery. Set into one wall was a fire, with a spit stretched across its glowing embers. From the ceiling hung rows of copper pots, capable of holding everything from an ant to a whole water buffalo, giant legs of ham, dead pheasants and rabbits. The walls were lined with racks housing knives, large and small, serrated and razor-edged, for filleting, chopping, dicing, gutting, pricking, slicing and disembowelling. Ranged on sturdy shelves were jars containing honeys, jams and pickles in every colour from lime green, banana yellow and mandarin to crimson, purple and black.

'Sit,' commanded the Gastronome, pointing at a rustic wooden chair.

He lumbered purposefully towards the Aga and opened one of the lower doors. Using a filthy tea towel, he pulled out an earthenware pot and removed the lid.

He bashed the surface of the stew with a wooden spoon, replaced the lid and put it back in the oven.

'One,' he counted. 'Now,' he said, wheeling round. 'What would you care to drink? An aperitif, perhaps? Or shall we move straight on to red?'

I would impress him with the knowledge I had gleaned from my father.

'Do you have any Mateus?' I asked.

The Gastronome looked puzzled. Then it dawned on him. 'Oho,' he laughed. 'Trying to catch me out with one of those obscure Chilean varietals? Sorry. In this household, it's French or nothing. And since this week I am essaying the cuisine of the Languedoc and the Roussillon, I think we might try a – yes, why not? – a Château de Nouvelles.'

After a foray into his cellar and a challenging search for a corkscrew and two clean glasses, my uncle joined me at the table.

'Your health,' he toasted, swirling the wine round his glass and sniffing at the rim.

I copied him.

He sipped his wine pensively. 'Not an especial favourite, Fitou, but it will suffice for the moment, don't you think?'

It must have gone straight to my head because I soon lost track of what my uncle was saying. Every now and then, he would break off from his puzzling speech about *cépages*, *appellations*, bouquets, length and finish, Carignan, Syrah, Mourvèdre and Grenache to visit the oven, where he repeated the mysterious process with the wooden spoon.

'You do like cassoulet, don't you?' he asked suddenly.

'Oh yes.'

He took a long draught of wine and smacked his lips.

'You're not just saying that to please me?'

He still looked slightly wary. 'Just that when you mentioned that book – yes, I know we don't talk about it, but since you brought it up I might as well explain. That book represents a period of my life which I am trying to forget. A time of decadence. Of depravity, even.'

He eyed me shrewdly.

'Let's just say, shall we, that I thought you had come here under false pretences. Expecting me to be someone I no longer am. Perhaps you hoped to be stirred by tales of "antres vast and deserts idle. Of men that do each other eat, of anthropophagi."'

'Actually, I sort of hoped you might teach me a little bit about . . . um . . . food.'

'But what sort of food? Did you hope to sup on juicy dorado

bladder with its sapid tang of ocean spray and urine? Or blackened strips of Atabascan fire newt griddled over fragrant mesquite wood? Or blood drunk fresh, rich and warm from the pulsing neck of an ox as the Maasai do? Or a bouillon of Seychellois fruit bat, its wings leathery yet tender?'

'Well . . .'

'I know what you young fellas are like. Never satisfied with the classical. Yearning for the rare, the exotic . . . the forbidden . . . Convinced that somewhere over the horizon, just waiting to be savoured by you and you alone, is that special dish. The Dish That Dare Not Speak Its Name. Am I right? Course I am.'

He made his final journey to the oven and slopped the cassoulet into two bowls.

'Do you believe in magic?'

I took a reluctant mouthful. It looked like something the dogs had brought up. That, at least, was what I thought until I tasted my first mouthful.

'I take it the answer's yes?'

'But . . . it's just . . . amazing!' I stammered. 'I mean . . . how do you . . . ?'

'I dare say the unimaginative might claim it was in all in the ingredients. The best lingots — soaked overnight — cooked just so, firm to the bite, yet just soft enough to meld with the confit d'oie and to set off that savoury tang, that grainy meat which you'll only find in the finest Toulouse sausage. And they'd be right, up to a point — if you had any idea of the trouble I have getting the right ingredients. Can't even find 'em in Exeter, for heaven's sake — but trust me, boy, this dish is never as good without that final touch.'

'The magic?'

He nodded.

As we worked our way through the cassoulet — the Gastronome refilled his bowl twice, but I could only manage one helping as it was so rich — he expounded dreamily on the origins of the dish. Invented by the Spanish and Romans; perfected 'inevitably' by the French who had given us the Holy Trinity of Cassoulets. 'Le Père — that's Castelnaudary; Le Fils — Toulouse, and Le Saint Esprit — Carcassonne.'

'Only in France,' mused the Gastronome, 'would they elevate a simple peasant dish like this to a religion. And, as in all religions, they have their schisms. In this case, it concerns the addition of mutton. Some, like Prosper Montagné, would have you believe that it is indispensable. To me, however, there is no place in *le vrai* cassoulet for any meat but sausage, pork rinds, goose and – at a push – duck, as I shall point out in no uncertain terms when I come to write my book.'

'It's just about French food, then?' I ventured.

'Are you suggesting it's not a fit subject for a book?'

'Not at all.'

'Thirteen years it has taken me to research this book. And yes it is "just" about French food.'

'I didn't mean to –'

'Don't you see? It's exactly that form of . . . of ignorance I am fighting against. I hear it from my publisher. From my agent. Is it any wonder I go out so little when all the world wants to talk about is *ethnic* food, about *trends,* about *A* bloody *Discourse on Divers Cuisines*?'

The Gastronome banged his fist on the table. A tottering pile of saucepans cascaded noisily on to the floor.

I made to pick them up.

'Leave it,' said the Gastronome. He studied me wistfully.

'Forgive me, Giles. You're not to know the agonies which this book has caused me. It was worse at the beginning, of course. My first few months in France seemed to last an eternity. I'd be sitting in some auberge, chomping my way through the prix fixe – gésiers de canard, perhaps, or a succulent boeuf en daube – and I'd find myself wishing I was in the Moroccan fleapit across the esplanade, supping on couscous or – if I was really lucky – a sheep's eyeball. But I couldn't, you see. I knew that that one sheep's eyeball would be the first step to perdition. So I stuck with those gésiers and that boeuf en daube. And little by little, the longing dwindled until one day, I awoke to find myself salivating at the prospect of my next French luncheon. A true, honest, French luncheon. Omelette nature. Cassoulet. Tarte Tatin. Good Lord, that reminds me.'

The Gastronome went to the fridge, removed a circular baking tray and put it in the oven.

'Now,' he said. 'Salad?'

This comprised three green leaves apiece in a sort of oil-and-vinegar soup. As we ate (with forks and spoons), he told me more about his project. It was to write the definitive guide to the Cuisine of France, set out region by region, heavy on anecdotes, imperatives and historical detail, light on fiddly weights and measures.

'Had the most fearful rows with my agent about that one, I can tell you,' he said. 'Silly woman wants to bring in some ghastly inter-fering food technician to convert everything into litres and what not. I ask you. Did Boulestin have to put up with that? Did Brillat-Savarin? Did Taillevent?'

The Gastronome slapped the table.

'Course not. And d'you know why? Because they understood, as I do, that cooking is not a science. It's an art. And that is why it's quite impossible for me to teach you how to cook. But what I can teach you, my dear boy,' he added, 'is something infinitely more valuable. The Art of Good Taste.'

That night, in a dank, musty bedroom, between mildewed sheets, I dreamed of my new-found loves; of cassoulet and Tarte Tatin; of honeys – sainfoin, lavender, thyme and pine – such as my uncle had shared with me at tea-time, on home-made bread toasted before the fire which I helped him kindle with the pages of *Cuisine Minceur* (a whole stack of which the Gastronome had bought for just this pur-pose); of dinner's moules farcies and a garlicky fish casserole called bourride; of fine white wine ('Never tried a Premier Cru Chablis? Then, just this once we'll forgo the niceties of research and skip the Picpoul de Pinet'); and of rasping Arabica so strong I had to wreck it (so my uncle griped) with three spoonfuls of sugar.

The sun had long risen when the Gastronome shook me awake. Downstairs, in a clearing amid the dirty pots and pans, I found a 'modest breakfast' of herby, home-made sausages, dry cured bacon, scrambled eggs, fried bread, grilled tomatoes, piles of toast and a pot of hot Darjeeling.

The Gastronome was oddly melancholy over breakfast. He grew even more disconsolate when I asked whether he couldn't drop me back at the station in time to catch the midday train as my parents were expecting me back by late afternoon. They believed I was staying with Eric.

He sent me into the sitting room to stoke the fire. He'd be with me in a moment

After a few minutes of dutiful prodding with the poker, I decided to have a nose round the room. Already, the Gastronome had shown me his library of rare first editions – early cookbooks mainly – and his souvenirs from his foreign travels (an ebony devil's head from the Upper Volta; a Pygmy quiver made out of spotted Zairean jungle-cat; an Aboriginal crocodile painting; the bright, South American Indian rug disguising the threadbare sofa). But for some reason he'd by-passed the photographs on the wall above his writing desk.

I soon saw why. The early ones – in which he beamed, slim, tall and handsome, from school-team portraits – were a sad reminder of how much he'd gone to pot. And the later ones, snapped in sundry foreign locations, were too embarrassing. The Chinese Mao suit and the black Vietnamese pyjamas weren't so bad, though they were obviously too small; and I suppose he looked dashing enough in his flowing Arab jellaba; but the African ones were plain awful. Especially the one where he towered above a gaggle of Pygmies, dressed, like them, in nothing but a loincloth. And as for the one which showed his tribal scars – hideous whorls carved on to his stomach, presumably by one of the similarly disfigured natives standing next to him – it hurt to look at it. I'd just moved quickly on to an out-of-focus picture dominated by a black splodge where someone had put their thumb over the lens when I felt a presence behind me.

'It's the only one I have of him,' said the Gastronome.

I studied the picture more closely.

Behind the splodge, you could just make out the head of a smiling boy with darkish skin and tightly curled black hair. The Gastronome, wearing a toga-like garment, had an arm draped over his shoulder.

'Can't have been much older than you when that was taken.'

'Was he a good friend of yours?'

'My friend, my guide. And in all my travels, by far the most faithful companion I met. Ibrahim is his name. Or rather was.'

I turned round. The Gastronome was dabbing at the corner of his eye with a dirty spotted handkerchief.

'Would you rather not talk about it?'

'I *must* talk about it. But, first, I think you should sit down.'

I sat on the sofa. The Gastronome warmed his back by the fire.

'Perhaps I should begin by telling you how my book came about. You may think that what I have to say is irrelevant. The ramblings of a disappointed old man. But let me tell you, Giles, that it is vital you listen to me if you are not to make the same mistakes as I did . . .'

He had started working on *A Discourse on Divers Cuisines* in the summer of '52, just after leaving Wellingborough.

'Grim times indeed. And I ain't talking about rationing. That was bad, but worse – much, much worse – was to come. I'd seen the writing on the wall during the war, when the GIs came over with their chocolate and bubblegum . . .'

He winced.

'. . . and the promise of a threat to our freedom almost as great as the Nazi menace they helped us defeat. I refer, of course, to the hamburger. The thick shake. Convenience food. Pre-packaged dinners, embalmed with preservatives and wrapped in plastic. What I foresaw, Giles, was the death of all that I held most dear.'

He gazed out of the window, misty-eyed for a few seconds, before pulling himself together.

'That was when I resolved to do my bit to stop it. Like the monks of the Dark Ages, I would transcribe the world's finest recipes before they were trampled underfoot and forgotten by the New Barbarians.'

He had started out, full of high hopes, with a modest advance from a publisher. On a two-year tour of Europe, he managed to track down what he believed were the ur-recipes for osso bucco, paella, kleftiko and boeuf bourguignon.

'But there came a time when I began to grow weary of these delights. My palate had grown jaded. I must travel further afield in search of more challenging fare. But do you know something? No matter how exotic the dish – be it the hottest curry, the spiciest sambal, however rare or barbarically bizarre its ingredients – it was not enough. Never enough! I wanted hotter, spicier, rarer, stranger.'

'The Dish That Dare Not Speak Its Name?'

The Gastronome pursed his lips and nodded.

'It was, in retrospect, a quest that could never be fulfilled. My publisher saw this long before I did. And bugger me if one day – I'm just in the middle of my Northern African phase, quite my favourite bit of my travels because by now I've met dear little Ibrahim – bugger me if my publisher doesn't turn up on my doorstep. If I don't polish off the book *tout de suite*, he says, he's going to want his advance back . . .'

I made noises to the effect that this was extremely unreasonable.

'Well, that put me in a bit of a quandary. You see, it so happens that a few days before, I'm hanging around the Royal Geographical Society when I bump into this fellow who gives me this rather useful lead. In the Western Sudan, so his story goes, there's this tribe fabled for their cuisine. Like nothing else on earth, he says. And if I were to pay a visit to this mountainous region by the name of Jebel Mara –'

'The place you named this house after?'

'Just so . . . Anyway. As you'll imagine, my first instinct was to forget the publisher and trog off to Jebel Mara straight away. Problem was, by now I didn't have a penny to my name. No book, no Jebel Mara. So, of course, I dash off the manuscript in a couple of months. My publisher likes it. And after a lot of grovelling, I manage to get him to advance me enough money for the sequel. And, the minute he does, though I'm feeling pretty rotten from a dose of flu your wretched mother's given me, I make a beeline for Egypt. Back to little Ibrahim who has been working as a tourist guide at Giza. Bloody waste, of course. D'you know that boy could speak seven languages? And that's not counting all the Arabic dialects. Soon as I'd scraped enough moolah together I was going to pay for him to have a proper education. And a damned fine career he'd have had ahead of him. So brave! So intelligent! So handsome! That boy, Giles, was destined for –'

The Gastronome cut himself short.

'Or he would have been if I hadn't dragged him along on that half-baked expedition . . . You see, Giles, as so many times before, I was tilting at windmills. We got to Jebel Mara sure enough. We found the tribe too. And a pretty rum bunch they were.'

He looked at me for a moment, as if trying to decide whether to elaborate.

'But I'll spare you the details. Suffice to say that they were splendid from an anthropological point of view, but distinctly lacking on the gastronomic front. Couldn't find hide nor hair of this fabled cuisine of theirs. So back down the volcano young Ibrahim and I went.'

'What volcano?' I was beginning to feel a little cheated. Instinct told me that the Gastronome was editing out the exciting bits.

'Eh? Oh. This tribe lived slap bang in the middle of a volcano.'

'Didn't they get a bit hot?'

'An *extinct* volcano,' he said.

'And this tribe . . . what were they called?'

'The Gonda.'

'The *Gonda*?' No wonder he was getting so touchy. He was making it all up as he went along.

'Somethin' funny about that?'

'Er . . . no. I was . . . I was just thinking that, um, I could do something on them for my geography project next term.'

'You'd be wasting your time. You won't find anyone who's heard of 'em.'

'Oh.'

'Wiped out. Every man jack of 'em. Your mother's fault . . . Now –'

'It was *Mother's* fault?'

'Yes, your mother's fault,' he snapped. 'Now will you stop asking any more of your damned fool questions?'

I bit my lip.

'The point was,' continued the Gastronome, 'my mission, to all intents and purposes, had been a failure. Not that I saw it that way at first. Any time spent in the company of dear little Ibo, I reasoned, could not be counted a waste.'

He sighed.

'And then, as we were making our way down the volcano, it happened. Just a few rocks at first. Then a few more. Bigger this time. And suddenly, half the bloody mountain was falling down on top of us.'

'An avalanche!' I enthused.

'The avalanche,' said the Gastronome slowly, 'that crushed the life out of my little Ibrahim.'

There was a long silence, broken only by the spitting of the logs in the fire and the Gastronome's stertorous breathing.

'It was my fault,' he whispered at last. 'All my fault.'

'But . . . it wasn't really your fault . . . I mean . . . avalanches . . .'

'Are acts of God?' The Gastronome shook his head. 'No, dear boy. I was to blame. If it hadn't been for that idiotic quest of mine, he'd never have been there. And it was that terrible knowledge which drove me to the brink of madness.'

He stared blankly into the fire. I glanced at the clock on the mantelpiece. If we left it much longer, I was going to miss my train. But I still had an important question to ask. The problem was how to raise it tactfully.

'Uncle.'

'Mm?'

'Was it when you were on the . . . um . . . brink of madness that you came to my christening?'

His eyes narrowed.

'Might have been. Why do you ask?'

'Oh . . . nothing really . . . it's just that, well, um . . . somebody told me . . . and, and I'm sure they got it completely wrong . . . but they said you were behaving a bit . . . oddly.'

'Did they, now?'

57

'So . . . er . . . I was sort of wondering . . . what were you doing . . . exactly?'

'Giles, it was really so long ago that –'

'Was it,' I persisted, 'some sort of magic spell?'

Only with difficulty, I could see, was my uncle resisting the urge to explode.

He jabbed a log viciously with a poker.

'I . . . I . . . have simply no idea what was going through my head at that time. Maybe it was a spell . . . or maybe . . . maybe . . .'

'If' – I was treading on very, very thin ice now – 'If it was a spell, can you remember what sort it might have been?'

'I think,' said the Gastronome, 'that's quite enough questions for one morning, don't you?'

'But –'

'Enough, damn it!' He flung the poker on to the stone flags by the fire. It landed with a dull clang.

'You've . . .' the Gastronome began to pace in angry circles, 'you've completely missed the point of my story, haven't you? Completely missed the point?'

'I . . . I didn't mean to . . .'

'The point about that bloody story,' he growled, 'is that the only sort of magic you should ever concern yourself with, Giles Fripp, are the seven whacks a chef gives with his spoon to the crust of well-made cassoulet!'

CHAPTER SEVEN

'Don't say it,' I hissed.'Whatever you do, *don't say it!*'

It had taken the waiter an hour just to bring our starter. At this rate, we wouldn't escape before midnight.

'But I want one,' said Rodney, petulantly sloshing his spoon around his bowl of watery clam chowder. He glanced over his shoulder. 'Where is the bastard?'

'It's only a garnish, for God's sake.'

'It's a point of principle,' said Rodney. 'Would you go to Mont Saint-Michel without trying one of Mère Poulet's omelettes?'

'She's dead.'

'You know what I'm getting at.'

'But omelettes are edible.'

'And flies aren't?'

'Now you're being stupid.'

'Waiter! WAITER!'

I speared another morsel of the slimy, orangey-pink flesh masquerading as smoked salmon. I was not remotely hungry. But I had seen what happened to those diners foolish enough to leave a full plate.

Three hours earlier, our cab had pulled up in a dilapidated stucco street at the seedier end of Ladbroke Grove. If it hadn't been for the queue of people snaking down into the stone stairwell, we might have missed the entrance altogether.

'Some sort of club, is it?' the cabbie asked as I paid the fare.

'A restaurant,' I said.

The taxi driver raised his eyebrows and jerked his head back to where Rodney lay slumped in the back of the cab, clutching a hip flask.

'He going to keep his dinner down?'

'You don't come here for the food,' I said. And as if on cue, a queasy-looking fellow in a grey pinstripe staggered up the stairs and retched violently into the gutter.

'Charming,' observed the cabbie.

I asked for a blank receipt.

Once I had coaxed Rodney out of the taxi, we joined the queue. It resembled those you see in the West End late on a Friday night: whispering couples, boisterous lads in designer sportswear, flashy young execs in expensive suits. Many of them were speculating as to whether Stronzo really was as bad as their friends had made out.

'Come on,' said Rodney, partially revived by the fresh air. 'We don't have to put up with this.'

He tugged me towards the doorway.

''Ere. You on the guest list?' grumbled someone as we brushed past.

'We *are* the guest list,' replied Rodney, with worrying conviction.

Before setting out, we had fortified ourselves with a bottle or two of Pomerol. Light-headed, I had mentioned one of my stranger theories as to Stronzo's genesis. Rodney had seized on it with great enthusiasm.

'You know, Giles,' he said, gazing into the inky depths of his glass, 'if you played your cards right, you could be drinking this stuff every day for the rest of your life.'

'Mm-hmm?' I too was examining the wine for colour and clarity. A difficult task since by now everything was looking rather blurred.

'All you've got to do is prove these Stronzo people stole your idea. Then you can sue 'em for breach of copyright.'

'And who's going to pay the legal fees?'

'You could get one of those no win, no fee lawyers.'

'If my case was strong enough, maybe.'

'Cast iron, if you ask me.'

'The problem is, Rodney, the jury won't be reaching their verdict after three bottles of Bordeaux.'

Experience had taught me to take extra care whenever Rodney became enthusiastic about something. Indeed, I was beginning to wonder whether we shouldn't call off the trip to Stronzo, lest he do something stupid.

It was, in retrospect, a mistake opening a fourth bottle. Not only did it propel Rodney towards that level of drunkenness where he often became obstinate and unpredictable. But it also dulled my senses sufficiently for me to mention my other theory about Stronzo. The one I'd vowed never to divulge.

'What if it was more complicated than just plagiarism? What if it was something even weirder than that?'

Though Rodney knew about the Gastronome and the events at my christening, he had always pooh-poohed the notion that I might have inherited a special gift from my uncle. He'd seen precious little evidence of it so far.

What I hadn't mentioned before was the curious business of the café I had invented for the school magazine. And this, as far as Rodney was concerned, was the clincher.

'Just think,' he murmured, staring at the ceiling, his glass balanced on his chest. 'Anything you've ever wanted could be yours. Anything at all. Paf! Just like that.' As he gesticulated, the wine toppled on to my carpet.

'So you've changed your mind about suing Stronzo?' I asked, as I poured salt on the crimson stain.

'Eh? Oh. No need. This way's going to be much much easier. Like, say you wanted – I don't know – what do you want?'

'A clean carpet?'

'Think big!'

'Lots of clean carpets?'

'All right. Well, all you've got to do is write in your next column "And when I got home, what should I find but lots and lots of expensive, clean, deep-pile carpets."'

'What have carpets got to do with restaurants?'

'You can weave them in. Subtly. "The one thing that spoiled my dinner at this expensive restaurant was its hideous carpets. Frankly I would have been better off staying at home where . . ."'

I groaned.

'Just a suggestion. You could get all sorts of things like that. TVs. Video-recorders. Kitchen equipment. And wine of course. Loads and loads of wine.'

'Ah yes. I could write, "And blow me if I didn't have a rather wonderful surprise waiting for me on my doorstep. A case of 1947 Cheval Blanc."'

'Now you're getting the idea.'

'I was being sarcastic.'

'You got your restaurant.'

'But Stronzo *exists*.'

And its very existence was what finally convinced me of the sheer idiocy of my magic theory. How could I possibly have created something so solid? So real?

The people who cursed as we barged our way to the front of the queue were real. As was the black-painted door with the ornate gold 'S' at the bottom of the stairs. And the frustrated would-be diners congregating by the silken rope. And the doorman who was now saying to Rodney with very genuine menace, 'Oi. Can't you see there's a queue?'

He was a good six inches taller than Rodney. Blond. Muscular. Square-jawed. Had he been an actor, he would have specialized in Nazi villains.

'Suppose I were to tell you that my friend here invented this restaurant?'

The Nazi wrinkled his nose in distaste. 'I'd say you were drunk, cock. Now piss off. The pair of you.'

'Maybe we should,' I suggested, edging towards the exit.

'Shut up, Giles,' said Rodney. He fixed the doorman with a haughty stare. 'We're not going until we've seen the manager.'

'I am the manager. And if you don't go right now –'

'Giles Fripp,' said Rodney crisply, 'would never have put an abusive, supercilious oaf like you in charge of one of his restaurants.'

'Giles who?'

'Never mind that. Just get Mr Stronzo. At once.'

The doorman was unsure what he was meant to do. Unwilling to leave his post, he tried catching the attention of one of his colleagues. But Stronzo's rudeness training had not been wasted. They completely ignored him.

Having taken an imprint of my credit card – Rodney had conveniently forgotten to bring his – the doorman let us through the barrier.

The next staging post was the bar.

The stools, impossible not to slide off unless you had spectacular buttock control, afforded a reasonable vantage point from which to observe the dining area.

Rodney withdrew a crumpled piece of paper from his inside pocket.

'Aluminium tables. Rude waiters. Disgusting food –'

'Put it away.'

Rodney tasted his Bloody Mary and nodded with satisfaction. He consulted my review: 'Devoid of celery salt, dry sherry, Tabasco or Worcestershire sauce.'

I snatched the paper from his hand.

Rodney shrugged. 'Coincidence?'

'Obviously.'

'Him too?' Rodney nodded towards the trestle table near the kitchen hatch, where a dishevelled individual was garnishing the soup bowls with flies.

'And him?'

We watched the proprietor buzzing from table to table like an angry wasp. He was small, greasy and balding. He had a down-turned mouth which glistened with spittle. I was sure I'd never seen him before. But the odd thing was, he looked exactly like the Guido Stronzo I'd imagined when writing my piece.

Even the details I hadn't mentioned in the review seemed uncannily familiar: the peeling wallpaper, the cockroaches scurrying beneath the diners' feet, the layout of the bar and tables. It was as if I had re-entered an old dreamscape.

'Maybe I have been here before,' I suggested. 'Maybe the experience was so terrible I blanked it out.'

'Maybe,' said Rodney, deeply sceptical.

I sighed. 'All right. Suppose I did have these magic powers. Why would I waste them on somewhere as horrible as this?'

'Who am I to judge the workings of your warped psyche?'

'Come on! It stands for everything I hate. It's even worse than one of Eric Talbot's places.'

From nearby came a shriek of outrage.

Stronzo was venting his spleen on a young woman who had complained about her casserole.

'Of course it is vegetarian!' he screamed. 'It has carrots in it, no?'

The woman whimpered something back.

'Meat stock? Of course it is made with meat stock! How you expect it to taste of anything if it is not made with meat stock? Stupid bitch!'

'Another couple down,' said Rodney, as the tearful woman was led away by her boyfriend. 'Shouldn't be long, now.'

'I've had enough,' I said, making to leave.

'Giles, I risked my life to get you in.'

'Well, I'm sorry but I've got better things to do than sit here being poisoned and insulted.'

'We should be so lucky.'

'You want to be poisoned and insulted?'

'I don't know why I'm explaining the rules – you invented them – but that's the whole point of coming here. It's a challenge. Can you stay the course? Or will you end up skulking out half-way through like that worthless, snivelling, boring, cowardly couple?'

Rodney was still in the middle of his first course when I realized quite how seriously he was taking these 'rules'. I had already finished my smoked salmon – less through hunger than terror of what might happen to me if I didn't – when our waiter finally deigned to reappear.

'What?' he snapped.

'You forgot my fly.'

'Tough.'

'If you don't bring my fly right now, I'll tell Mr Stronzo that you have been polite and efficient.'

The threat worked. The waiter returned with a bowl of flies and a liquidizer, into which he emptied the clam chowder. Then he added a handful of flies and whizzed them into a crimson, foaming pulp. He slopped it into Rodney's soup dish.

The waiter flounced off, clearly confident that there would be no more trouble from this particular table.

'Wait!' said Rodney. 'I haven't checked it for seasoning.'

I looked at him in disbelief. So did the waiter. Rodney dipped his spoon into the black-flecked redness and raised it threateningly to his mouth.

'Don't!' I pleaded.

'I was just kidding,' said the waiter. 'Let me get you something else.'

Rodney shook his head, an evil smile on his lips.

I turned away. But I couldn't shut out the muted slurp as the fly-and-clam chowder went in; nor Rodney's ostentatious belch; nor the gagging noise made by the waiter, just before he hurried off, clutching his mouth.

'Was that really necessary?' I asked, struggling to control my nausea.

'Absolutely,' said Rodney, wiping his mouth. 'We've got to show these scumbags we mean business. It'll strengthen our hand at the negotiating table.'

Rodney had been thinking. It made no difference whether I'd conjured Stronzo from thin air, or whether it was simply a case of plagiarism. Someone, he had concluded, was making a fortune from my genius.

I suppose it was the 'genius' bit which kept me listening.

'As you said yourself, this place is ten times worse than anything Eric Talbot could have dreamed up. And a thousand times more profitable. All we have to do is grab our share of the takings and –'

'We?'

'Management fee. Face it, Giles. If you'd been left to your own devices, you wouldn't stand to make a penny.'

Rodney's plan was simple. I would continue to devise imaginary restaurants, making sure someone witnessed the date on which I had written my reviews. Then, when the restaurants appeared, I would present my evidence to the alleged owners and demand my cut of the profits.

This, he added, was the worst-case scenario. If my powers were as effective as he believed, there would be no need to bother with the restaurant side at all. A brief mention of, say, the £16 million I had won during a roll-over week in the National Lottery would suffice.

'That settles it, then,' I said. 'We needn't stay in this roach pit a second longer.'

'Not necessarily. There's always the worst, worst-case scenario.'

'Which is?'

'We'll cross that bridge if we come to it.'

And we did come to it. Just after our waiter had brought our main courses – two slabs of carbonated meat.

'Excuse me,' said Rodney. 'We wanted our steak well done.'

'So?'

'It *is* well done.'

'Stronzo's orders. We've changed our policy since that tosspot wrote his review.'

'That tosspot happens to be –'

I kicked Rodney hard under the table.

'Just what we wanted. Thank you.'

'No, it isn't. Bring Mr Stronzo. At once.'

'My pleasure.'

'Er, Rodney. I think we should leave.'

'Trust me. I know what I'm doing.'

I scanned the room for an escape route. There was certainly no way I could get past the doorman. And there did not appear to be any fire exits. The kitchen was the only possibility. It was sure to have its own entrance.

I picked up my jacket and made quickly towards it. But I hadn't gone far when I noticed three grim-faced figures moving swiftly towards me. In the middle was Stronzo; flanking him were the waiter and a long-haired man in a chef's uniform with – he was now so close I could see his pectoral muscles rippling underneath – the name Jules embroidered on the front.

I retreated to my chair.

'You wish to complain, yes?' asked Stronzo.

'I . . . I think there's been a dreadful mistake,' I said, regarding the pair of anacondas writhing under Jules's sleeves.

'No, there hasn't,' said Rodney. 'You owe us an explanation.'

'Not at all,' I said. 'If we could just have the bill –'

'We're not paying them a penny,' said Rodney. 'Now look here, Mr Bastard, or whatever your real name is. My friend Giles here is an important restaurant critic. And you owe him a great deal of money.'

'I do not understand,' said Stronzo.

'Don't pretend you don't know,' said Rodney. 'If it wasn't for *Knob*, this place wouldn't exist.'

'*Knob*?' said Stronzo, exchanging an evil smile with Jules. 'Now I remember. I remember it well. So does Jules. You said his cooking was not so good.'

Jules nodded.

'Look,' I said, 'I'm really, really sorry if I misrepresented –'

'Please,' said Stronzo. 'It is I who must apologize.'

'That's all right,' said Rodney. 'Pull up a chair and we'll come to an arrangement.'

Stronzo chuckled raspingly.

'I heard about the flies. Your friend, he has a good sense of humour, no?'

I nodded.

'But my chef, my waiter, and I, Guido Stronzo, we do not.'

The back of my neck was raw. My arm, which had been half-twisted out of its socket, ached horribly. And my buttocks glowed from the hefty kick with which, ignoring my squeals for mercy, Jules had propelled me brutally down on to the pavement, bruising my right shoulder and grazing my hand.

I turned my attention to the battered, limp form at my feet. When I kicked it, it shuddered slightly. Thank God. The last thing I needed was to spend all evening in a casualty ward. I bent down and gave it a vigorous shake. Rodney groaned. I hauled him up, pleased to see he was even more bruised and bedraggled than I was.

I had half a mind to toss him back into the gutter and leave the vultures to pick at his bones. But innate generosity prevailed. Pulling one of his arms around my shoulder, I heaved him along the street and dumped him on some steps.

We sat there in silence while I recovered my breath. Rodney stirred back into life.

'You idiot,' I said. 'You stupid, stupid idiot. What the hell did you have to go and do that for?'

'What do you mean?' he mumbled. 'They were scared shitless.'

'I'd hate to see them when they were feeling brave.'

'Giles, I promise you,' he said. 'We had 'em by the balls. All we need to do now is go back –'

'Are you mad?' I screeched. 'Are you completely off your head? They'll murder us!'

'Not if you tell them what you'll do.'

'Oh yes? And what will I do?'

'Kill 'em. Kill 'em all. Just write a piece saying how Stronzo gets burned down in a terrible fire and . . . Hey, where are you going?'

The bruise on my shoulder had metamorphosed from deep purple through pale yellow to a dull grey, and the scabs had almost dropped from my grazed hand, when I came upon two pieces of evidence suggesting that maybe, just maybe, I had been wrong to dismiss Rodney's magic theory so hastily.

The first was an outraged *Daily Mail* article with the headline, 'It's Come to This!' It described how a white male waiter had applied for a job at a restaurant in Bath only to be rejected because he wasn't black.

The second was when I tried ringing the number which had been printed beneath my review of the same restaurant. A voice at the other end answered in Latin.

CHAPTER EIGHT

Lucullus

'*Accipe Lucullo,*' said the man in the purple toga.

'*Er ... tavola per due persone?*' suggested my companion.

'*Tabula duobus?*' corrected the maître d'. '*Certe, magister.*'

'Must have got the wrong dialect,' my companion, who fancied himself as a bit of a linguist, muttered in my ear.

'Wrong millennium, actually,' I explained. For Lucullus is the only restaurant specializing in Neapolitan cuisine from the first century BC.

The dining area is situated in a russet-roofed, pillared cloister, surrounding a courtyard in which fountains play and exotic fish swim. There are no windows to protect customers from inclement weather, but they are kept warm by braziers which, *caveat emptor*, have been known to smoke out the restaurant when the wind is blowing in the wrong direction.

There are no proper tables. Instead, diners recline on couches, picking with their fingers (Roman cuisine predates the fork) at the delicacies which are served on metal platters. Though I found that eating while recumbent can play havoc with the digestive system, and though – despite the finger bowls – one's hands soon become frightfully messy, I suppose it pays to do things properly. When in Rome ...

The menu – painstakingly inscribed in Latin and English on a slate – struck me as being highly authentic. Too authentic, judging by the response of my companion.

'Dormouse? Hedgehog? Fried cicadas? I thought the Romans were civilized.'

'Wait till you try the garum,' I warned.

If there is anything that illustrates the gap between Roman tastes and our own, it is this extraordinarily unappetizing condiment, made from the fermented juices of decomposing fish. The Romans smothered their food with the stuff to disguise the flavour of rotten meat.

The version at Lucullus, apparently derived from a mackerel-based Carthaginian recipe, tasted appropriately disgusting. I suppose the nearest equivalent to its briny, anchovy tang is the nuoc mam sauce used in Vietnamese cuisine.

My companion chose to forgo this pleasure, but grudgingly agreed to sprinkle his dishes with the Romans' other favourite condiment, asafoetida. To my taste, this resinous Oriental plant extract is even worse than garum. Despite its pleasant odour of extra-strong garlic (the Germans call it *Teufelsdreck* – 'devil's dung'), its bitterness tends to overwhelm all other flavours.

But on to the dishes themselves, conveyed to our couch by a muscular, bare-chested, dark-skinned gentleman got up as a Nubian slave. (I foresee trouble with the Commission for Racial Equality here.) He said nothing, partly for reasons of authenticity, partly – one assumes – because his Latin wasn't up to much.

The cicadas were more unpleasant to look at than they were to eat. If you can get over the awful crunching noise the insects make when you chew them, you might be pleasantly surprised by their chickeny flavour. My companion contented himself with a bowl of green olives.

Offal next. And yet again, my companion cheated – this time by opting for the foie gras. Maybe the Romans were the first to feed their geese *à la gavade*, but I did think that an original menu like this called for a little more adventurousness.

My own warm terrine of pike liver, pheasant brains, peacock brains, flamingo tongues and lamprey roe, struck a suitably decadent note. Flamingo tongues, as everyone knows, are almost impossible to get right. Cook them too long and they lose that delicately fishy flavour; too little and they turn out hard and tend to lodge in your throat. The chef at Lucullus had timed his tongues perfectly, though a little more of that green pike's liver would not have gone amiss.

Baked hedgehog, which I selected from the abundant meat platter heaved, from couch to couch, on the shoulders of the 'Nubian slave', is an unfairly maligned dish. At its best — as the Romans and later the Romanies recognized — the hedgehog has a savour which happily unites the gaminess of wild rabbit with the sweetness of suckling pig. Sadly, the one at Lucullus was a disappointment. The quality of the meat was indisputable. But, oh dear, the chef had gone overboard with the garum.

Infinitely more satisfying was the chestnut-fattened dormouse, roasted and coated in an unctuous sauce of honey and poppy seeds. The restaurant breeds its own mice in special mud containers, feeding them through holes too small to let them escape. Let's hope the practice catches on, because the intense flavour — hare is the closest I can think of — is well worth the effort involved.

My companion spoke very highly of his fillet of young fig-fed sow. Its diet, he said, had perfumed the tender flesh to an 'unimaginably divine' degree, though he found the cream sauce in which it was drenched just a little too rich. This, it must be said, is a common drawback in late Roman cuisine. Dieting was not high on the list of their priorities.

By this stage, neither of us felt able to contemplate a pudding, though the purple-togaed maître d' was most persuasive. He said, if my schoolboy Latin serves me correctly, that we were welcome to vomit up what we had just eaten and start all over again. He meant well, but we decided not to take him up on his suggestion. To console him, we nibbled at a few lumps of hard cheese, flavoured with powdered thyme.

There is little to say about the wine list except that variety and quality have been sacrificed for authenticity. We were assured that our pitcher of chilled red wine — heady, heavily spiced and so thick I had to break my usual habit and water it down — had been made in traditional fashion from the finest pre-phylloxera Sicilian grapes.

At least, at £5 a pitcher, the wine is inexpensive. The food is not. Put it down, if you will, to the cost of importing flamingo tongues, or of employing fluent Latin speakers, but I fear that – at £187 for two – this is a restaurant which will send all but the fattest wallets into decline and fall.

Lucullus welcomes bulimics.

Of course, I knew it couldn't last for ever. One day, Andy would decide regretfully that the joke had gone on long enough. But that moment was still far hence. I could tell from the impressive pile of correspondence on my desk.

The letters asking for further details as to the whereabouts of Stronzo or Hunters went straight in the bin. Those congratulating me on the liveliness of my copy would – if I could spare the effort – receive a polite formal reply.

I tried to spin out my letter-opening session as long as possible. Then I scanned the morning papers to see whether anyone had followed up my reviews. This had become a habit since I'd chanced upon a clueless tabloid diary item which repeated, almost verbatim, the paragraph about the airborne, underwater and clifftop restaurants in my Hunters review.

The dailies dealt with, I might have gone on to look at the latest issue of *Zed*. But I was put off by its cover story: 'Eric Talbot: We Lift the Lid on Britain's Culinary Sex Pot'.

Time to do the crossword.

Today's was a really fiendish one. Eight across. 'Bird found in ring of fire?' Eight letters. What kind of clue was that? A hidden word maybe?

'Rupert.'

Rupert shuddered. For some reason he had grown quite edgy of late. He would react violently whenever there was a sudden noise. Telephone calls were the worst. I was getting a little bored with picking him up off the floor whenever the phone rang.

He looked up from his keyboard, wild-eyed.

'Is there a bird called a "Ringoffi"?'

'Probably,' he said.

I pencilled it in, uncomfortably aware that he was still staring at me. This was another thing that had begun to get on my nerves. He had grown almost pathetically eager to please me, as if his job depended on it. I would have preferred him as he used to be, cold and aloof.

'Giles?'

'Yes.'

'W-would you mind awfully having a look at my copy?'

'I'm a bit busy right now.'

'I'd be very grateful. It's just that I'm not sure whether I've struck the right note and, well, you seem to know what it is Andy's after.'

'Go on, then. Send it over.'

I read through Rupert's account of his latest jaunt. It was called 'Sarajevo High Society: Glamour amid the Ruins'.

Rupert fidgeted so much it was difficult to concentrate.

'Is it all right?' he asked, when I'd finished.

'Fine,' I said. 'But you could probably lose all those paragraphs about this Count Stanislaw's genealogy.'

'Righto.'

'Then there's his morphine problem. You don't go into enough detail.'

'Ah, well, you see, he's a frightfully nice chap and if his family were to hear . . .'

'Do his family pay your salary?'

Rupert shook his head.

'And the bit at the end. It's not at all clear what happened when you both drove over the mine. Did he die?'

'Fortunately no but –'

'Make him die. In detail. More poignant.'

'You think?'

'I know.'

'Thanks, Giles.'

'Not at all . . . oh, hello, Jessica, Aurora.'

'Hi, Giles,' simpered Aurora. 'We were wondering whether you were fixed for lunch.'

'Love to, but as you can see I'm tied up right now. Monday week, maybe?'

Now. Where was I? Two down . . .

Behind me there was a cough. Now the chief sub had come to pester me.

'You've forgotten the contact address for your review. *Again.*'

I didn't like his tone and told him as much by staring pointedly at the crossword.

'Are you going to give me this address or not?'

I pondered this at suitably irritating length.

'Give me five minutes.'

When the sub had stomped off, I typed out an address. 'Number One, Pump Room Cloisters, Bath, Avon.' Bath did have a Pump Room, didn't it? Then I looked up the code – 01225 – and invented a six-figure number.

It occurred to me that when I next saw Andy I could suggest a useful cost-cutting measure. In the overstaffed subs' department.

Andy was always finding some feeble pretext to invite me into his office. Today, he wanted to introduce me to his 'new friends'.

One, a frizzy-haired brunette with emerald-green eyes, was perched on his knee. The other, a sultry, coffee-coloured girl, leant against the back of his chair.

'Jaffa. Fluffy. Meet my star columnist.'

Jaffa surveyed me imperiously. Fluffy yawned.

'Up you get, sugar pops,' said Andy, squeezing Fluffy's bottom. 'Can't have you missing your beauty sleep.'

Before the girls left, Andy handed each of them a fat envelope.

'Don't even think about it,' said Andy, mistaking my indulgent smile for a leer. 'They're well out of your league.'

'I'm sure.'

'Course, if you were really keen, we could probably come to some sort of arrangement.'

'They'd eat me for breakfast,' I said, blushing.

'You wish.'

However great our *rapprochement* over the last few weeks, there remained a cultural gulf between Andy and myself which no amount of alcohol-induced mateyness could quite bridge. I had recognized this one night at the Groucho Club when, debilitated by too many Gimlets, I had accompanied Andy to the gents for 'a quick sharpener'. One expensive sneeze later, I had decided that cocaine was a drug best left to the professionals. On another evening, I had endeavoured to introduce Andy to the pleasures of steak tartare. He had ordered it 'well done'.

Still, my lessons had not been completely wasted on him. His shelves were now laden with a choice selection of fine spirits. Highland,

73

Lowland and Islay single malts. XO Cognac. Andy had blagged them all from the manufacturers, supposedly as prizes for reader competitions.

'Vodka?'

'Why not.'

He opened his miniature fridge. 'Lemon grass? Buffalo? Chilli? Or Stolly?'

'Stolichnaya.'

He pulled the frozen bottle from the freezer compartment, together with two frosted tumblers. They steamed as he filled them with the syrupy spirit.

'To Jaffa and Fluffy!' Andy toasted.

We downed our drinks in one.

Andy lit a cigarette.

'Had quite a job clearing them with accounts.'

'You got them on expenses?' I wasn't sure whether to be shocked or impressed.

Andy shook his head. 'On the pay roll. New column starting next month. "Celebrity shag".'

Apparently, the Geezer had been so delighted with the latest circulation figures – 200,000 and rising – that he had given Andy more money to spend on hiring and firing. Jaffa and Fluffy were the latest recruits. Each month, they would try to bed as many famous people as they could. Then they would write up their adventures in juicy detail. Or rather – since literature was not their forte – I would.

'Why me?'

'You've earned it. I'm well pleased with the way your reviews are going. So's the Geezer. Sent me some very complimentary E-mail about your Roman place.'

'That was quick.'

Andy nodded. 'Spooks me out, I can tell you. He's usually read your copy before I have.'

'How come?'

'Remote access.'

I might have inquired further, but Andy had moved on. He was telling me about his night out with the girls.

'Started out at that new Italian joint. You know, the one run by your mate.'

'CuFu.'

'That's the one. Incredible place. They've got this –'

'I know. I've read all about it. Everywhere.'

'Yeah. Pity, really. It might have been quite nice to give it a plug. Eric being a friend of yours and everything.'

'Wouldn't that defeat the object of the exercise?' I said.

'Eh?'

It was a shame Andy refused to discuss business outside office hours. Not just because it had prevented my taking advantage of his inebriated state to discuss my pitiful salary, but because I'd never been able to ascertain how much he knew about my restaurants.

'Well . . .' I chose my words with care. 'You know . . . being . . . *inventive*. I mean, surely the whole point about what we're doing at the moment is that none of the opposition can possibly get there before us.'

'Funny you should say that.'

Andy pushed a copy of *Zed* across his desk. 'Check out their food pages.'

I flicked past the paean to Britain's brightest restaurateur. Blinked. And looked at the page again to make sure I had seen what I thought I'd seen.

'Bloody hell!'

They'd made it into a two-page spread. One side was taken up with a picture of an enormous bearded man carrying a rifle. At his feet were a dead boar and a couple of liver-coloured hunting dogs. On the other side, someone called Susannah Hobbs had composed a long interview with the man in the picture. A man who, so the story claimed, was none other than Rob Hunter, the pioneer of pick-your-own-boar farming.

'What d'you reckon?' Andy beamed. 'Desperate or what?'

'I'll say.'

It confirmed my profound cynicism about journalism. Surely *Zed* had discovered that my original piece was a hoax. Yet they'd actually chosen to promulgate the lie by dressing somebody up as Rob Hunter and rigging a fake interview. Why they'd gone to all the bother, I couldn't imagine. And I certainly wasn't going to speculate in front of Andy. Especially not now that I had thought of a rather useful opening.

'In fact,' I said, as nonchalantly as I could manage, 'they're so desperate, they actually rang me the other day.'

I paused to allow the significance of this to register. Andy made a bad job of looking unconcerned.

'Nothing concrete as yet. Just a . . .' I searched for the right phrase, 'a baseball figure.'

'Ball park,' said Andy.

'Right. But I'm really not sure whether they were serious or not.' I was buying time while I thought up something suitable. Couldn't be too greedy. Then again, I did have a cellar to maintain.

'How much?'

'Twenty K,' I said. A nice touch, the 'K' bit. It was the sort of language Andy understood.

'I'm sure we can match it,' said Andy.

Damn! Should have gone for twenty-five.

'Expenses,' I said. 'That was the other thing we talked about.'

'And?'

'Well, you might have noticed that I haven't put in for my last three reviews and I was wondering –'

'Sure,' said Andy, apparently relieved. 'Bung 'em in when you want.'

'There is a slight problem, though,' I said.

'Yes?'

'No receipts.'

'Well, it's OK by me if you file without. But I might get a few funny questions from accounts. Tell you what. There's quite a useful print shop just off Marsh Wall and er . . .'

I nodded. He didn't need to say any more.

'Great!' Andy rubbed his hands. 'What do you reckon? Couple more Stollys and a bite to eat?'

'Lunching with Tamsin, I'm afraid. I'm already late.'

Andy was hurt.

'Better not keep you, then.'

I rose to leave.

'And Giles . . .'

'Mm?'

'Mind she doesn't bitch about me.'

'Not getting on?'

'Thought you knew,' he said. 'Everyone else seems to.'

'What?'

'We split up last week.'

'I'd almost given up on you,' said Tamsin, killing her cigarette. Before I could apologize, she'd grabbed her jacket and was accelerating out of her office towards the lift. I just made it inside before the door swished shut.

Tamsin stabbed the ground-floor button and huffed impatiently all the way down.

'Easy,' I said. 'We've plenty of time.'

'You may have,' she said tersely.

It was all I could do to keep up as she scuttled determinedly across the marble-floored atrium. She sped on until we reached the shopping arcade at the western end of Canary Wharf, where we stopped for a breather.

'Booked us somewhere nice?' I asked.

'Mm-hm,' said Tamsin, lightening up a touch. 'Charming riverside location. Dining al fresco. And very reasonably priced.'

'Brilliant!'

Tamsin turned to look at the menu of a nearby sandwich bar.

'Well?' she said. 'What are you having?'

'But I've just had some really good news. And I thought we might . . .'

Tamsin was already ordering.

'One mixed salad, no dressing, one Perrier and – Giles?'

I clutched my pastrami and mustard, prawn and avocado and roast beef sandwiches, and breathlessly pursued Tamsin as she bustled down one of the paths leading to the river. Because it was a sunny day, all the benches were occupied by *Knob* employees. We sat on the edge of the dock and kicked our heels above the turgid, oily waters of the Thames.

'So,' said Tamsin, picking at her leaves, 'what's this good news?'

'Well,' I said through a mouthful of sandwich, 'as long as you don't tell anyone.'

'Spit it out.'

'I've just got myself a pay rise.'

'How much?'

'I'm not sure that I –'

'*How much?*'

'Twenty,' I whispered.

Tamsin let out a stream of curses.

'I thought you'd be pleased for me.'

Tamsin glanced behind her. The Rock editor and the Dangerous Sports and Fast Cars editor were feigning extreme interest in the fisherman casting his line just to our right. Tamsin lowered her voice.

'What are *they* going to think if they find out? Working their balls off while you . . .' She shook her head. 'Just what is going on between you two?'

'I don't know why you're getting so upset. It was you who told me to suck up to him.'

'That,' said Tamsin, 'was before I'd seen where he was taking the magazine.'

Against my better judgement, I muttered, 'Before you split up with him, you mean.'

Tamsin whipped round to face me.

'Say that again,' she commanded.

I stuffed my mouth with more sandwich.

Tamsin reached furiously for a cigarette.

'When have you *ever* known me to mix business with pleasure?' she asked.

The sandwich bite went down my throat in a dry lump.

'All I meant was that . . . er . . . Andy can't be doing all *that* badly. I mean, for one thing, sales are well up.'

'Short-term blip. Always happens after a relaunch. It's subscriptions you should look at. They've gone through the floor.'

'Give it time.'

'It'll only get worse. There're already far too many magazines competing for the same niche.'

'Andy seems to have plenty of ideas.'

'Too many. It's bang! bang! bang! Change this. Change that. The mag's got no identity. It's just a collection of gimmicks.' Tamsin gestured despairingly. 'Celebrity fucking Shag, indeed! Little wonder staff morale's hit rock bottom. And as for poor Rupert . . . !'

'He's doing rather well.'

'Are you blind? He's about to have a nervous breakdown!'

'Maybe you should tell Andy.'

'He wouldn't listen when we were an item. He's hardly going to now.'

Tamsin flicked her cigarette into the river. A water rat swam past the butt and clambered on to the wall below our feet.

'At least when the crunch comes,' she added softly, 'everyone will know that I've had nothing to do with it. *You* on the other hand . . .'

Tamsin regarded me darkly.

'Let's just say that there have been rumours going round about your copy.'

'It's that bloody sub, isn't it?'

'I'm not naming names.'

'The shit! Don't listen to him, Tamsin. He's got it in for me.'

'So there's nothing in these rumours?'

'Of course there isn't . . . I mean . . . Come on . . . You're not seriously going to take his word over mine?'

Only after staring at me hard for what seemed like thirty seconds did Tamsin reply.

'I'm wasting my time,' she said.

We threw away our lunch wrappers and sauntered back towards the office.

'By the way,' said Tamsin, 'how was Bath?'

'Bath?' I said. 'I haven't been there in ages.'

Tamsin nodded grimly.

Before returning to the office, I paid a trip to the printer on Marsh Wall. He provided me with three sheafs of blank restaurant receipts, printed on stiff card and complete with VAT numbers and plausible letterheadings. I only wanted one of each; but he couldn't do them in batches of less than fifty. Stronzo was printed in aggressive, trendy type on red card; and Lucullus, in Roman-style lettering with 'V's substituted for 'U's, on a white background. Hunters presented a bit more of a problem.

'Not much call for boars,' he said. 'Pig do you?'

The result wasn't wholly convincing. To me it looked very much like a pig's head with two tusks superimposed on it. But I was sure such niceties wouldn't trouble the accounts department.

CHAPTER NINE

The inaugural tasting session of the Wellingborough Wine Society was not what its founder, G. Fripp, Esq., had hoped when he dreamed it up during a particularly dull French lesson.

Although, naturally, I had secured myself the plum job of president, with the title of secretary going to my scholarly chum, Horatio Burgess (whose distinguished nose alone qualified him well for the task, I thought), I was galled to find that all the executive and legislative power had been devolved to the society's unelected chairman, Mr Drought (pronounced Drew).

I suppose it was inevitable, really. Any school society involving something so volatile and dangerous as alcohol had to have a master in charge. But if I had had any choice in the matter, I would certainly not have opted for a chairman as small-minded as the school's third-string French teacher (you know the sort: good on grammar; an atrocious accent; not much cop above O level standard).

I should have guessed that things were going to go awry when Horatio, Mr Drought and I met to plan our first meeting. Even a simple matter like choosing which vintages we should taste turned out to be far more difficult than I had ever expected.

To set the ball rolling, Mr Drought suggested that we each put forward a few thematic options for the first few tastings. This seemed a perfectly reasonable idea, so I composed a list guaranteed to enlighten the palates of the large numbers of boys who had expressed an interest in joining the society.

I jotted down a few obvious ones. Week One: The Côte de Nuit; Week Two: The Côte de Beaune. That should start things off nicely. A few complex reds to separate the wheat from the chaff. Some of the applicants for membership, I felt sure, had joined the society under the delusion that it was going to be some sort of grand piss-up.

I carried on scribbling. Week Three: White Burgundy – Meursault, a couple of Montrachet villages (I doubted our budget could run to

Montrachet itself); Week Four: Back to the reds: Claret One; Week Five: Claret Two: By now I was getting into my stride. Week Six: Alsace – Gewürztraminer, Muscat, Pinot Gris; Week Seven: Côtes du Rhône Un: Châteauneuf-du-Pape and its prelates (witty, eh?); Week Eight: Côtes du Rhône Deux: the masterly Côte Rôtie (on which I considered myself quite an expert. I had tasted a bottle once *chez* Le Gastronome).

Looking up from my adventurous programme notes, I saw that Horatio had completed his own, rather simple-looking list of suggestions.

Mr Drought cleared his throat.

'When our resident Hugh Johnson has finished . . .' he quipped. I stopped writing. '. . . Good. Let's start, then. Burgess. You first.'

'Yes, well, um, I don't know as much about wine as, um, Fripp does, sir, but I had an idea we might start with some champagne. There's more than one sort, isn't there?'

'There is. Continue.'

'Well, I thought that would make a nice start. Then I thought we might taste some Bordeaux; then some claret.'

'It's the same thing, Horatio,' I interrupted.

'Oh, is it? Well, in that case, we'll taste the Bordeaux and the claret at the same time. Then maybe move on to a bit of German, a bit of Spanish, and, um, some white.'

'Good. Good. I can see that the next few weeks' lessons are not going to be wasted. And what about our young Master of Wine?'

Ignoring his sarcasm, I languidly began to reel off my suggestions. 'And it's not quite finished yet,' I said, rounding off my list. 'In Week Eight, I thought it might be time for a little Côte Rôtie,' I rolled the 'r' flamboyantly in a way that I thought would make Mr Drought just a little envious.

'Côte Rôtie,' he repeated, pronouncing his 'r' as you would for the English word roast. 'From the Rhône, isn't it?'

'Yes, sir. The upper region. Near Vienne.' I had done my homework.

'I see.' He paused for effect. 'A little *ambitious*, isn't it, this list?'

'Yes, I suppose it is, sir.' And then, trying to say the sort of thing that schoolmasters like to hear, I added, 'But you see, I wanted to make it quite clear what this society is about. It's about learning; about good wine; about developing taste. It's not about getting drunk, you know.'

'Quite so. And how much do you think this modest excursion through the *vignobles français* is going to cost?'

'I'm not sure, sir. But I'm not suggesting we go for the best vintages. As long as there's just a bit of age on the red burgundies, I'm sure none of us will really mind.'

'That's most generous of you, Fripp. I suspect, however, that your parents will not prove quite so obliging. Nor will the parents of all the other boys when they write to complain that I have been nurturing a society of sybarites.'

'But –'

'No, I'm sorry, Fripp,' he said unapologetically. 'For the moment, I fear we may have to set our sights a little lower. Burgess, your suggestions were slightly more appropriate, though I think we may have to forget about the champagne. Sparkling wine will do quite nicely. As an end-of-term treat, perhaps.'

I studied my list miserably.

'Let's not run before we can crawl, gentlemen. As chairman with the casting vote I propose that we limit our weekly budget to 50p – no, let's call it 75p – a head. And let's start with something simple. Agreed?'

Four days later, at 6 p.m. sharp, the sixteen members of the new society milled expectantly in the uncongenial surroundings of Mr Drought's classroom. 'You'd have thought the bugger could at least have invited us to his home,' the society's secretary observed, justly.

Eric Talbot hadn't turned up, despite my entreaties. Too cool to join anything so conformist as a society, I suppose.

In one corner of the room, Monk and Norville, two louts whose interest in wine was even smaller than their minuscule brains, swung their feet under a desk in time to the merry drinking tune they were singing softly: ''Ere we go, 'ere we go, 'ere we go.'

I marvelled that they could remember the words.

''Ere we go, 'ere we go, 'ere we go-o. 'Ere we go, 'ere we go, 'ere we go-o. 'Ere we go-o. 'Ere . . .'

With a flourish of his briefcase, Mr Drought had finally arrived.

'Do you need any help with the crate, sir?'

'The crate, Fripp? No, no, it's all here, thank you. In my bag.'

Reaching into his brown leather bag, he confirmed my worst suspicions. There were four bottles of wine, brought for the delectation of seventeen people. Monk and Norville were almost as disappointed as me.

We gathered round the table and watched him unwrap the first fruits of the Wellingborough Wine Society. A bottle of Liebfraumilch. A bottle of white Sauvignon. A Lambrusco. And a low-grade Chianti.

Horatio looked at me quizzically. I could not meet his eyes.

'Now, how many are we? Fifteen?'

'Seventeen, sir. A bit less than a quarter of a bottle each,' I said bitterly. Mr Drought tossed me a dark glance.

'Right, gentlemen. As some of you may know, Fripp here is something of a wine expert. The rest of you, however, probably don't know a claret from a burgundy. Eh, Burgess?'

I was probably the only one who appreciated the ineptitude of his jest.

'So, we're going to start things off nice and gently. I don't want any of you going back drunk to your housemasters.'

Titters from the more sycophantic members of the group.

'In front of you, you will see four bottles of wine.'

'Is that each, sir?'

'That will do, Monk. As I said, in front of you, there are four bottles of wine. A Lambrusco – a lightly sparkling red wine from . . . Anyone know where Lambrusco is from?'

'Spain?' came one suggestion.

'Alaska?'

'No. Close, Roberts. Definitely not, Norville. Fripp?'

'Italy, sir,' I hissed.

'Correct. A Lambrusco from Italy which also happens to be the home of our second bottle of red, a Chianti, which hails from Tuscany.'

'I thought you said it was from Italy, sir,' said Norville.

'Chianti *is* in . . . oh shut up, you wretched boy. Now, where was I? Ah yes. The whites. We have first a Sauvignon Blanc – and as you will have been able to tell by my exquisite pronunciation . . .'

More titters.

'. . . this one is from France. Finally, to round things off, we have a German Liebfraumilch. Any questions? No? Then, let us begin.'

Everyone took a glass. Mr Drought passed me a corkscrew.

'White ones first,' he said. 'As our Master of Wine here will tell you, the reds need time to breathe.' Actually, the Master of Wine would have said, if consulted, that they did not deserve to breathe. They should have been smothered at birth.

Mr Drought dribbled a scant mouthful into the glasses I had laid out on to the table earlier.

'It may help if you take a pen and paper and mark down what you think are the special qualities of each wine. Hold it up to the light first. See if you note anything peculiar about its colour. Then smell it. What we call the wine's nose is just as important as its taste. Then try and isolate in your mind the individual flavours. Butter. Tar. Whatever you think it is that makes this wine special. You'll see why in a minute.'

Petulantly I scrawled, 'Fart. Rancid sick.'

'Sir! Sir! Aren't we meant to spit it out after we've tasted it?'

'My, what an expert we are, Norville. Swallowing it will be quite sufficient here, thank you.'

And so it went on. Syrupy plonk. Sharp plonk. Sweet, fizzy plonk. Acidic plonk. Some members of the tasting group earnestly sniffed above the rims of their glasses, rolled the wine appreciatively round their mouths and took diligent notes. Others sipped, looked puzzled, sipped again. And tentatively wrote down a few approximate adjectives. Three of us – me, Norville and Monk – downed ours as quickly as possible. They were doing it in a vain attempt to get drunk. I was being merciful to my palate.

'All finished?' asked Mr Drought. 'Then on we shall go to the next step, in which we shall put to the test your powers of memory and your sense of taste. A blind tasting.'

'This will be a tough one, sir,' I said sarcastically.

'All right, all right, Fripp. Give everyone else a chance. I shall blindfold you one by one . . .'

'Is that legal, sir?' asked Monk.

'. . . laying down four glasses of wine in front of you. I'll pass them to you, one by one. It's your job to guess which one is which. You won't have the advantage of being able to judge the wine's colour, which is another crucial part of any tasting. But I am sure you'll enjoy the challenge.'

'Eurggh. We've got to drink out of the same glasses as everyone else. Bags I go before Drabble,' commented Norville. Mr Drought ignored him.

'One more thing. To spare anyone any embarrassment – Monk and Norville – you don't have to say what you think it is aloud. You can turn round and make a few notes after each glass. Then at the end, you can write down the name of each wine in the order you drank them. Good luck, gentlemen. Fripp – excuse me, I should address you, should I not, as Mister President – why don't you lead?'

I swaggered over to the tasting table, and let Mr Drought tie a black length of cloth round my eyes. 'See anything, Fripp?'

'No, sir.'

'Carry on, then.'

I accepted the first glass, raised it to my lips, without dignifying the wine with a preparatory sniff, and sipped a tingling mouthful.

'Lambrusco,' I noted perfunctorily.

The rest were equally easy to identify. Chianti, cloying Liebfraumilch, and the spicy Sauvignon, I scrawled in conclusion, ripping off my blindfold.

'Burgess, you next,' said Mr Drought. And everyone laughed as he poked his giant proboscis over the first glass.

I distanced myself from the rest of the group, a prince among paupers, and watched them all, snorting and tasting their way through the list. Monk and Norville both adjusted their blindfolds after they had been put on, claiming unconvincingly that they were trying to close up a crack of light at the bottom. No less implausible was their complaint that they needed four slurps of each glass before deciding what it was.

After what felt like an age, it was over. Anyone would have thought that this was an international wine-tasting competition. What did Burgess think he was doing taking so long over that stuff? I would have expected better from my secretary.

We exchanged our numbered lists for marking purposes. I swapped mine with Horatio, whom I could trust not to get things wrong.

'Right. Everyone got a pen? Here Norville, take this. Ready. Number One: Lambrusco.' I nodded as he ran through each one. Chianti. Tick. Sauvignon. Tick. Liebfraumilch. Tick. Horatio had got four out of four. Thank God he had not disgraced me.

I passed Horatio back his list. 'Easy peasy,' I said, accepting my own piece of paper in return. I would have tossed it away immediately, had there not been something in Horatio's expression which made me look down. Two out of four, he had written. There were two crosses on it. Idiot! I thought I could have trusted him to pay attention.

'Sir,' I put up my hand.

'Hang on, Fripp. Let's find out how you all did. Who are our budding masters of wine, then? Hands up who got four out of four?' I kept mine half up and half down.

'And who got two? I see.' I lowered my arm slightly, cocking it behind my head as if it were simply a position I found comfortable. 'And who got them all wrong? Nobody. Splendid. There's some promise in you yet. Now, what is it, Fripp?'

I stepped over to his table, while everyone discussed how easy or difficult the contest had been – 'I knew the third one was the Sauvignon because, you know, like when you're eating a fruit salad and it's got lots of pears in it which you don't want to eat, and then you eat one by mistake', 'I thought mixing your drinks was meant to get you pissed quickly','It had to be a red, so it was just fifty fifty after that', 'I don't mean to sound pretentious but to me, the Liebfraumilch reminded me of . . .'

'Would you mind just letting me see the correct answers again, sir?' I said sotto voce.

'Pass me your list, Fripp. Let's have a look. Two out of four, hmn? Rather embarrassing for our president. Let's check them against my list. Lambrusco. Yes. Chianti. Yes. Liebfrau . . . Hold on. The third one's meant to be Sauvignon. You've got it the wrong way round. Fripp has got it the wrong way round!'

'Sir,' I pleaded through gritted teeth. But there was no depriving Mr Drought of an opportunity for a cheap laugh.

'Ohohohoho. Dear me. Two out of four. Well, I never. Our Master of Wine cannot tell the difference between a Sauvignon and a Liebfraumilch,' he continued, his voice growing louder.

All ears were tuning in to Mr Drought's burbling. What was he on about? Who had got it wrong? Fripp? The sharper swots cottoned on first and led the chortling. It would only be seconds before the slowest got there too. And sure enough, the beefy laughter of Norville and Monk soon swelled the chorus. Even Burgess's mouth had creased in a guilty grin.

The President and Founder of the Wellingborough Wine Society, try as he might to convince himself that there had been some hideous error, that everyone else had been cheating, that the wines had been served at inappropriate temperatures, that the glasses had not been cleaned properly, had been unable to differentiate between a Liebfraumilch and a Sauvignon Blanc.

Within seconds of handing in his resignation to the society chairman, he had disappeared into the night.

My belly growled as I pondered the vexed question: 'Reading and rereading *Emma* are two totally different experiences. Discuss.' It should have been easy. All I had to do was find a few of choice Austenian paragraphs which I'd previously marked 'D.I.' (dramatic irony), string them together with some plausible linking paragraphs, and I'd turn out a model, mock A-level essay. Unfortunately, even so simple a task was impossible on an empty stomach.

Still, I didn't regret my decision to skip supper. Going hungry was preferable to seeing Burgess grinning at me across the prefects' table. I couldn't avoid him for ever, of course. But for now, the best place to come to terms with my humiliation was the semi-darkness of my study/bedroom.

It could have been worse. At least Eric hadn't turned up. Not that that had ever been likely. Though we'd tried to keep our friendship alive during the first couple of terms at Wellingborough, we'd slowly drifted apart. It didn't help that we were in different houses. Nor that he was sporty and I was academic. In our final year, the differences between us had grown even more marked. I was in the Oxbridge set – he'd be lucky if he got more than one A level; I had kept my nose clean and become a school prefect – he'd gone the other way, experimenting with pot and girls, dropping out of the school teams and hanging around at night in seedy pubs that no master would dream of entering.

I was just about to switch off my table lamp and try to sleep off my misery when the window rattled. I put it down to the wind blowing outside. But it rattled again.

Pulling back the curtain, I saw a face staring in at me.

'Quick,' hissed Eric, his breath frosting the glass. 'It's freezing.'

I lifted the sash-window so that Eric could squeeze through and clamber across my desk. A blast of cold air sent my papers flying on to the floor.

'That's better!' he said, brushing the brick dust and drainpipe rust off his long DMC (Dead Man's Coat – essential wear for the cool set).

'You're mad,' I said.

'Drunk,' he corrected. 'Tampon done his rounds yet?'

I nodded.

'Good-oh.' Eric took off his coat and sat on my mattress, blowing into his hands. 'Well? Are you going to bung the kettle on, or what?'

Though the risk of being discovered by our lax housemaster, 'Tampon' Rodgers, was slim, I still felt uneasy about the situation. A confirmed reprobate like Eric had little to lose if caught in another

87

boy's house after the 9 p.m. curfew. I, on the other hand, risked being stripped of my prefecthood, not to mention my rights to walk across the school lawns, to make toast in the prefects' common room and to wear whatever shirt I wanted with my uniform.

'Er . . . Eric . . .' I said. 'It's not that I'm ungrateful for your dropping in like this . . . but, um, actually, I've had a pretty awful day and I was about to turn in.'

'Pissed off about the wine tasting, I'll bet,' said Eric.

'You . . . ?'

'Monk and Norville were laughing about it in the Vulture,' he explained. (The Eagle and Child, popularly known as the Vulture and Foetus, looked kindly on under-age drinkers.) 'Guessed you might be on a bit of a downer, so I thought I'd come and cheer you up a bit.'

'It's very kind of you but –'

'Lighten up, will you? And put the kettle on. You won't get your present otherwise.' He tapped the bulging pockets of his overcoat.

I put the kettle on.

'Hungry?' he asked.

'Starving,' I said.

'Just as well I brought these, then.' From his pockets, he retrieved a pair of Pot Noodles. 'Chicken and Mushroom or Spicy Beef?'

'On second thoughts, I think I'll survive till breakfast.'

Eric rolled his eyes.

We waited silently for the kettle to boil. When it did, I filled up both pots and found Eric a fork.

'You know,' said Eric, stirring his bowl of rehydrated additives and preservatives, 'I'm glad at least one of us has got a bit of taste.' He looked up. 'I mean, it's quite important if anything's going to come of it.'

'Come of what?' I said, trying to hold back my nausea at the synthetic stench emanating from Eric's pots.

'Don't tell me you've forgotten. Our restaurant.'

'You're still serious?'

'Aren't you?'

'Well, yes . . . but . . .'

'Thought I'd lost interest?' Eric wolfed down a large mouthful, brown juices trickling down his chin. 'Mmm. To tell the truth I had. But then, it all came back to me at that careers fair the other day up in big school. Looked round the stalls. Couldn't find anything that suited me. Not enough O levels for most of 'em, anyway . . . And that was when I got chatting to this bloke about catering and hotel management.'

Eric reached for the other pot.

'And?' I said.

'That's it, basically. Soon as I've done my As, I'm off to catering college.'

'Well, I never.'

'Jealous, eh? Give me a couple of years and I'll know more about cooking than you do.'

'You'll probably learn a lot about conference catering and ordering up stock and . . . the technical side of things but –'

'Give us a break, will you? I couldn't learn in two years what you know about food and wine . . . but don't you see? That's why we're the perfect match. While you're at Cambridge –'

'Oxford.'

'Oxford, then . . . I can learn all the practical stuff. Get a bit of experience maybe. And we can team up after that.'

'Sounds good to me.'

'Thought you'd like it. Let's drink a toast to it, then.'

'All right. Tea or coffee?'

'Don't be silly!' Talbot reached into his coat again and pulled out a bottle. Of Liebfraumilch. 'There,' he said, displaying the Blue Nun label. 'Have to do things properly, eh? Got a corkscrew?'

Fortunately, I hadn't.

'Never mind,' he said. 'These corks go in easily enough.' He began unwrapping the blue foil at the top.

'You sure this is a good idea?' I said.

He answered by pushing in the cork.

'But I haven't got any glasses.'

' 'S'all right. A mug'll do.'

'A mug?'

'Straight out the bottle, then.' He took a long swig and passed me the bottle.

I wiped the lip and, trying not to think of all the bits of spit floating around in it, drank the tiniest sip I could. Sweet, warm and yellow.

'More than that!' insisted Eric.

I took a tiny bit more.

'There!' I said, making a face. 'No point wasting it on me. You can keep the rest for yourself.'

'You're hardly going to get pissed on two mouthfuls,' said Talbot.

He glugged another draught appreciatively. 'Anyway, I bought it for you. Have some more. Quicker you drink, faster it'll work.'

'But I don't want to get drunk . . . I've got work to do for the morning and – '

'Giles,' chided Eric, 'this is a historic moment.'

I took a breath and had another mouthful. Already I detected signs of deterioration.

'Really,' I said, 'that's quite enough for me.'

'What the hell's wrong with it?' said Eric, eyeing up the Blue Nun label. 'I'll have you know this stuff set me back almost a quid.'

'You've just explained what's wrong with it,' I said.

'Oh?' he sneered. 'Like that, is it? So how much does a bottle have to cost before you can drink it?'

'I'm sorry . . . I didn't mean to be . . .'

'No, I'm the one who's sorry. I didn't have to come round . . . and let's face it, it's not as if you can tell the difference, anyway.'

'And what's that supposed to mean?'

'Just what I said. I'll bet if you hadn't seen the label . . .'

I stood up, shaking with rage and disbelief.

'You little shit. That's why you came here, isn't it? You just wanted to take the mickey like Monk and Norville and all the rest of them.'

'Well, you're a fine one to talk, aren't you? Sneering at my wine like that.'

'If you call an objective critique of your wine sneering – '

'Don't try to impress me with your long words.'

'All right. I'll put it into ones you'll understand.' I snatched the bottle and waved it in front of him. 'This wine is complete crap. OK?'

Talbot sat on the bed, studying me bitterly.

By the time I realized I might have over-reacted, he had already risen and put on his coat. He removed the bottle from my shaking hand, took a last, contemptous draught, and put it on my desk.

'You were right,' he said, quietly. 'I was mad to come here.'

'Look – '

''S'all right, Giles. Better now than later, eh? I mean, can you imagine it? Us setting up our own restaurant together. Wasting all that time and money. And then me suddenly discovering that my partner's a complete and utter jerk.'

'Eric, I – '

'Don't worry. I'll find my own way out.'

He opened my study/bedroom door a fraction and peered into the darkened corridor.

'And Giles,' he said, just before he slipped out, 'no more of this Eric stuff, OK? The name's Talbot.'

CHAPTER TEN

'Can't we just divide it by ten?' I proposed.

And, for the first time all evening, everyone noticed me.

Voices which, for the last two hours, had been rising in a self-righteous crescendo of Chianti-fuelled bile to denounce lecherous tutors, impossible two-hour-a-week workloads, the Evils of Thatcher, the extortionate beer prices in the subsidized college bars and (a few seconds ago) the ludicrously expensive bill which had just been presented to us by the *padrone*, fell suddenly silent.

Nine pairs of eyes, registering various states of horror, embarrassment, loathing and incomprehension, watched me across the red, wax-spattered tablecloth.

Three weeks. Three weeks now since I'd arrived at Oxford. And not for the first time in my brief university career, I wondered whether I'd ever quite get the hang of being a student.

OK. So Brideshead was a myth. But surely there ought to have been enough similarly nostalgic folk keen to recreate the pleasures thereof. Where was my invitation to join the Buller? Where was my gilded aristocrat with the gazelle-like wine cellar? And what had become of all those drowsy, sun-drenched picnics I was supposed to enjoy on the banks of the Cherwell with beautiful undergraduettes. Like the ones in this basement trattoria, perhaps.

Any one of them would have done. The gamine Audrey Hepburn lookalike at the far end of the table; the green-eyed, Amazonian blonde; even the fey 'hippy chick' (as I'd heard somebody call her) with the dyed black hair and patched 'ethnic clothes'. But a fat chance I stood of getting anywhere with them. Not when *he* was holding court.

' 'Ere's a better idea,' Eric Talbot announced in his fake London accent, *de rigueur* among most privately educated undergraduates (not that the latter term strictly applied to denizens of the local catering college). 'Let's order a bit more vino, while we work out oos 'ad what.'

This suggestion met with more enthusiasm than mine. Talbot, nauseatingly cool Eric Talbot, with his new extra-short haircut, two-day-old stubble and greasy suede jacket, smirked.

I scowled back at him and turned to my neighbour. It was thanks to Emma, the blonde with the Alice band, whom I knew vaguely from the English faculty library, that I'd come to this dreadful trattoria in the first place. I'd been chatting her up in the Turf when one of her friends had tactlessly asked whether she fancied something to eat. 'Absolutely!' Emma enthused. 'Er . . . Garry, isn't it? You probably won't know anyone but . . . er . . . do feel free to tag along if you want.' Well, I couldn't turn down a come-on like that, could I?

Now Emma was ignoring me. She was engaged in animated conversation with Rick, a pony-tailed law student from Bradford.

'Well, I certainly didn't eat twelve pounds' worth,' she was saying. 'I only had the mozzarella salad and a couple of spritzers.'

Rick agreed. 'My carbonara were no more than £3.50,' he said. 'And I only 'ad a few glasses of the red. I'm putting in seven. Don't see why I should pay for them as went through the whole bloody menu.' He glanced slyly in my direction.

'Service isn't included, you know,' I said.

'Quite,' said a supportive voice on my right. It belonged to a chap in a bright-coloured waistcoat, the only person besides me who'd ordered pudding.

Emma threw a glance of pained non-comprehension at us both and resumed her discourse with Rick.

'So what's the law library like anyway?' she continued seductively.

Chastened, I turned to my right. My insistence that we should sit boy girl boy girl might yet pay off. Gertrude – or was it Geraldine? – the redhead whom I'd ignored for most of the evening, was doing exactly what she had been doing when I'd last noticed her – staring dreamily into the middle distance, elbows astride a plate of half-eaten veal.

'They might at least have cleared your plate,' I opened, solicitously. Wasn't that what girls were looking for? The caring type?

'Biology,' she murmured.

'No. Your plate,' I said. 'They might at least have bothered to clear it. Some of us have already had our pudding.'

Much to my irritation, my fellow pudding eater – sitting the other side of Geraldine/Gertrude – was eavesdropping.

'Oh . . . Right . . . yes.' Geraldine/Gertrude smiled weakly.

I'd made my mark.

'So, er, you didn't rate your saltimbocca alla romana?'

'Eh? Oh. Not bad . . . *He* chose it.' She nodded towards the eaves-dropper. He interpreted this as an entrée.

'I was just telling her the only place you're going to find it done properly is in Brescia. The ham there is –'

'Brescia?' I interrupted. 'I think you'll find it's a Roman dish, hence the name.'

'Yes. Yes. *Alla romana*' – the interloper pronounced it in an absurdly affected Italian accent – 'I know that. But the dish itself actually originates in . . .'

'Excuse me,' said Geraldine/Gertrude, rising from her chair.

'You're not going?' I said.

'Off to the ladies,' she explained.

Once she'd gone, I had a chance to assess my rival. He had floppy, unkempt hair with grizzled streaks in it; his face was angular, bony, ferret-like; his pale grey eyes were lazily decadent; his mouth – from which a high-tar cigarette drooped – was slack and moist. All in all, he looked pleasingly revolting. Well dressed maybe (he was the first undergraduate I'd seen wearing a suit) but far too louche for a nice girl like Geraldine/Gertrude. Still, you couldn't be too careful.

'You and . . . um . . . wotsername . . .' I nodded towards the ladies, 'you're not, um . . . going out with her or anything. Are you?'

'God, no!' said the interloper.

'Oh. Not your sort?' My relief was tempered by a certain trepida-tion. The vehemence of the interloper's denial seemed to suggest that you'd have to be blind before you contemplated going out with a girl that unattractive.

'Not sure that I have a sort,' mused the interloper, casting a lazy eye towards the far end of the table. 'I mean, why bother?'

I laughed self-consciously. 'Well, you know. University . . . sexual freedom. It's what we're here for, isn't it?'

'Is it?' he asked, in a way that implied he had never heard quite such an absurd notion. He took a hard swig of his wine, pulling a sour face as he did so.

'And even if I did want to waste my time with that sort of thing,' he added, 'I dare say types like old Suedehead over there would muscle in.'

We both watched Eric being lionized by his pride of adoring females.

'Eric Talbot.'

'Friend of yours?'

'God, no!' I said.

'So who is this Eric Talbot when he's at home? I'm sure this isn't the first time I've seen him schmoozing around.'

'Probably in the Union.'

'Political hack?'

'Barman, actually. He's not even a member of the university. Goes to some scrofulous catering college.'

'Then he really has no excuse,' said the interloper. 'I mean, what in God's name possessed him to order up muck like this?' He clutched his wine glass gingerly as if it held some sort of unspeakable medical sample. He drank its contents all the same. And he was just extending a hand for a refill when he shook his head and muttered, 'No. No more gut rot for me this evening. I've had enough!'

He rose, unsteadily, from his chair.

'Come with me if you like,' he said. 'Maybe I can show you what university's *really* about.'

'Er . . . no,' I said. 'Thanks all the same but . . . um . . .'

Geraldine/Gertrude was making her way back to the table.

The interloper slapped a twenty-pound note on the table. 'There. That should cover me. The name's Holmes, by the way. Rodney Holmes.'

I told him mine. Rather distractedly, since the new love of my life was now lowering her delectable bottom on to her chair.

Rodney steered his way round Geraldine/Gertrude and whispered in my ear. 'Good luck,' he said. 'And if, ah, things don't go according to plan, why don't you drop round?'

He jotted his address on a piece of paper and put it into my breast pocket.

'Yes, yes,' I said, waving him away. His breath reeked of alcohol and my mind was set on more important matters.

'More wine?' I asked Geraldine/Gertrude.

'Thanks,' she said. I filled her glass to the brim.

'So, er . . . your saltimbocca alla romana . . .'

'Are you reading Italian, then?' she asked.

'Coffee?' she asked and, despite my haze of drunkenness, I knew what that one meant.

'Please,' I said, wondering how long it would be before her friend took the hint and left us alone.

'Polly?'

'Love one, Geraldine, thanks.' So it was Geraldine. Lucky I hadn't committed myself to Gertrude. It's amazing how little it takes to scupper one's chances.

While Geraldine bustled around in the kitchen, Polly and I settled into chairs – as far apart from each other as possible. We each pretended to be thinking of something so earth-shatteringly important that we could not spare the time to acknowledge each other's presence.

'How would you like it, Giles?' called Geraldine. Well, there was a come on, if ever there was one. Still, perhaps best to maintain the social pretence of it all.

'Black, please,' I said.

'And mine's milk with two sugars,' said Polly. They weren't that intimate, then. I'd been beginning to wonder. Dungarees. Fat. Short hair. I knew all the signs.

The object of Polly's slavering lust emerged from the kitchenette, clutching two tannin-ingrained mugs. So Polly really was going to stay. The naivety of some people! Had she not been aware of the coded significance of my exchange with Geraldine?

Maybe where Polly came from, they had yet to evolve towards that sophisticated level of social interaction where the *double entendre* was properly understood. In her sad, benighted way, she actually imagined that when a young female undergraduate said, late at night, to a reasonably attractive member of the opposite sex, the word 'coffee', she really did mean a cup of freshly ground Blue Mountain, Java or Kenya AA. Or a cup of pre-ground supermarket own brand. Or, let's get really disgusting, some ordinary Nescafé instant.

'Uggh,' I exclaimed involuntarily. It really was Nescafé instant. Not even Blend 37 or Gold Blend.

'Something the matter?' asked Geraldine. Another sign! She cared. She couldn't bear to see me in pain.

'No, it's nothing. It's just a bit hot, that's all. Er, actually, I've suddenly remembered. I do take sugar. Three spoonfuls will do. And could I just have a dash of milk to cool it down a bit?'

Was it for this that the first wild *arabica* beans made their way from the Sudan and Ethiopia to the Middle East? Was it for this that the Viennese, in their courageous battle against the Turk in 1683, liberated the precious beans for the West? Was it for this that slaves had died, that dinky little home grinding machines and cappuccino makers with lots of knobs on had been developed? For this, this brand, which would disgrace the very word ersatz?

'Mm. Lovely coffee,' said Polly, catching my eye.

'Mm. Yes. Delicious,' I said, trying to hold it down. But I wasn't going to give up that easily. In return for Geraldine's sexual education, I could easily tutor her in the ways of gastronomic righteousness.

The object of our attention nodded coyly. Coquettishly, even. It was going to be a long struggle, but it would be worth it.

Geraldine put a scratched record on to her budget turntable.

On the floor by my feet was a three-month-old edition of *Cosmo*. 'The G-Spot. Does it Exist?' I was just reaching for the dog-eared copy when I decided that this would be counter-productive. I pretended I was checking to see whether my shoelaces were undone and sat back. Only the pop music filled the void.

'Fancy another cup?' asked Geraldine.

'Not for me, thanks,' said Polly, draining the dregs of her mug.

'I'm fine too, thanks,' I said. Victory! I still had half a cup to go.

'In fact,' said Polly, 'I ought to be off. I've got an essay on Hardy to finish off. Will you be all right, Geraldine?'

The cheek of it. Of course, the woman would be all right. She had me to look after her.

'I should think so,' replied Geraldine, head bowed.

The door closed behind her.

'Shall we play the other side?' I said, edging towards the record player in such a way that she could not glimpse the awkward bulge developing in my cords.

'If you like.'

I fumbled with the record, hoping for my tumescence to die down enough for me to make a clean approach.

Half-doubled over, I made my way back – not to the armchair which I had previously occupied but to the faded sofa, next to Geraldine.

'So, you live here on your own, then, do you?' I said, looking at her properly for the first time all evening. She had, admittedly, been prettier in the gloom of the restaurant, through a blur of *vino rosso*.

'No. There's three of us altogether. But Sue's at her parents' for the weekend and Barbara's staying over with her boyfriend. So . . .'

Despite the fact that she was still half-masked by the flattering gloom of two side-lamps, her features had come sharply into focus. Caffeine was beginning to win its way over alcohol. What I had mistaken for a rosiness of complexion turned out to be a gentle smattering of acne; the reddish-brown hair was even wispier and more bedraggled than I had given it credit for; and the lips were thin and unvoluptuous. I would have to work fast.

'So,' I said, draping my arm casually over the back of the sofa, within caressing distance of her red locks, 'when you offered me coffee a moment ago, that wasn't what you *really* meant – was it?' I could scarcely believe how manly and forthright I had become. University had clearly invested me with a new maturity.

'No,' she admitted. 'I really wanted to give you tea but I didn't think anyone would fancy it at this time of night. I forgot to get a new jar of coffee when I went shopping this morning so I had to borrow some of Barbara's. She'll kill me if she finds out.'

I let my hand rest near the back of her head. 'You're right, you know. You can't beat a really nice cup of coffee at this time of night.' I punctuated the last three words with a couple of gentle strokes of her hair.

She jerked her head slightly, like an excitable young filly.

'Coffee,' I said.'You'd never guess that for thousands of years its magical, restorative powers went completely unrecognized by man. Even in the place where *Coffea arabica* – the regions we now know as Ethiopia and the Sudan – is actually indigenous.'

She gazed ahead in rapt silence, the stiffness of her neck (which I was now smoothing with the back of my hand) indicating the grip my tale had exerted on her imagination.

'They say that its discovery came quite by accident. One day, a goatherd noticed how, when his flock fed upon certain shrubs, they became suddenly animated and excitable . . .'

She let slip a brief, passionate sigh. Seizing the advantage, I steered my free hand on to hers, which she had clenched in her lap. Sweaty, but promisingly warm.

She flinched. But I knew from the way her hands trembled what her secret desires were.

I teased out the delicious anticipation a few minutes longer. Soon, she would be unable to control her passion any longer. She would be weeping. Pleading with me to make love to her there and then on that creaky sofa.

And I would, but not before completing the miraculous tale of the drink which I told her, with a sexy rasp of the throat, the Arabs call *qahwah*.

By now, I had found my voice. Spurred on by her eager silence, I tripped fluently through the history of coffee-drinking. From Aden to Constantinople we travelled, Geraldine and I. Thence to Venice in 1615 and so on and on, to that glorious moment in the reign of George I when Pasha Rossi, servant to the home-coming ambassador, Edwards of Smyrna, popularized the bean in our own fair country.

It was no good. I would have liked to have taken her further, to the plantations in Mexico, Costa Rica, Java and Brazil, soaring higher and ever higher into the Blue Mountains of Jamaica, but finally I could contain myself no longer and with a final gasp of air, I pressed my mouth against hers, thrusting my tongue between her lips.

It was blocked. Her teeth were in the way. Less experienced than I thought, but no matter. My tongue pushing on with the determination of a Panzer division, I tried prising her teeth apart.

Her mouth opened a fraction and I felt the rough flutter of her responsive *langue de chat*. Dry, tannic and heady. Clearly not a *grand vin*, but it might open out given time. I probed further, aiming for the tonsils.

But her defences were too strong. At the very instant when I was preparing to lend her my precious body for a night of slavering oblivion, she yanked herself from my grasp. She leant towards the far end of the sofa.

'Look, I'm really sorry,' she said, 'but I don't think we should.'

I blinked, uncomprehending.

'I mean, I hardly know you . . .' Oh God, not that line. Please. Anything but that line.

She stood up and moved towards the light switch.

'But you do, Geraldine. You DO. And I promise you, you'll get to know me better. Just . . .'

The room burst into brightness.

'No, Giles, really. You're a really nice bloke and everything. But I just don't think, you know . . . it's just not right.'

Were all female undergraduates issued with the same phrase-book?

She could see I was hurt. Hadn't I a right to be? The woman had done enough to lead me on all evening. I had a bulge the size of a prize gourd to show for it.

'Giles, seriously, I'm going to bed now . . .'

I stood up. Would it be too forward simply to seize her and drag her into the bedroom?

'. . . alone.'

My dreams shattered, all resistance beaten, so brutally, out of me, I shambled towards the door.

'Some other time,' she said, kissing me chastely on the corner of my drooping lips. 'Soon. For coffee, perhaps?'

This was more like it. An oak-panelled room looking out on to the neo-classical splendours of Peck Quad. Ancient portraits in heavy gilt frames. Leather chairs. A *chaise longue*. A magnificently rich Persian rug. The scene illuminated by at least two dozen candles.

'Just in time,' said Rodney without looking up. 'Your d'Yquem's on the sideboard.'

He was squatting on the floor, crouched over a gas burner. Something very delicious was sizzling in the skillet.

I made to pick up the goblet of wine. But honesty prevailed.

'Actually it's me. Giles. From the restaurant.'

'Mm-hm,' said Rodney, plucking two morsels from the pan. He laid them on a saucer.

'Toast should be ready any second – now.' The toast popped up just as he said 'now'.

'Quick,' he added. 'Can't eat foie gras cold.'

I scooped one of the glistening, oyster-sized pieces on to my toast and ate it in one go. The exterior was hot and crisp. The inside molten, velvet-smooth and gorgeously rich. I followed up with a sip of cold, syrupy, golden Sauternes.

'Not a patch on the '76, of course,' said Rodney.

Château d'Yquem and real, fresh foie gras. Not even my uncle had ever run to such extravagances with me.

I decided that I would like to see more of Rodney Holmes. Especially once I'd learned that before coming up to Oxford, he had spent a year working under the legendary French chef Luc Piccholine. I didn't want to show my ignorance by admitting I'd never heard of him. Fortunately, Rodney was too modest to elaborate.

'So which one was it?' he asked. ' "I hardly know you" or "I don't on the first date"?'

'Both.'

'And I expect you picked up the tab for her dinner?'

'She only had one course. And a glass of wine.'

'You're sounding like your chum Suedehead. Big difference being, he won't have had to fork out for his pair of floozies. That sort never does. As for the likes of you and me, my advice is, stick to tarts. Inexpensive and infinitely more effective.'

I grunted in manly agreement, wondering how best to steer the conversation towards an area in which I could compete with any proficiency.

We had dispensed with women, the vulgarity and small-mindedness of the modern student, and the laziness of the average scout when I saw an opening.

Rodney had a particularly fine collection of classic cookery books. Browsing through them, I noticed a copy of *A Discourse on Divers Cuisines*.

'First edition,' observed Rodney, as I pulled it out. 'Terribly rare.'

'Didn't they only print one?'

Rodney nodded. 'Scandalous. Never got over it, you know. He was telling me only the other day –'

'But that's amazing! You know my uncle?'

Rodney looked vaguely perturbed.

'By repute certainly. I've long been an admirer of his. From afar.'

'I thought you –'

'But you're talking to the wrong man. It's my room mate who's the real expert on the – on your uncle. Utterly obsessed, he is.'

'Really? I must meet him.'

'Doubt you'll ever get the chance. Keeps himself very much to himself does –'

Behind me I heard the door open. Looking round, I saw a tall figure in a dark green overcoat and broad-rimmed hat. His mouth was muffled with a pink scarf, which he made no attempt to remove.

He nodded curtly at Rodney. Glanced quickly past me towards the Sauternes and half-eaten foie gras, and then stomped towards his bedroom. A gloved hand pulled the door shut.

'Time you were off,' said Rodney softly.

CHAPTER ELEVEN

Cruel Cuisine

'Is the tuna dolphin-friendly?' I asked the man in the shark-skin suit.

'Good Lord, no!' The maître d' was mortified. 'Our seafood is caught in drag nets. Never with rod and line.'

He glanced nervously towards the tinted bullet-proof window. On the other side, a baying mob of protesters was chanting slogans and insulting would-be customers. Perhaps the maître d' was thinking that I was an animal rights terrorist who had come to plant a bomb in his restaurant. Or worse still, a Customs officer gathering incriminating evidence.

'Don't worry,' I said. 'I'm on your side.'

The maître d' was visibly relieved. I could understand his concern. You'd need nerves of steel to cope with a job like his, running Britain's most politically incorrect restaurant.

For obvious reasons, the establishment's owners prefer to remain anonymous. But they are said to comprise a cabal of right-wing entrepreneurs, vigorously opposed to the creeping menace of PC. Pro-smoking, pro-field sports, pro-fur and anti-everything that smacks of leftist ideology, Cruel Cuisine is not so much a restaurant as a political statement.

Three times since it opened earlier this year Cruel Cuisine has been forced to move premises because of its enemies' unwelcome attentions. Yet you would never guess it to look at the decor, which maintains a deceptive air of permanence.

The tables, solid and apparently immovable, are made of rare tropical hardwood inlaid with ivory. The chairs, upholstered with baby-seal fur, are bolted firmly to the mahogany parquet floor. On the wall hang paintings from a better, happier age when men were not afraid to participate in such harmless pursuits as bear-baiting, cock-fighting and bare-knuckle boxing. *Eheu fugaces* runs the restaurant's motto.

From our raised position near the window, my companion – who, despite the summer heat, was giving her sable coat a rare outing – enjoyed a fine view of our fellow diners. An Arab potentate was being spoonfed mouthfuls of foie gras by his blonde mistress. A gang of shiny-suited barrow-boys made good in the City raised their rhino drinking horns in a toast to another successful deal. Chirruping groups of Chinese stuffed themselves with house specialities such as 'Sizzling Szechuan Dog', 'Braised Hock of Panda' and 'Tiger's Penis, Pan-fried in Its Own Juices'.

The menu changes daily, partly to accommodate the ever-changing rarities chef has secured through his black-market contacts, partly to waste unrecycled paper. Though the list of dishes is extensive, many of them will be ruled out as unpalatable by all but the most adventurous diner. Other dishes, like the 'Cruel-reared Escalope of Veal', are less attractive than they sound. As a rule of thumb, steer clear of any meat that hasn't been stewed for a long time. All the livestock which ends up at Cruel Cuisine is factory-farmed and inhumanely slaughtered. Unhappy animals make tough meat.

Instead of the tuna sushi (too boring), I opted for the turtle soup. I can highly recommend it: plump morsels of flesh and fat (leatherback, I would guess), swimming in a glossy, pale green soup, whose fishiness had been nicely offset by a good measure of rump steak, and finished with a delicate hint of cloves, cinnamon and port.

Even better was my companion's exquisite osprey egg soufflé (expensive, but that's the price you pay for native Scottish eggs). Deceptively light, with an interesting, frothy, amber tinge, it proved so rich that it was all I could do to help her finish it.

My steak tartare was sweet but rather chewier than I might have liked. But I suppose this was to be expected of meat derived from a muscular thoroughbred which had taken a fatal tumble at the Grand National. Still, I had to give it full marks for presentation. Stuck on top of my pile of raw mince was a charming miniature flag, decorated with the racing colours once sported by the dead horse.

My companion was unimpressed by her blue-whale steak, which she complained was blubbery and insipid. She blamed me. What she'd really wanted was the chargrilled okapi, but I'd refused on the grounds that, thrilling though it might be to eat such a spectacularly rare antelope, it was simply beyond my price range at £1000 a steak.

Fortunately, she was distracted from her misery by a loud roar from the pavement outside. It was the animal rights protesters, harassing a couple of new customers. The couple entered shortly afterwards — escorted by a phalanx of the restaurant's private security guards — the woman still trying to remove the red paint which had been flung on to her fur coat.

The maître d' dispatched a minion to wipe off the paint. The minion scrubbed at the stain for a few seconds. Then he stopped suddenly and examined the fur. He beckoned to the maître d', who ruffled the fur between his thumb and forefinger and shook his head. After a curt exchange with the woman's boyfriend, the maître d' sent the couple packing, with the admonition that they should never darken his door again.

'What was that all about?' I asked the maître d' when he came to take our pudding order. He sniffed. 'Fake fur.'

Though I had been most impressed by the restaurant's determination to serve nothing but the cruellest food — even the rice accompanying my companion's whale meat, had been selected from Cambodian paddy fields viciously supervised by the Khmer Rouge — I doubted that they would be able to maintain their standards on the pudding menu.

The maître d' agreed that it had been very difficult finding examples of unjust desserts. But he strongly recommended the bananas flambé, assuring us that the fruit had been gathered by slave labour on Haiti. We followed his advice, and concluded with two cups of strong coffee made from despotically harvested South American beans, together with a pair of (compulsory) Havana cigars.

A word about the wine. Most of it is wholly unpalatable, owing to the lack of vintages which are truly politically incorrect. The electoral changes in South Africa have, of course, meant that Cape wines are no longer a valid option. After a few sips of our Serbian Merlot – a violent, unpredictable number – I found myself longing for a bottle from that case of Cheval Blanc 1947 which a generous reader kindly sent to my home.

Dinner for two at Cruel Cuisine came to £452.30. Expect to pay considerably more for rarer items. At the time of writing, Cruel Cuisine can be found at 50, Cheyne Crescent, London SW1. It is more than likely, however, that it will since have changed address.

Never had Canary Wharf Tower looked so beautiful. Nor the clouds reflected in its metallic blue glass so exquisitely fluffy and white. Nor the still waters of the Thames so – so what? Deep? Dark? Opalescent? Majestic? Spenserian? And what did it matter anyway?

What did anything matter on this, the best, best day of my whole life?

'Good morning!' I said, skipping past the receptionist. She looked doubtful. But I meant it. I really did.

'Hi guys!' I called out to Oriole and Sherman.

'Check out his pupils,' murmured Oriole.

'He's on one. For sure,' agreed Sherman.

'Goooall!' I yelled at the sports desk, punching the air with my fist.

'Prat,' said the soccer correspondent. And for once I didn't mind.

'Lovely dress,' I told Aurora, squeezing her arm gently.

'I've had it for six weeks,' she replied, looking askance at Jessica.

'Well, it has aged *beautifully*.'

'And how is our intrepid war correspondent?'

Rupert did not reply. He just slumped deeper into his chair, his sunken eyes staring blankly at the screen.

He had been like that since returning from his latest assignment. Unshaven, still dressed in his dirty boots and sweat-stained fatigues. Smelling ranker by the day.

Andy was concerned. If this went on much longer, he wouldn't have any copy to go with all those gory shots he had commissioned for the 'My Seven Days in Hell' feature. A pity, since it was meant to be the next issue's cover story.

I had first heard of it a few days earlier.

'What do you reckon?' Andy asked.

Pinned to his noticeboard was a selection of especially nasty mock-ups for the September edition of *Knob*. One showed a head impaled on a spike. Another, a napalm victim. Another, a burned-out armoured vehicle, surrounded by charred bodies.

'Very . . . arresting,' I conceded.

'Or what? If this doesn't get us noticed, nothing will.'

The 'Big D', Andy went on to explain, would be devoted to a subject no other magazine had ever dared cover. Death.

'Now I know what you're gonna say. It's sick. It's tasteless. It's disgusting . . .'

I nodded.

'. . . which is why we're going to print 200,000 extra copies to cope with the demand.'

I still wasn't wholly convinced. But Andy's enthusiasm, and a couple of chilli vodkas, soon won me over.

Arts would cover Death Metal, snuff movies and any celebrity who had died in particularly interesting manner; Sports would deal with football tragedies (Heysel, Hillsborough, the Manchester air crash, etc.) and all-time great motor-racing disasters; the Sex section would interview necrophiliacs (unless Jaffa and Fluffy were prepared to co-operate); Features would include an investigation of the best places to be buried and a top-ten chart of the most prolific serial killers; Fashion were modelling shrouds and winding cloths; and Food . . .

'Tricky one, that. Any ideas?'

It hadn't taken me long to dream up an appropriately morbid theme for my next restaurant. In a fit of enthusiasm and unwonted efficiency, I wrote it up that afternoon – long before the copy deadline.

My diligence was to cost me dear. If I had known then what I was to discover a few days later, I would certainly never have invented something quite so irresponsible as Morgues.

But on the happy day when I was finally presented with cast-iron proof that I really did have magic powers, I was simply too far gone to care. For me, their existence meant one thing above all else: the chance – no, not the chance, the absolute certainty – that I would win the heart of Tamsin May.

'Traitor,' she said when I bounded into her office bearing a huge bunch of red roses. 'Goodbye,' she added, once she'd tossed them into the bin.

'I know things haven't been going too well between us lately –'

'Are you still here?'

'But I want to make it all up. You see, something absolutely incredible has happened. Something that will completely change your opinion of me.'

'You've decided to sign the petition?'

Tamsin had composed a missive, urging the Geezer to scrap the 'suicide issue'. Everyone, save Andy and I, was convinced that it was doomed. The advertising department was up in arms, so desperate to fill space that it had cut rates by three quarters. But still no one was interested in having their products splashed next to pages and pages of relentless gore.

'No,' I said.

'Then I'm not interested.'

'Please, Tamsin. We don't have to talk about it now. I thought maybe if we had dinner this evening –'

'I'm busy.'

'Tomorrow night, then.'

'Ditto.'

'Friday?'

'Goodbye, Giles.'

'You won't regret it. I swear. Let me cook for you on Friday and I'll do anything you want. I'll sign the petition. I'll talk Andy out of it. I'll –'

'OK.'

'You'll come? You'll really, really come to dinner?'

'I said OK, didn't I?'

'Tamsin, you've made my day.'

Though in truth, what had really made my day was the wooden case that had arrived just after breakfast.

There was no indication on the delivery note as to where it had come from. But it scarcely mattered. It was the contents that counted.

I carried the case into the kitchen, prised off the lid and removed one of the bottles. I wiped the label with my sleeve and kissed it three times. Once on the word 'Cheval'. Once on 'Blanc'. And once on the date.

Then I placed the bottle on the table and – I simply couldn't help myself – knelt before it in reverence.

Château Cheval Blanc 1947. One of the century's greatest vintages. Cabernet Sauvignon, Merlot and Malbec grapes, ripened to fat perfection by the long, hot summer of '47.

And I knew then that anything I wanted – anything at all – was mine for the asking.

'Giles,' purred Tamsin, 'that was just . . .' She trailed off, shaking her head in silent ecstasy. No superlative, it seemed, was strong enough to describe the ineffable wondrousness of the dish she had just consumed.

As she lay back in her chair, stretching luxuriantly, her nipples pressed against her blouse. A button had come undone and, through the gap in the dusty-pink silk, I glimpsed a curve of firm, white flesh. She was not wearing a bra. And when she realized that I knew, she blushed and reached instinctively for her button. But instead of doing it up, she smiled, took my hot hand and guided it towards her breasts.

The cassoulet had worked its spell.

It had taken me two days to prepare. On the first, I had purchased from my organic butcher two fatty pork cutlets, a length of thick, coiled, additive-free Toulouse sausage and a handful of hairy pork rinds. From the delicatessen, I had bought a packet of lingot beans, a couple of scarlet Provençal tomatoes, a giant clove of garlic and – in preference to the overpriced tin of goose confit imported from Carcassonne – a pair of cuisses de canard nestling in their own white fat. That evening, I rough-chopped the garlic, leaving it to infuse with the duck grease. I covered the beans in cold water and left them to soak overnight.

On the second day, while the now-swollen beans bubbled in their pan of salted water, I sealed the pork, duck and half the sausage in sizzling, garlicky duck fat, added the peeled, deseeded, chopped tomatoes and left it all to simmer. Once the beans were blanched and drained, I poured them into my cherished *marmite*, covered them with fresh water and threw in the meat, tomatoes and a bouquet garni. Finally, I coiled the remaining sausage on top of the dish, sprinkled the thickly greasy surface with breadcrumbs and slipped the pot into the lukewarm preheated oven. I left it to cook all day.

By six it was done to near perfection. Both the sausage, bursting grainily out of its caul skin, and the crispening breadcrumbs were turning a delightful golden brown. I smashed the crust with a wooden spoon, pushed the cassoulet back into the oven and waited for the crust to re-form. In the next hour, I repeated the process six times.

As soon as I had removed my cassoulet for the final time, I plunged in a large spoon for my first taste. The beans, though soft enough to enrich and thicken the sauce, had yet to disintegrate into a messy goo. The pork and duck, voluptuously flaky, still clung – but barely – to the bones. So simple and yet so fatly decadent.

The charm was sealed.

Powerless as she was against the combined forces of magic and culinary genius, Tamsin fought a valiant rear-guard action.

'Strictly business, all right?' she said, eyeing the candlelit table with deep suspicion.

'I won't do anything you don't want,' I replied, half-filling her balloon glass from the decanter of Cheval Blanc.

She swigged it as if it were any old red. Looked up. And tried it again, more thoughtfully this time.

'Not bad.'

'Glad you like it.'

'Expensive, I imagine.'

'About £1000 a bottle.'

'No!'

I nodded.

'But it's wasted on me. I don't know the first thing about wine.'

'Never too late to learn.'

At first Tamsin pretended not to be interested. Wine was wine, she said. She could tell that this one was better than anything she had tasted, but she didn't want to know why. Buffery was boring. It got in the way of 'naked pleasure'.

'Watch it, Giles,' she said, catching my lecherous 'mm'. 'I came here for one reason.'

But as the Saint-Émilion began coursing through her system, the conversation turned away from office politics.

Together, we agitated our balloons, and I showed Tamsin the glaucous, translucent legs of glycerine trickling down the side. We inhaled the bouquet – 'Do you get those violet and chocolate aromas?' – and I explained how scent, most fickle of all our senses, is so easily bored that the initial sniff will always be the most vivid.

'First impressions,' I said. 'So important . . . That's why I knew from the day we met on the *Courier* that you were special.'

'Giles,' groaned Tamsin.

I showed her how to roll the wine around your mouth, so that its body caressed your tongue – 'Oh really, Tamsin. What a dirty mind you've got' – and how to draw in air as you slurped it down, causing a chemical reaction with the oxygen. 'Like this,' I said. 'Urrggh,' said Tamsin.

I taught her about tannin – 'You know that taste when you drink tea?' About fruit – 'Strawberries, raspberries . . .' 'Grapes?' queried Tamsin. 'Rarely,' I said. About balance – 'Difficult to judge. This is where experience counts. But if it feels right . . .'. And about length – 'With a great wine like this, the taste lasts for ages after you've drunk it.'

Tamsin sighed.

'I'm not boring you, am I?'

She shook her head. 'I was just thinking what an idiot I've been. I've always thought of you as, well, just an ordinary friend. And now –'

'Yes?'

Tamsin blushed. 'Let's try this cassoulet, shall we?'

It was all I could do to finish my plate. The way her legs brushed, ever so gently, against mine under the table. Her murmur of pleasure as she tasted her first mouthful. The beany splodge which she let me wipe from her chin. The tightening knot of anticipation in my stomach. Then, at last, the warmth of her breasts against my palm.

Feverishly, I unbuttoned her blouse.

'Gently,' Tamsin rasped.

But already I had swooped down to suck and lick her breasts, encircling her hardened nipples with my tongue.

'Slowly,' she begged, as my hand drifted down her warm belly and beneath her knickers. I fumbled for the moistness within her pubic mound, and eased a finger between the slippery crack. Tamsin's back arched. She parted her legs wider.

I wanted to move somewhere more comfortable but I didn't want to stop.

I thrust my middle finger in deeper and, passing my other arm around her lower back, I guided Tamsin up out of her chair. We crabbed across the kitchen towards the sitting room. We had got as far as the fridge when Tamsin whispered, 'Wait.'

Kneeling before me, she unbuttoned my trousers and pulled them to my ankles. Then, with agonizing slowness, she unhooked my underpants and eased them down just far enough for the waist band to press against my scrotum and for my buttocks to feel the cold, vibrating metal of the fridge.

Tamsin looked up, wide-eyed.

'It's huge.'

I nodded. 'It's an original Cold Spot. 1952 model I think. I bought it . . . uunngghh!'

Tamsin's hot mouth had closed around my swollen member. Up and down her head bobbed, and each time, her lips plunged further down the shaft until it seemed that she must surely choke.

I was ready to explode. I tried pulling away from Tamsin. But she responded by pushing me hard against the fridge and sucking ever more vigorously. The fridge's humming merged with the squelching of Tamsin's saliva.

Any second now. But maybe I could stave off the moment by running through the contents of my fridge. In the freezer compartment, my Stolichnaya; my stocks — a pheasant, a couple of fonds blancs, an ineffably intense meat glaze, a fumet de poisson; some home-made pistachio ice-cream . . .

No. No. Just let me get down to the . . . tub of costly, rich, organic crème fraîche from Neal's Yard, and the half-finished tin of truffle-studded foie gras, and the shard of crumbling parmesan, and the chocolate mousse, and the Toblerone . . . No . . . No . . . There are plenty of shelves to go before the wine at the bottom, the . . . Puligny Montrachet and . . . No. No! NO!

YES!

Tamsin gulped. She wiped her mouth with the back of her hand and kissed me beneath the ear.

'Delicious *amuse-gueule*. What's next?'

I was removing the mousse and the crème fraîche when Tamsin checked me.

'Not yet,' she said, reaching towards the salad tray, wherein lay a large cucumber. 'There are another four courses before pudding.'

CHAPTER TWELVE

Iain Cowan, bald, Scottish, embittered, had never fulfilled his ambition to edit a national newspaper by the time he was forty. Certainly, he had been given his first editorship a few months before he reached the magic year. But, with a readership of around 25,000, none of whom lived further away than Bath, the *Avon Courier*'s circulation could hardly be termed national. Indeed, whether it deserved the name newspaper was, to my mind, a matter of some debate.

A small-minded malcontent of no significance, you might think. And, but for a couple small details, I would agree. The first is that he presided over the two worst years of my life, when, immediately after Fish Show, I headed to Bristol to serve my 'indentures' as a trainee reporter. The second is that, one morning, six months and nine days into my sentence on the *Courier*, he set in motion the events that would destroy the last vestiges of my friendship with Eric Talbot.

It began like any other day. A summons from the *Courier*'s grubby, smoky newsroom, where I toiled alongside my only friendly colleague Tamsin May; a trip to Cowan's office; and another long lecture on the deficiencies of my copy.

Today, Cowan's spleen was directed at the fifth draft of a report I had composed following a particularly humdrum Parish Council meeting. He read it with ill-disguised contempt, disdainfully enunciating the words he found particularly repellent.

'"Eschewed" . . . "Prolonged" . . . What's wrong with "rejected" and "long"?'

He looked up. His irises, a piercing, almost electric blue in the middle, grew paler at the edge, like the meniscus in a glass of well-aged claret. They were the sort of eyes that only mad Scotsmen have.

'. . . "Responded" . . . "replied" . . . "intoned" . . . the words ye were looking for when ye got lost in your thesaurus, I believe, were "said", "said" and "said",' he said mirthlessly.

Scowling, he replaced the pages carefully on his desk and waved his regulation cigarette towards a small plinth. At its base, it bore the legend of Cowan's alma mater the *Dumfries Bugle* and, jutting out from the top, was a long stainless-steel spike.

'See that, laddie? That is where, by rights, I should have stuck that drivel ye've just given me. What do ye think this is? *The Times Literary Supplement*? *The Oxford English Dictionary*? The *Echo*?' He named the last one with so much venom he almost choked. 'Well, it's nae good enough for the *Avon Courier*, laddie, make no mistake aboot that. Nae mistake at all.'

He scooped up my typewritten copy and looked at it again, as if unable to comprehend its sheer awfulness.

'Ye've wasted it, that's what ye've done,' he muttered. 'Ye've completely wasted . . . No! I'm not going to let ye do it! I'm not going to give ye the satisfaction of bringing down this paper's reputation just because of your childish incompetence . . .'

He leaned over to one side so that he could see past me into the newsroom. 'David,' he called. 'David, could ye just come in here a minute?'

David Tomkins, who sat two desks away from me and Tamsin, loped nonchalantly into the office.

'Iain?'

'David, dear boy, I hate to do this to you but' – he handed Tomkins my copy – 'try and make something of this, will ye? Ye'll find the real story buried in the last par.'

Tomkins skimmed through the piece and nodded.

'Twenty pars?'

'Aye, that should do it.'

Tomkins scuttled out, shooting me a look of pure loathing as he brushed past.

Cowan studied me wearily. 'Laddie,' he said, 'I've nae idea why I'm doing this. But I'm going to give ye one last chance to prove yourself worthy of this newspaper. Ye may have heard that Bob is indisposed.'

I had indeed. Much to my delight, Bob Potter, the paper's regular restaurant critic, had gone down with food poisoning after a visit to The Golden Chopsticks.

'So,' said Cowan, writing something down on a piece of paper, 'I'd like you to stand in for him. There's a wee restaurant I want you to investigate.'

★

'ET's' was its name. It was located on the corner of a leafy square in Clifton, a chichi village of bistros, cafés and student pubs, which I rarely visited. My pay was so pitifully low that I didn't dare expose myself to its manifold temptations. And only rarely was I sent there on assignment. Cowan took the lofty view that any goings-on in this bastion of middle-class respectability were of little interest to the majority of his readers.

Which begged the obvious question: What on earth was he doing sending me to review one of Bristol's pricier restaurants?

My suspicion only deepened when I went inside. Here was an identi-kit picture of the sort of place guaranteed to offend against Cowan's left-wing principles: the decor – spider plants and wicker chairs – was redolent of country-house conservatories; the customers – young, upwardly mobile couples and rich undergraduates, mostly – were well dressed; and the handwritten menu called chips 'pommes frites'.

Tamsin, who accompanied me for moral support, agreed that there must be something suspect about Cowan's motivation. But, beyond suggesting that Cowan was probably a friend of the proprietor's, she refused to speculate.

'It's a trap!' I insisted. 'It has to be.'

Tamsin signalled the waitress for an ashtray.

'We'll just make sure you don't fall into it, won't we?' she said, briskly calling an end to the debate. 'Now. What are you having?'

I studied the menu. Standard bistro fare which, in flusher days, I'd probably have dismissed as too downmarket for my tastes. Amazing how six months of poverty can change your appetite.

'Huh,' I said. 'Well, it's got nothing to do with what I want, has it? It's what that tight-fisted little Scotsman can afford.'

'You're really determined not to enjoy this evening,' muttered Tamsin, lighting her cigarette to signify that if her ashtray didn't come soon, she'd just flick her ash on the tablecloth.

The waitress arrived in time to save the linen, apologizing for the delay. Her white cotton shirt was unbuttoned almost indecently low. As she bent over, I glimpsed a sturdy white bra and a tantalizing hint of voluptuous flesh. When I caught her eye, she smiled back.

Tamsin noticed the romantic exchange and smirked.

'I'm allowed to flirt,' I protested. I could have added, 'Since you insist on keeping our relationship platonic.' But I didn't because it would only have prompted another Tamsin diatribe on the perils of mixing business with pleasure.

'I didn't say anything.'

'Good evening, sir, madam,' said a male voice behind me. 'Have you decided?'

'Almost,' said Tamsin. 'Could you just tell me what this foie de veau is?'

'I could have told you that,' I interrupted. 'Foie de veau – it's calf's liver.'

'Ha ha ha,' said the waiter behind me. 'Still not sure whether we should have printed it all in French. Some of our customers do find it a bit pretentious but' – the voice dropped into a flatteringly conspiratorial whisper – 'I think most of them like a menu they can't understand.'

Tamsin's dark eyes sparkled back at the unidentified smoother. She could, I belatedly remembered, speak perfect French.

'I'm glad madam was brave enough to ask.'

Tamsin was enjoying this shameless fawning. The waiter was evidently a spectacular tart.

'Is there anything you can recommend?' I said brusquely.

'An excellent question, sir. And that's another thing people don't ask often enough.' OK. So he was quite good at his job. 'I'd go for the steak or the cod if I were you. Sounds a bit boring, I know, but they're both looking really good this evening.'

'Fish and chips?' I asked, wheeling round in surprise.

'Yes, sir, it's – Good Lord! Giles, isn't it?'

'Talbot! What are you doing here?'

Talbot had reinvented himself since his scruffy student jeans and suede jacket period. Now, he wore a sharp, teal-coloured suit and a floral tie. His shoes were polished. His hair was slicked back. It could only mean one thing, I thought, with a delicious *frisson* of *Schadenfreude*. His trendy café venture had fallen through and he'd been forced to take on a job as someone else's head-waiter.

'I might ask you the same thing,' Talbot said brightly. 'The last time I heard from you, you were –' He checked himself just in time.

'And, er, your café . . . ?' I asked.

'Sold,' said Talbot.

'Oh, I *am* sorry.'

'I'm not!' said Talbot. 'Got way over the odds for it. More than enough to get a loan for this place.' He swept his arms around the room. 'So, what do you think of ET's?'

'You own this place?'

'Well, strictly speaking, the bank does. But not for long, I reckon. The way business is going . . . But enough of me. Tell me about yourself. What have you been up to since, er . . .'

'This and that,' I said. 'Working for the *Courier*, as a matter of fact. Can't blame you for not noticing. Never seem to use my byline.'

Talbot laughed sympathetically. 'It'll come, I'm sure.'

'That's what I keep telling him,' said Tamsin.

'You must be Giles's –' began Talbot.

'No. Just friends. Colleague actually. Tamsin May. Pleased to meet you.'

'Eric. Eric Talbot. Listen, I'd love to chat. Loads to catch up with Giles but, as you can see, things are pretty hectic at the moment. If I can just take your order for the moment and I'll be back later . . . Promise.'

We followed Talbot's recommendations. Tamsin had the cod and chips, preceded by crab salad. I opted for the soup of the day and the steak au poivre. We agreed to have a bottle of house red, because whereas I certainly couldn't drink white wine with steak, Tamsin didn't mind red with fish.

As we ate, Tamsin asked all the obvious questions: How did I know him? Why did I call him Talbot? Was he attached? And I responded, despite a twinge of jealousy at the last one, with a fulsome tribute to my old chum's qualities. It was almost as if I had missed his company.

Dearly though I wanted to find the food to be disgusting and the wine undrinkable, both were more than up to scratch. The home-made carrot soup tasted carroty and home-made. The seafood was fresh. The steak as *bleu* as I'd ordered. The chips were proper pommes allumettes – thin, crisp and hot. And the vegetables, served in crescent-shaped side-dishes, were all cooked nicely au point.

My main objection was that I had no real objections. Of course, I reminded myself that such dishes were far less challenging than anything I'd ever prepared, and that any chef worth his salt knew how to cook a courgette properly au point, but it didn't make me feel any better. Talbot's kitchen was depressingly competent.

Once we'd finished our puddings – a good crème brûlée and a fruit salad heavy on interesting things like mango and lychees – Talbot joined us for coffee. He brought with him three large measures of Armagnac.

'These are on me,' he said. 'It *all* is.'

'Are you sure?' asked Tamsin. I gave her a gentle tap under the table lest she protested her way out of our freebie. 'That's *very* kind of you.'

'Yes, well, my bank manager would kill me if he caught me at it, but Giles and I go back a long way, don't we?'

'Certainly do.'

'Sorry by the way about . . . Fish Show, wasn't it?'

I frowned.

'You probably don't want to –'

'If you don't mind,' I said, ignoring Tamsin's inquisitive glance.

'And, er, so what brought you to Bristol?'

'Experience, mainly,' I said, as breezily as I could. 'The *Courier*'s got an unrivalled training programme.'

Tamsin sniggered.

'Am I missing something?' asked Talbot.

'Office joke,' Tamsin said.

'I see. Paying you all right, are they? It's unlike you to order a house wine.'

'Good value, though. Rhône, was it?'

'Australian, actually. It's the coming thing, or so my supplier tells me. Reckons in five years' time, we're going to give up on French wine altogether. Apparently the Aussies are producing stuff just as good at half the price. I should get in there quick, if I were you.'

'I don't know. You know what these trends are like. Once in a blue moon perhaps some chap with corks on his hat is going to strike it lucky, but they're never going to be consistent. No tradition, you see.'

'You haven't changed that much, then.'

'By the way,' I said – I'd been looking forward to this bit – 'you'll never guess why we're here.'

'Word of mouth?'

'I'm reviewing ET's for the *Courier*.'

Talbot laughed. 'Lucky I let you off the bill, then, eh? No. Seriously. Was it all OK?'

'Excellent,' Tamsin and I agreed.

'Oh good. That'll be two in one week.'

'Really?'

'Yeah, we had a chap in from the *Echo* in the other day. Cheeky devil. Came out with his press card straight away just so's I'd give him a freebie.'

'And did you?'

'Just a brandy on the house. Don't want to be too prof . . . what's the word I'm looking for?'

'Profligate.'

'That's the one. Just like old times, eh?'

'Just like old times.'

Rare were the days when I failed to dread the interminable bus journey from my cramped flat above a main-road launderette in Cotham, on the outskirts of Bristol, to the *Courier*'s city centre offices.

Rarer still were the instances when I could stride up the stairs of that ugly Sixties block to face, with cheerful equanimity, the cacophony of telephones, battered typewriters and macho reporter-speak, the scowls of my pallid, polyester-suited colleagues and the familiar newsroom odours of stale beer and tobacco. But such was my happy state of mind the morning after my dinner at ET's.

I whizzed through my first assignment – an interview with a 'plucky, have-a-go pensioner', typed it up with unwonted professionalism, and settled down to a bit I'd been really looking forward to: my review.

That finished, I removed one of the three pieces of triplicate paper from my typewriter and showed the result to Tamsin.

As she read, her forehead creased into a frown.

'It's nice, Giles,' she said, eventually. 'Very nice. And normally all I'd suggest would be for you to lose the pretentious stuff. Like "aroma of young blackcurrants" which will convince the readers that it smells like Ribena. And "bleu", too. They'll just think it's a misprint for blue and assume the meat's off.' Tamsin swigged from a plastic cup of fake coffee and added thoughtfully, 'Under the circumstances, that may be no bad thing.'

'What do you mean?'

Tamsin shrugged.

'Just that it may be in your interest to play down your enthusiasm for the place. Knock it, even.'

I stared at her, aghast.

'But Tamsin, I liked it. We both did. It's the best bloody meal I've had in ages.'

'No. I agree totally with what you've said but' – Tamsin grimaced – 'I take it you haven't read this morning's *Echo*?'

'Hardly!'

At least some of Cowan's prejudices had rubbed off on me. In his eyes, the only possible excuse for any of his staff to read the *Bristol*

Echo was to read it in 'inverted commas', laugh at it, mock it, revile it, spit on it – and occasionally lift its stories, if they were good enough.

'Better see for yourself.' Tamsin tripped off to retrieve it from the long bench where all the daily editions were stored. Remarkably it had not been filched or defaced. 'There,' she said, flicking to the right page. 'Read that.'

'ET's . . .' it began. I read on. The *Echo*'s reviewer and I seemed to be pretty much in agreement.

'So?' I said. 'This chap has got taste, that's all. What are you looking at me like that for?'

'Giles' – she drew emphatically on her cigarette – 'have you really not twigged yet? Can't you see why Cowan sent you to ET's?'

And as the realization dawned, those newsroom noises and smells to which I had temporarily been immune came crashing, with sudden intensity, into my ears and nostrils.

'Never,' I said. 'There are some principles which I am simply not prepared to abandon. One is loyalty to one's friends. And the other is the inviolable right of a talented restaurateur to serve well-prepared, reasonably priced food without misguided, vindictive criticism from some chippy little newspaper.'

'I'm not going to argue, Giles. Just ask yourself one question: What's more important, your honour or your career?'

Some time later, after a friendly admonition for me to wipe the shit-eating grin off my face, Iain Cowan settled down to read my 'latest pile of twaddle'. But within a few minutes, I could see that his customary anger had mellowed into a comfortable state of only moderate irritation.

He tried harrumphing occasionally at the more tortuous grammatical constructions, but I could see that his heart wasn't in it.

'Nae bad, laddie,' he said, looking up at me less contemptuously than usual. 'Ye've written it in your usual pretentious way, I see, but I've nae doot the subs will be able to iron that oot well enough. I might even run it.'

I beamed.

'Ye'll no have seen that piece in the *Echo*?' he asked, as I turned to leave.

I turned round. 'Never touch it,' I said.

'Och, I can understand that,' he said, almost smiling. 'Well, awa' with you. I've nae doot ye've got some other work to be getting on with. And when ye have a minute, ye might try to think about which restaurant ye'll be doing next week. I think its aboot time Potter handed over his column to a younger man.'

Heart pounding, cheeks flushed, I bore my review triumphantly to the subs' department. And in that brief, joyous moment, I was too excited to contemplate the price I would have to pay for my good fortune.

Even had I been able to predict the consequences, I doubt I would have acted differently. That review, the work of half an hour, was to cost me the eternal hatred of Bob Potter, whose position I had usurped; it would result in my being sent to Coventry by all Potter's friends; it meant that once a week I would have to visit restaurants with names like The Avon Gorge, Big Daddy's Family Diner and Hungry's Burger Emporium; my reviews would be printed without a byline (Cowan believed that it would strike a loftier tone if they read: 'by the *Courier* Food Critic'); and, of course, it would mean that every morning I would awake filled with nausea and self-loathing, as I remembered the heinous act of betrayal I had committed against my old friend Eric.

But still, it was worth it. I had demonstrated that I had the makings of a real journalist; I had taken the first step towards a bright future as a restaurant critic; and, most importantly, I had averted starvation by guaranteeing myself at least one square meal a week.

Eric would understand. Wouldn't he?

ET'S

Those of us fortunate enough, either through birth or choice, to live in Bristol rather than that brassy, money-minded bastion of greed and licentiousness a couple of hours away up the M4, have hitherto had cause to congratulate ourselves on dwelling in a town where honest home cooking is prized more highly than the more fanciful excesses of the yuppie bistro.

Plain cooking, simple and true, has been the West Countryman's watchword. We may not smother our ingredients in rich sauces and extravagant garnishes, but we do not need to. Unlike the unfortunate Londoner, we have no fear of allowing the full flavour of our fresh local produce to emerge on to the plate, round, unvarnished and undisguised. Plain, but filling and piping hot.

This, I had thought, was still the case until I suffered the misfortune of visiting a new restaurant in Clifton End, which enjoys the offensively yuppie name of ET's.

Those of our readers not sensible enough to have been put off by the pretentious menu outside – written in French with no English translation and accompanied by a price list which would make even Croesus pad his wallet nervously – might do well to heed the *Courier*'s advice and refuse to fill this establishment's rapacious coffers with their hard-earned pennies.

The fact that children under the age of five are pointedly discouraged from visiting this restaurant is a good indication of the sort of clientele it hopes to attract: the sort that are rich enough to be able to afford the services of a baby-sitter.

For all this reviewer knows, such people may well appreciate having their steak served undercooked to the point of rawness and smothered in an overbearingly peppery cream sauce. They may well even think that it is worth burdening the restaurant's hapless washers-up with a needless extra plate – used, mark you, to separate the main dish from its accompanying vegetables.

But of one matter this reviewer is sure. The readers of the *Avon Courier* will not be gracing this restaurant with their presence for many years to come. Not, at least, until it learns that £5.50 is an absurd price to pay for a plate of grilled cod and pommes frites – fish and chips to you or me; and certainly not until it appreciates that an extra £1.00 is an extortionate demand for a plate of carrots and greens so raw you would barely think they had been cooked.

There is only one variety of lager, served on tap at a pricey £1.50 a pint. The wine list, meanwhile, is well beyond the financial reach of all but the most spendthrift snobs. At £5.00 a bottle, we might just have recommended the house red. But since it smells and tastes like peppery Ribena, even this seems a dreadful imposition on the right-thinking customer.

The bill for one person, with wine, came to £22. If this seems reasonable to you, then by all means pay a visit to ET's. You should have little difficulty finding a table. The rest of us will be content to stay at home, secure in the knowledge that that is truly where good value and honest, plain cooking will always be welcome.

———

CHAPTER THIRTEEN

Of course, it could all just have been my imagination. Since the moment I had smelt the burning beans, I had passed the morning in the grip of an increasingly virulent paranoia.

But the looks my colleagues were giving me today seemed unusually significant, their laughter especially cruel, and the tone of their whispered remarks particularly bitchy.

Did they know something I didn't?

Was it pure coincidence that Sherman had a large cucumber on his desk?

No. There was definitely something wrong. Because if there wasn't, why was I in the office when I was meant to be taking Friday off? And why had Tamsin sounded so nervy on the phone?

'No, it can't wait until this evening,' she'd said. 'I've got to talk to you now. In person.'

The day had started well. A leisurely breakfast of dry cured bacon and scrambled egg. A quick vacuum. A deep, relaxing bath in which I scrubbed and loofahed my body until it glowed.

Then, all of a sudden, that whiff of burning. It seemed to be coming from the kitchen. I ducked under the bubbly water, trying to shut out the smell. But when I resurfaced, it had not gone away. It had grown stronger.

By the time I reached the stove, it was too late to save the beans. They had boiled down to a thick black crust, studded with white blobs. It took me ages to scrape off the mess, and, when I had, I discovered a large crack in the earthenware.

Strange. Though I had tried to make the piece as realistic as possible, I didn't recall having mentioned burned beans. Let alone a ruined *marmite*.

Nor – and there wasn't time now to soak another batch of dried beans – had I said that the dish would be made with tinned haricots blancs. And if I used tinned beans, then it wouldn't have the right consistency. And if it didn't have the right consistency, it wouldn't be perfect. And if it wasn't perfect, then why should any of the other things I had predicted . . . ? No. The possibility was simply too awful to contemplate.

Only the sight of my Cheval Blanc arrested the downward spiral. Solid, expensive, reassuring – those twelve bottles were all the proof I needed that things were going to work out.

Whenever I had any doubts – and I certainly did after Tamsin's phone call – I thought of my miraculous wine. And, at once, my fears slipped away.

I rapped on Tamsin's door.

Today she was looking especially gorgeous. At first I couldn't discern why. Had her skin grown softer? Her dark eyes more piercing? Her mouth more voluptuous?

Then I realized. She was wearing that pale pink silk blouse.

'All ready for tonight?'

'Oh yes,' she said, with gratifying enthusiasm. 'Planned anything special?'

'Wait and see.' I tried to sound darkly mysterious.

'Because if it were – No. That would be too much to ask.'

'Tell me.'

'I was just thinking how wonderful it would be if you'd made me one of your cassoulets.'

'You like cassoulet?'

'But you know I do. I *adore* cassoulet! I *worship* cassoulet!'

'Then you won't be disappointed.'

'You haven't made one!'

'I have.'

'Then, I can't see us discussing much business this evening.' Tamsin dropped her voice to a conspiratorial whisper. 'If there's one dish absolutely guaranteed to get me wet between the legs, it's cassoulet.'

Had I heard her aright?

Tamsin smiled her confirmation.

Never had she spoken to me with quite such sexual directness. I was torn between embarrassment and extreme desire. My face had turned crimson; my throat was dry; and I had to cover my groin discreetly with one hand lest Tamsin see the burgeoning lump.

'You'd better sit down,' said Tamsin, eyeing it shamelessly. 'Both of you.'

This was almost more than I could bear. Now she was sucking suggestively on her cigarette.

'Cassoulet. God only knows what I'd do after a bowl of cassoulet. But I don't suppose you'll be short of ideas.'

I nodded weakly.

If she carried on much longer, I could see myself making a fearful mess of my underpants.

'Maybe,' Tamsin purred, 'we could smear ourselves with chocolate mousse and make passionate love on your kitchen table. Or – let's not get ahead of ourselves – I could suck you off first against your fridge.'

Incredible. Our desires coincided exactly.

'And then, we could look inside your fridge. A Cold Spot, isn't it? God, I love Cold Spots. They're so big. So cool. And maybe we could find some crème fraîche. And a cucumber. And you could fuck me until I begged you to stop.'

She was psychic. Had to be.

'But you'd show no mercy, would you, big boy? You'd slide out that cucumber and find something even more exotic to pleasure me with. Like a – yes! – how about a huge, huge bar of Toblerone? I'd love that, wouldn't I?'

And all of a sudden I felt rather ill. Maybe it was the mention of the Toblerone. Or the note of sarcasm, of menace even, which had crept into her voice. But something had alerted me to the possibility that Tamsin was not being wholly sincere.

'From behind. My back slippery with Tuscan Extra Virgin Olive Oil. My head in your oven so that I could inhale the sweet residues of your sublime cassoulet as you thrust your –'

'Tamsin.'

'You're putting me off my stride. Thrust . . . oh yes . . . thrust your throbbing manhood into my moist –'

'Tamsin. This isn't funny.'

Tamsin dragged hard on her cigarette. She studied me seriously for a moment.

'You should have thought of that before you wrote it.'

'Wrote what?'

She tutted and pushed some sheaves of computer print-out paper towards me. I read the first lines to myself.

' "Giles," purred Tamsin. "That was just . . ." She trailed off, shaking her head in silent ecstasy . . .'

I looked up, blushing.

'Extraordinary. Some practical joker must have hacked into my file and –'

'It won't wash, Giles. This is your imagination at work here. No one else's.'

I reddened more deeply. Were my perversions really so peculiar?

'Mind you, you've given me a couple of ideas. Might try them out tonight . . .'

Tamsin's eyes narrowed. Mine lit up.

'. . . with the new man.'

'Oh.'

'Come on, Giles. You don't seriously think I'm still coming to dinner after all this. Sure, I'm flattered that you can be bothered to fantasize about me in such graphic detail. But you can't believe the feeling's mutual, surely?'

I shrugged.

'If it wasn't so absurd, I think I'd have had you sacked. In fact, that's exactly what I was going to do when I found your little essay pinned to the general noticeboard last night. But I think you've learned your lesson. Don't you?'

Tamsin shook her head and tittered to herself.

'I mean, really. I know I've had some strange men in my time. Iain Cowan and Andy Bell, to name but two. But you, Giles? I'd rather eat worms.'

There were cheers when I emerged from Tamsin's office. Sherman and Oriole were re-enacting the cucumber scene.

'No! No!' Oriole gasped. 'Give me something triangular.'

'Like this you mean?' cried Sherman, grasping a Toblerone.

'YES!'

I took the rest of the day off.

It might well have been the greatest cassoulet in the history of cuisine but I wasn't going to give it the benefit of the doubt. I scooped the last spoonful on to the remains of its charred predecessor, enjoying the misery and waste. This was to be an afternoon of sackcloth, ashes and rare malt whisky.

I diluted my 21-year-old cask-strength Bruichladdich with a drop of peaty Islay water, put a Jacques Brel record on the turntable and was just sinking into my least comfortable armchair when the buzzer went.

It was a motorcycle courier with a box wrapped in brown paper. My address was written in thick black marker ink. I carried the package into the kitchen and tore at the shiny sealing tape. The contents stank to high heaven. A truffle maybe?

Trying not to inhale the noxious odours, I prised apart the cardboard flaps. No truffle had ever smelt this bad, surely? I peered inside the box. Lurking at the bottom was a translucent plastic envelope. It contained something soft and squidgy.

Gagging, I carried the box towards the sink and slipped on a pair of rubber gloves, lest I end up with rabies or anthrax. Then, holding my breath, I peeled back the envelope and inspected The Thing.

If it had ever been edible, it was now well past its prime. Fat white and yellow maggots writhed on the surface of a mauve sphere, gaping with dark holes and tubes and swimming in dark, putrid blood. A piece of dead animal, perhaps. The heart by the looks of it.

After a good gulp of whisky, I felt brave enough to examine it more closely. I lifted the object free, brushed a heap of maggots into the waste-away and held the quivering lump up to the light. A pig's heart, perhaps. Only it must have come from a pig bigger than any I had ever seen.

I put the heart to one side. There was something else at the bottom of the box. Another plastic sac, containing three pieces of paper.

One was a copy of the Hunters interview in *Zed* magazine. Another was a cutting of my own Hunters review. The passage where I had suggested that Rob Hunter was a con man had been circled in red ink.

But it was the other piece of paper which was the most frightening thing of all. Even more chilling than that hideous lump of putrescent flesh. It was a sheet inscribed with the familiar gothic logo. Written in a jagged black scrawl was the message: 'You lie, Fripp. Here be boars. Now you have proof.' It was signed Rob Hunter.

Rodney slammed his third empty pint glass on the butt-strewn table and belched loudly.

'So you've given up on your magic powers theory?' he asked.

'If you'd been paying any attention to me this last half hour, you'd have realized it's got nothing whatsoever to do with magic.'

'Someone's stealing your ideas.'

'There's no need for that sceptical tone.'

'Well, I'm sorry, Giles. But I thought we'd ruled out that theory ages ago.'

I wished there had been someone else in whom I could confide. And I could certainly have settled on a better location than the Duke of Clarence, a pub at the rougher end of Ladbroke Grove. Just to get inside, you had to run the gauntlet between several pairs of jaws belonging to the assorted pit-bulls, Alsatians and Rottweilers tethered outside. They belonged to the drug dealers, car thieves, burglars and junkies within.

Yet, in its odd way, the place felt safe. Rodney was known here. And because I was in his company, I too was accepted.

'Do you mean I've got to go through it all again?'

'If you wouldn't mind,' said Rodney. 'Once I've had a top-up. What are you having?'

I thrust another note into his hand.

Rodney returned with a pint of bitter and a gin and lime. Not Tanqueray. Or Rose's.

'Fire away,' said Rodney.

'OK. But this is the last time. The reason we ruled out plagiarism, you'll remember, is that we worked out that there simply wasn't enough time for anyone to copy my ideas. The restaurants opened within days of my reviews being published.'

'With you so far.'

'That's the easy part. Now. As I explained, the reviews are the last pages to go. So there are only two weeks between my writing them and their appearance in print. Not very long, I admit. But if someone were to hack into my computer file, and copy my piece as soon as I'd written it, they'd have just long enough to get the restaurant finished in time.'

'And you think this someone is your editor?'

'I know it is. Apart from the accounts department – and I think we can safely rule them out – he's the only person who got to see my Hunters receipt.'

'So?'

I pulled from my pocket the two bits of paper. One had on it the nasty message purportedly written by 'Rob Hunter'. The other I had taken from my pile of faked receipts. Both were emblazoned with the identical pig's head logo.

'Can't you see? They're exactly the same. Even down to the fake tusks.'

Rodney swigged at his beer.

'I see the similarity. But if this Andy character is so clever, what's he doing giving the game away?'

'That's what I've been wondering. And I've got two theories. One is that it was a mistake. He can be pretty puerile, Andy. Maybe he wanted a bit of fun and went over the top. But I think the more likely explanation is that it was a warning.'

'A warning!'

'Shh!' I looked round the pub to check no one was eavesdropping. But the punters were more interested in getting drunk, playing pool or exchanging banknotes for little squares of black stuff wrapped in clingfilm.

'A warning to keep away,' I said in a low voice. 'They know we're on to them.'

'They?'

'I'll come to that in a minute. But yes, there's definitely more than one of them. A whole network of them. As soon as we were seen sniffing around Stronzo, it must have been reported straight back to headquarters.'

'But how did they recognize us?'

'I think it may have had something to do with the fact that you were blundering around shouting, "My friend Giles Fripp invented this place and we want our money!"'

'Oh yes.'

'But there's another reason for the warning, too. It's only a theory, mind, but what I reckon is that they were just a little bit peeved about my last review. It was too clever for them.'

'Really?'

'Don't sound so surprised. You see, the problem with Cruel Cuisine, unlike my other inventions, is that it's actually quite difficult to do. Think of the trouble they'll have getting hold of a tiger's willy, let alone endangered species like okapi.'

'Maybe they won't bother.'

'Of course they will. It'll be a matter of pride.'

'You sound very sure.'

'If I know anything about the evil genius behind all this . . .'

'Andy, you mean.'

'No. At least I don't think so. Though he's certainly got the motivation.'

'Money?'

'Sure. There's plenty of money involved. Has to be. But I was thinking more of his reputation. You see, well, look at it from his point of view. He wants his magazine to be packed with sexy copy on things that no one else has ever written about.'

'And the easiest way to do that is to get you to make things up.'

'Right. But sooner or later, he's going to be exposed. So he hits on the bright idea of making these made-up stories come true.'

'Fairly complicated way of doing things.'

'And very, very expensive. That's how I know he couldn't possibly be working on his own. I mean, just imagine how much it must have cost to set up these places. Take Lucullus. They'd have had to buy up the site on exactly the same address I'd given in my review and do it up in a fortnight. The builders must have been working day and night. Just think of all that overtime! And when they'd sorted all that out, there'd be awkward details like the phone number and finding a regular hedgehog supplier and getting the togas made and recruiting a head-waiter who could speak Latin.'

'I'd say it was impossible.'

'Me too, if there hadn't been so much evidence to prove me wrong. It just goes to show what a determined person we're dealing with. Determined, clever and incredibly rich.'

'Not for much longer. He must be losing money hand over fist.'

'You think so? You saw how popular Stronzo was. And it wouldn't surprise me if all my other places were doing just as well. How could they fail after all the publicity?'

'Even so. It must have been quite a risk for this chap to take. Surely it would have been a lot cheaper for him to think up his own ideas?'

'That's the whole point. He can't think up ideas as clever as mine. And that's why he's doing it. The money he makes out of it all is just a perk. The main reason he's doing it is because he's jealous.'

'Of *you*?'

'Yes, Rodney,' I said, patiently.

'He can't know you very well, then.'

'He knows me very, very well. Probably even better than you do. And if you haven't guessed who it is by now –'

Rodney nodded slowly. 'I think I've got it.'

CHAPTER FOURTEEN

By midnight, everything was ready. I locked the kitchen and lingered in the dining room, enjoying the soft bubbling of the three fish tanks and the way their phosphorescent light shone blue upon the glassware. Tomorrow, this room would be filled with the sounds of contentment: the chink of silver on porcelain, the spit and crackle of an open fire, the splosh of fine wine in crystal glass, and the cheerful murmuring of twenty or more satisfied customers.

I paused to admire the brass plaque outside.

The sign was incomplete, of course. By rights, it should have had three rosettes embossed next to it. But for now those two words would do.

I polished them with my sleeve.

It was Rodney who had thought up the name. And despite my initial preference for something more sophisticated and French, I had eventually come round to his way of thinking.

'Fish' – that bit was obvious. And 'Show'? Well that, in a sense, was what it was. A spectacle, a performance, a flamboyant demonstration of all that was best in the British culinary tradition.

Fish Show. Two words on which my reputation would stand or fall.

'Good morning. Fish Show . . . Rodney? What the . . . What? . . . How? . . . You fell asleep at the wheel? You bloody . . . Never mind about you. What about the fish? . . . Missed the collection? . . . You incompetent . . . No. No . . . All right. I'm sure it was dreadful but . . . All right, I'm sorry I shouted . . . I said, I'm SORRY. OK? . . . I see . . . Well, just get back as soon as you can . . . Yes . . . Yes . . . I'll deal with that . . . Bye . . .'

The fishmonger was just pulling up his shutters as my cab arrived, half an hour later, in Sodding Woodbury.

'Well, well, well,' he said. 'Mr Fripp, isn't it? Supplier let you down?'

'No. Well, yes. Kind of . . . So if you wouldn't mind, I'd like to buy, um . . .' I consulted my list. 'Six lobsters, eight sea bass, five Dover sole . . . Here . . . It's all written down.'

The fishmonger looked at the list. 'Twenty coquilles Saint-Jacques. Could be tricky. Frozen ones do you?'

'FROZEN?'

'The thing is, Mr Fripp, if you'd been a regular customer, we could have had it all ready and waiting. But with a bulk order like this . . . Conger eel, dear me, I don't think I'm going to be able to help you there either –'

'I can see some, right there,' I said, pointing to a length of dark-skinned eel coiled next to the mackerel.

'I've got some all right. Got plenty, in fact. But your conger's quite a popular commodity these days. Wouldn't be right, now, would it, for me to disappoint my regular customers?'

'It's my house speciality.'

The fishmonger shook his head. 'I can do you the rest. But not the conger.'

'How much do you want?'

'It's not a question of money, Mr Fripp. It's my reputation that's at stake here.'

'What about *my* reputation?'

'Tell you what, Mr Fripp. Seeing as how it may not be the last time your supplier lets you down, I'll do you a favour. I'll give you one conger steak. Now I can't say fairer than that, can I?'

Back at Fish Show I was greeted by my flustered sommelier, Marcus, who muttered that something horrible was going on inside.

It was my parents.

'Just checking the fish have settled in,' said my father, holding a net over one of his unsightly aquaria. In vain had I argued that the three tanks would destroy the dining room's refined ambience. Now he had compounded the sin by putting a vulgar placard on the wall. 'Interested?' it said. 'Then, why not come down to Fripp's Garden Centre. For all your tropical, marine and freshwater requirements.'

Mother was placing a series of name cards on the long table I'd set up for my guests. Or, rather, *her* guests, whoever they might be.

I handed Marcus the fish and went to read Mother's name cards. Something soft squashed beneath my foot. A corpulent dirty yellow elderly creature scurried from under the table, closely followed by another.

'I want these health hazards out of here.'

'No need to take that tone of voice with me, young man. I'm seeing to it that my guests are properly looked after.'

'*Your* guests? What do you think this is? A private dinner – No!' I had caught sight of the names on Mother's cardboard rectangles. 'How could you? How could you invite the Schrecks, of all people?'

'I think it's only right that you should thank them for all those years they spent putting up with you.'

'*They* put up with *me*?'

'I hope you're going to be polite to them this evening. They're our guests. And since your father has put seventy-five thousand pounds into this restaurant –'

'Out, Mother! And take those bloody dogs with you.'

'Darling, did you hear what your son just said?'

Mother and I glared at Father. I won.

'Er, maybe we should be getting out of his way,' he said. 'He is opening in a few hours . . .'

'You never support me,' Mother whined at her husband.

'Daphne! Mortimer! Come to Mummy.'

The dogs did not come.

'Darlings!' called Mother.

From beneath the floorboards came a muffled bark.

'The fish!' I cried, dashing downstairs to the kitchen, where – sure enough – the dogs were fighting over a sea bass.

Mother grabbed them both before I could inflict as much damage as I'd have liked and dragged them into the street.

'And don't come back before seven,' I shouted after my fleeing parents. I picked up the fish – still fairly intact – and gave it a good rinse. Marcus, emerging from the wine cellar, frowned.

By midday, my hands were raw and calloused. On a wooden board stood an orange mountain of painstakingly chopped carrots. Nearby soared two even higher peaks made up of unprepared courgettes and intact mange-touts. Next to them was a half-filled ashtray. In a bin at my feet, ten pounds of King Edwards awaited peeling. In the fridge sat twenty pints of muddy, barnacled mussels, a grilse, five Dover sole, eight sea bass, six lobsters, half a cod and a solitary conger-eel steak. Ahead of me lay hours of filleting and cleaning. And not for the first time in my brief culinary career, I wished I had chosen a product slightly less labour intensive than fish.

Scrape scrape scrape with the back of the knife. Scales all over the sink and the front of my apron; scales clinging to the hairs of my arms and the palms of my burning red hands; scales on my face when I scratched my nose; and under my nails and in my mouth. And slime. A thin coating of it which, scrub as you might, never quite goes. It lingers, rotting all over your clothes and body. After a while, you forget it's there. But nobody else does.

'Pooh,' said an acneed youth in a denim jacket, holding his nose. He was followed by another, similarly repellent specimen. Ben and Tom, my washers-up.

'Pooh, *chef*!' I replied, pleased that in the midst of a crisis I was still keeping my good humour. 'Now. Is either of you familiar with the term *julienne*?'

They shook their heads.

'You will be.'

At six forty-five Holmes finally lurched into the kitchen. His face was pale, his hands were trembling.

'Jesus, Rodney. You look dreadful.'

He opened his mouth to say something. His breath stank of alcohol.

'Yes, yes, I'm sure it was horrible but I haven't got time to hear about it now. I've left you some mussels to clean – in that bowl over there. So hop to it. You'll feel much better.'

Rodney shook his head.

There was no time to sober him up now. What he needed was the hair of the dog.

'Mandy,' I called to my waitress. 'Fix Rodney a stiff Bloody Mary, would you? Plenty of Tabasco and Worcestershire sauce.'

'Eh?'

I reminded her how to make it. One part vodka to four parts tomato juice.

'There,' I said, forcing the glass to Rodney's lips. 'You'll be right as rain after that.'

He glugged it down, shuddering.

'Right,' I said, slapping him on the back. 'Off you go. I'll be in the dining room if you need me.'

Rodney slouched over the chopping board, looking sick.

★

Shortly after seven, the first guests arrived. Marcus was stationed by the entrance with a tray of kirs Royale. Mandy tended the bar. I watched from a discreet distance.

'No . . . not . . . ahem . . . Asti Spumante. Veuve Cliquot,' Marcus was explaining to a muscular, grey-haired gentleman and a tanned, terrifyingly coiffured harpy with a gold jumper and too much make-up, jewellery and perfume. I recognized them as Mr and Mrs Briggs, about the only two of my father's friends Mother had failed to expunge from his Black Country past.

'Ooh, look who it is, Harry!' cooed Mrs Briggs. Her wrists jangled as she nudged her husband. 'Doozn't 'e look posh?'

'Doozn't 'e joost. Loike a proper chef, 'e looks,' said Mr Briggs.

I practised my slimy smile. 'How lovely to see you. Can I get you an aperitif?'

The Briggs were puzzled.

'A gin and tonic?' I suggested. 'A Noilly Prat?'

'A snowball for the woife,' said Harry. 'That'll be 'er lot for the evening. She's droiving. And I'll 'ave a, what did you say again, an Oily Prat? Sounds loike your dad, that dooz – Whoops. Speak of the devil. Joost been talking about you to ah kid 'ere, Barry.'

'Oh, ah,' said my father, advancing ahead of Mother, the Schrecks and the squire and chatelaine of the village manor, Mr and Mrs Kempe.

'Awroit?'

'Can't complain. 'Ow's yerself?'

I retreated towards the bar, closely pursued by Mrs Briggs.

'You've grown up quoite a bit, 'aven't you? A restaurant all of your own. Now when I last saw you –'

'Love to stop and chat but er – Mandy, would you mind making Mrs Briggs a snowball?'

I felt a tap on my shoulder. It was the Gastronome, unusually kempt in a port-coloured smoking jacket and velvet bow-tie.

'I think she's avoiding me,' he said. I followed his gaze to where Mother stood with the Kempe/Schreck nightmare ensemble.

'So then he kicked poor Daphne, right in her little tummy,' Mother was telling them. 'I had to ring up the vet, she was in such pain.'

'Do you think I should break the ice?'

'*She's* not going to, is she?'

Mother was still holding forth. 'Of course, his father and I did most of the work. But has he once said thank you?'

The Gastronome approached the group and hovered on the fringe.

The two men acknowledged him with embarrassed nods. The women huddled together more closely.

The Gastronome cleared his throat. But Mother had other plans. 'Now,' she trilled, 'I'd like you all to come and see my flower arrangements.' And, negotiating her brother as if he were an invisible obstacle, she led her friends towards their table.

Behind me Mr Briggs was complaining to my father. 'Tastes like bloody Martini, whatever 'is nibs loikes to call it.'

I began retreating towards the kitchen. But it was no use. Now Horatio Burgess and his girlfriend were vying for my attention. Since leaving Wellingborough, I'd gathered, he'd been doing great things in the wine trade.

'Horatio,' I said. 'Nice to see you looking so well. And this must be . . . Hello. Pleased to meet you. Giles Fripp. I run this little establishment for my sins. Both got drinks? Splendid. Splendid. I'm glad you could make it, Horatio. I want a word with you later about my drinks supplies. I'm sure I've just paid over the odds for my Mersault.'

Before I returned to the kitchen, I did a quick head count.

Only nine people? Maybe I should rearrange the seating. Should I keep them all spread out to make the restaurant look fuller than it was? Or would it be better to pile them into a corner so that it all felt more cosy? As if it were a deliberately small gathering.

Good. Another couple had just walked in. A sorry pair. He: balding and middle-aged, wearing heavy-rimmed spectacles and a 'cosy' patterned sweater. She: drab and morose, dressed in a pale brown synthetic jacket with matching drip-dry skirt. Friends of Mother's, perhaps? No. Too common. Father's, then? No. Not flashy enough. Critics, then? They were looking round the room, pretending to be lost but secretly trying to find fault with the decor. And what was that poking out of the man's trouser pocket?

A notebook!

Rodney was poised above the mussels, shivering like a rabbit with myxomatosis. Nearby sat the dregs of his Bloody Mary.

'Cheer up,' I said. 'Before you know it, we'll be ready for our DRC.'

Domaine Romanée-Conti. Empress of Burgundian vineyards. I had acquired, at considerable expense, a bottle of their renowned '78 vintage. We would drink it to celebrate the end of our first successful sitting.

'Rodders, we're going to have to get a move on. It's nearly –'

'Can't,' he whispered.

'Of course you can,' I said. 'You just take a knife, bash off the barnacles, pull out these tiny little Brillo pad things, rinse them and – Come on. You've done it thousands of times before.'

Rodney regarded me balefully.

'It's going to be a disaster, isn't it?'

'What on earth makes you think that?'

'Because . . .' He trailed off.

I snatched his glass of Bloody Mary and tasted a little. Roughly four parts vodka to one of tomato juice.

I grabbed the back of his chef's whites and gave him a good shake. 'Now look here, wretch,' I said, slapping his face with one hand while I held him up with the other, 'you're going to sober up and help me with this dinner if it's the last thing you ever do.'

Rodney had grown limp in my grasp.

Maybe I had taken the wrong approach. I lowered my voice and whispered soothingly in his ear.

'Rodney. I *need* you. You're the only one who knows how to run a restaurant kitchen.'

'I am?'

'Luc Piccholine. Remember?'

Rodney laughed sickly.

'What would Luc have done if he'd found you like this? You were the best commis–chef he ever had.'

'Oh . . . hee hee hee . . . you really don't know, do you?'

'Know what, Rodney?'

His body was convulsing with mirth.

'Luc P-Piccholine. I m-made him up.'

I slackened my grip on Rodney. He crumpled heavily on to the floor.

He did not get up.

'Shall I call a doctor, chef?' asked one of the boys.

'Certainly not. One of you help me drag him outside.'

'But he'll freeze to death.'

'No more than he deserves,' I said.

The boys looked shocked.

'Well, what are we supposed to do?' I said. 'We can't have him cluttering up the kitchen.'

One of the boys indicated the cellar.

'How about in there?'

'Quickly, then. Before Marcus stops us.'

I was just locking the cellar door when Marcus appeared.

'Ahem,' he coughed.

'Just, um, checking things are OK down there . . . er . . . Nothing to worry about but Mr Holmes is having a rest and if you could do your best not to disturb him too often . . .'

'Could I have a word,' said Marcus icily.

I moved closer so that no one else in the kitchen could hear.

'There's a lady just come in who claims to be Mr Holmes's mother. She wants to see him.'

'Well, she can't. Not now. He's indisposed.'

'A family trait, perhaps?'

Only one guest had yet to be seated: the flushed, middle-aged woman with the fur coat and crocodile-skin handbag whom everyone was doing their best to ignore. Rather difficult when she was blundering up to them, breathing fumes of alcohol into their faces and croaking, 'Have you sheen my little boy? He works here, you know. He's the chef. He's in the kitchen now. And that horrible man won't let me see him. Why won't he let me shee my little boy?'

Mandy was trying to take the critics' order.

'I think it means congealed . . . Hang on, I'll just check with chef – CHEF!'

'Tell him it's conger eel but that unfortunately it's off,' I hissed to her, my professional smile growing increasingly strained.

'Chef says the eel's off,' Mandy shouted to the customer.

'No, no, wait!' I said. If anyone was to taste the sole piece of eel, it should be the critics. 'There's one left.'

'The eel's off. But there's one left, chef says,' repeated Mandy.

I held Rodney's mother firmly by the arm. 'Hello, Mrs Holmes,' I said. 'If I could just take your coat and then we'll have you seated.'

'I don't want to sit down. I jusht want to shee my little boy. Go and tell the manager that I want to shee my little boy. *He*' – she looked daggers at Marcus – 'won't let me.'

Marcus was not faring much better with the Briggses. 'I don't care how bloody well chosen chef's wine list is. I'll have a pint of bitter or nothing.'

'Mrs Holmes,' I persisted, 'I am the manager. And if –'

'No you're not. My little boy's friend Giles is the manager.' She surveyed me blearily. 'What are you doing wearing my son's uniform? He's the chef. Not you. This is a disgrace.'

'I *am* Giles, Mrs Holmes. And I would be most grateful if you'd give me your coat and bag and sit down. You're spoiling it for the other customers.'

'I'm a customer too. And a shareholder. Don't I have any rights?'

'Of course you do, Mrs Holmes. Of course. But you can't see Rodney right now. He's busy.' She looked unconvinced. 'In fact, just a few moments ago, he said to me . . . he said, "Please don't let Mummy come and see me now because I wouldn't want to ruin that delicious dinner I'm making for her."'

Mrs Holmes grinned sloppily.

'Hear that,' she called out to the diners. 'That's my son Rodney he's talking about. My little boy. And he's making you all a delicious dinner.'

I whispered to Horatio that there was a decent bottle of wine in it for him if he could keep his new neighbour under control for the evening. 'A very decent one,' I added, when he looked unenthused.

Before I returned to the kitchen, I took the order slips from Mandy. Fourteen starters and fourteen main courses, all of which I would now have to prepare single-handedly.

I perused them as I went. Five fish soups – no problem there: just a question of thickening the stock; four coquilles Saint-Jacques – Rodney's bloody recipe. How did it go again? Bourride – meant to be a main course. Who the devil had ordered . . . Ah. Must have been the Gastronome; four moules marinières – easy, Rodney had been bearding them. No, wait a second, Rodney had been *attempting* to beard them, which meant . . . This was going to be impossible. The starters alone would take me all evening. I stopped at the top of the stairs and glanced back at my uncle.

With the Gastronome newly promoted to chef de cuisine, things took a dramatic turn for the better. The starters had been dispatched. And the main courses were well under way. My uncle took charge of the difficult bits – like the Briggses' lobsters à l'américaine and the four soles meunière, while I dealt with the less taxing chores – stirring the aïoli into the bourride, deep-frying my father's cod and chips, and making sure that Mrs Schreck's sea bass was the one the dogs had mauled. I needed to preserve my energies for Mr Critic's 'Congre à la Mode Fripp'.

Not that he was likely to appreciate it. Already he'd demonstrated a suspicious lack of discernment when he'd sent back his white wine. Marcus had returned, sour-faced, with the bottle.

'There's nothing wrong with it,' he'd grumbled.

Having sampled it, my uncle and I agreed.

'I endeavoured to persuade the gentleman,' explained Marcus, 'that what he had mistaken for oxidation was in fact the distinctive nutty quality one encounters in a good Mersault.'

I had gently chided Marcus for his presumptuousness. Surely he must be aware that critics were always right? He should apologize at once, I told him. Furthermore, he should replace the rejected Mersault with an even better one.

Pursing his lips, Marcus had obeyed.

But now, here he was again. Back with the second bottle.

'Imbecile,' he cursed, storming towards the wine cellar.

'Oi! Watch it!' snapped Mandy, whose pile of empty first-course bowls Marcus had nearly knocked on to the floor.

'Again?' I asked.

'AGAIN!' snapped Marcus.

I sniffed the rim of the second Mersault bottle.

'You're quite right, Marcus,' I said. 'But, um, I do hope you didn't tell him what you thought of his judgement?'

'I couldn't help myself, chef,' he said. 'I haven't been a sommelier for sixteen years to put up with that sort of nonsense.'

I gritted my teeth.

'Marcus, it may have escaped your notice, but this is not the bloody Toison d'Or. I do not pay you £15,000 a year to argue with my customers. Now, if you'd be so kind, perhaps you'd like to go back there, apologize to the man and get him something else.'

'I certainly will not,' said Marcus.

'You'd jolly well better or you'll be out of a job.'

'That might be the most agreeable solution for both of us,' said Marcus.

'I'm sorry?'

'Did I not make myself clear? Then, please, allow me to elaborate. I have worked in many restaurants in my time, Mister Fripp. Some small. Some large. Some in this country. Some abroad. But never in sixteen years of service have I had the misfortune to ply my trade in an establishment quite so ill-conceived, poorly managed, inept, shoddy –'

'Marcus!'

'– unhygienic, incompetent, and quite so obviously doomed to spectacular failure as this miserable excuse for a restaurant.'

'I take it you have certain reservations about Fish Show?'

'Reservations,' said Marcus, just before he slammed the door behind him, 'are a concept with which this restaurant is destined to remain eternally unfamiliar.'

'Well, everyone,' I said brightly, 'now that we're rid of him . . . Mandy. Where do you think you're going?'

'After him,' she said, retrieving her anorak.

'Mandy, wait. Please. You don't believe all that nonsense he just said?'

'It's not him. It's them upstairs. They're a bunch of animals,' she said.

'Who's a bunch of animals?'

'All of them. Specially him with the beer. If he feels my bum one more time . . .'

'But Mandy, if you're having problems, all you've got to do is tell me.'

'I am telling you.'

'But you can't go now. We've still got the main course to serve.'

'They can all stuff their main course. They'll only grumble like they did about the last one.'

'Complaints? Already? What were they complaining about?'

'What wasn't they complaining about, more like. The ones with the soup said it was too salty. The ones with them white things in shells said the potatoes was lumpy. The ones with the mussels was moaning that they hadn't been shaved properly –'

'What was that?' called the Gastronome, sweating over his sauce américaine reduction. 'Been complaints, have there? Who was complaining? Ungrateful buggers.'

'He's right, Mr Fripp. They're ungrateful buggers, that's what they are,' chipped in Mandy. 'And I've had it up to my tits with them.'

'Don't you worry, me young filly. I'll sort 'em out,' said the Gastronome, licking his lips.

'Uncle . . . Mandy . . . Wait. Mandy, look, if you have any more problems, I promise I'll deal with them. And I'll make sure there's a nice little bonus for you at the end of the evening. But please, I need you.'

'He may be right, dear girl,' said the Gastronome. 'Give the fellow a chance. And if he can't do anything about it, you can be sure that I will.'

Mandy replaced her anorak on the hook. 'All right, then. But any more –'

'Thanks,' I said, diving for the fridge, where I found our most expensive bottle of white. Montrachet. 'I appreciate this. I really do.'

The hubbub at the main table subsided into discreet chuntering as I approached my guests.

'Everything all right?' I said, smiling brightly and rubbing my hands together.

'Great, thanks,' chirped Horatio to the disgust of his neighbours.

'No, everything is not all right,' barked Mother. 'And whatever your polite young friend here says, I know I'm speaking for all of us.'

There was an embarrassed hush.

'Ah.' I glanced to see whether the critics were listening in. They were.

'Well?' Mother squawked, increasingly self-righteous. 'Are you going to offer us an explanation? Our starters were perfectly abysmal.'

'There's no need to shout,' I said, fighting my urge to throttle her. I lowered my voice and muttered in her ear. 'Please, Mother. I'm sorry you're having a bad time, but don't ruin it for everyone else. We had a little mishap in the kitchen, you see.'

'A jolly big mishap, I should say,' said Mother loudly. Mrs Schreck nodded in furious sympathy.

'Mother,' I pleaded, 'I'm trying to explain. Rodney had an accident this morning and –'

'Rodney? What's happened to my little Rodney?'

'It's all right, Mrs Holmes. He just had a slight bump in the van this morning. That's all.'

'Oh my God. Just like his father. Where is he? I must see him at once.'

'Mrs Holmes. Sit down. Please. I told you – he's perfectly all right. In fact, he asked me especially not to tell you about the accident because he knew you'd worry and he doesn't want to be interrupted while he's cooking your main course.'

'So we have Rodney to blame for this muck, do we?' said Mother.

'Did you hear that?' Mrs Holmes said to Horatio. 'That dreadful woman is insulting my son's cooking. You liked it, didn't you?'

Horatio gave me a 'this had better be a particularly good bottle of wine' look.

'Right,' snapped Mother. 'That's the last word I'm going to hear from that fishwife this evening. Giles, you must eject her at once. She's drunk!'

'Fishwife?' shrieked Mrs Holmes.

'Ladies!' I cried. 'Control yourselves. It's – '

'Either she leaves, or I do,' said Mother.

Before I could tell her that the latter option would make everyone a great deal happier, Father muttered in her ear. Something on the lines of putting aside pride for the sake of the family honour.

I took the Montrachet to the critics' table and, before they could say anything, I delivered a slobberingly sycophantic apology, gave them just long enough to approve the wine, and fled with what little dignity I could muster.

'D'you know, if you weren't such a damned fine chef, you'd make a bally marvellous diplomat,' the Gastronome said. 'Don't know where you get it from. Tact's never been a strong point with us Dantes. If I'd had my way, I'd have been out there and at 'em with my cleaver.'

It was the first time all evening we'd had a chance to relax. The Gastronome, dripping with exertion, was towelling himself down by the back door. I had propped myself near the oven, consolatory cigarette in one hand, glass of the critics' rejected Mersault in the other.

Then Mandy appeared. Mr Critic wanted to talk about my conger.

I flung the half-finished cigarette towards the bin, went wearily upstairs and, avoiding the mutinous remarks emanating from the main table – 'I wanted proper batter on me cod, not sodding breadcrumbs. And as for these chips . . .' 'Those are dog hairs. Those are *definitely* dog hairs . . . Waitress . . . WAITRESS!' – I Uriah Heeped towards the critics.

Mr Critic was scribbling.

'Chef arrived . . .' he noted in a suburban monotone. 'How many minutes is it now, Deirdre?'

Deirdre checked her watch. 'Five, dear. No, I tell a lie. Five and a half.'

'– Five and a half minutes after objection was raised regarding quality of aforementioned dish.'

Mr Critic looked up from his notes.

'Hello again, sir' – I bowed – 'madam' – I bowed again. 'I under-stand that the "Congre à la Mode Fripp" was not to sir's satisfaction.'

'Indeed,' said Mr Critic. 'I regret to report that, having essayed the . . . con-gree . . . the connnggree . . . the dish you mentioned just a moment ago, I found it to be . . .' Mr Critic consulted his notes, "too fishy" . . . And Deirdre thought so too. Didn't you, dear?'

Mrs Critic nodded. 'Indeed I did,' she said. 'Much too fishy.'

I swallowed. 'Very good, sir. It will be my pleasure to find a more agreeable substitute. Have you had time to decide what you would like instead?'

'I have,' said Mr Critic. 'What was it again, dear?'

'The lobster,' said Mrs Critic. 'You wanted the lobster.'

'Lobster' I wrote. 'But . . . um . . . I take it everything else was to your satisfaction?' I asked. 'The wine. You liked the wine, didn't you?'

Mr Critic furrowed his brow.

'Should I mention it, dear?'

'Oh, I think you should,' said his wife.

'You . . . you didn't like the Montrachet?' I asked.

'Oh no,' said Mr Critic. 'Deirdre and I found the Mont Ratchitt with which you furnished us to be most agreeable. Didn't we, dear?'

'Most agreeable,' agreed Mrs Critic.

'But what concerned us was whether,' droned Mr Critic, 'your most generous gift of this not inconsiderably costly bottle of fine wine might, so to speak, be construed as a *bribe*.'

'A bribe,' echoed Mrs Critic.

'A bribe!' I exclaimed. 'Heaven forbid! I would have done the same for any of my customers.'

'You would?' asked Mr Critic.

'Certainly.'

'Only, if we thought that you were endeavouring in any shape or form to . . . coax us . . . into securing a favourable report in the *Good Restaurant Guide* –'

'Careful, dear,' chipped in Mrs Critic.

'The *Good Restaurant Guide*!' I pretended to be spectacularly impressed. 'Goodness me. This really is an honour.'

Mr Critic was too busy beaming to notice his wife's anxious expression.

'Isn't that . . . now correct me if I'm wrong,' I said, 'but isn't that the splendid publication which, rather than trust the opinions of professional critics, takes the admirably populist line of asking ordinary members of the public to write in with their own reports?'

'The very same,' said Mr Critic, revelling in his power. 'And they never fail to write back to tell us how much our comments are appreciated.'

'I'll bet.' I licked my lips, relishing the moment.

Behind me, from the direction of my parents' table, came a startled male shout, quickly followed by some angry female squawking. I ignored it. Nothing was going to deprive me of the first fun I had had all evening.

'Unfortunately,' I told Mr Critic, with a note of subdued menace, 'your comments are not so highly valued at Fish Show.'

'Begging your pardon?'

'I mean, *sir*, that this restaurant has better things to do than waste its time pandering to the petty prejudices of idiots who quite clearly know nothing whatsoever about food or wine.'

'Does he mean us, Deirdre?'

'Out!'

'I surmise that he –'

'OUT!' I yelled, only just loud enough to be heard above the growing din at my parents' table.

Mr and Mrs Critic hastily grabbed their coats and followed the chef's recommendation.

I turned to survey my other diners. There'd be no more misbehaviour after what they'd just witnessed. Unfortunately, they had not even been watching. Their attention had been drawn elsewhere: to the corner of the room which Mandy, armed with two platefuls of food, was defending. Advancing on her was a party of discontented diners, led by Mr Briggs and closely followed by Mother and Mrs Schreck.

'I warned you,' squawked Mandy, flinging one of the plates towards them. It described an arc above their heads, spraying them with red juice and half-eaten lobster, and smashed near my feet.

The raiding party paused to wipe their clothes. And then continued their advance on Mandy.

I hurried between the two warring factions.

'Out of my way, Joiles. That little trollop's going to get the 'oiding of 'er loife,' warned Mr Briggs, rolling up the sleeves of a shirt whose front was dripping with thick red sauce.

'Any excuse to touch my bum, you dirty old sod,' taunted Mandy.

'Leave them, Giles. She deserves it,' screeched Mother, flexing her claws.

'She bloody well doozn't,' called Mrs Briggs. 'It's about time some-one put 'im in 'is place. Loike a bloody octopus, 'e is.'

'I'll 'ave none of that lip from you,' Mr Briggs snarled back at his wife.

Mother and Mrs Schreck edged closer.

'If either of those fat cows moves a step closer, they're getting this straight in their gobs,' said Mandy. 'Tell 'em, Mr Fripp. I won't miss again.'

'STOP. ALL OF YOU!' I shouted.

'After what she said to Hortense? Certainly not,' said Mother.

'Certainly not,' agreed Mrs Schreck.

'I think perhaps we ought to be going,' said the Kempes, beating a hasty retreat.

'For goodness' sake!' I cried. 'You're all acting like children.'

'What about moi shirt?' 'Dog hairs!' 'She told Hortense she could like it or lump it!' said Mr Briggs, Mrs Schreck and Mother simul-taneously.

'Right, that's it. I want you all sitting down again this minute,' I said.

'Not until that bitch apolojoises,' said Mr Briggs.

'Would you care to repeat that?' said a voice from the top of the kitchen stairs. All eyes turned towards the Gastronome.

''Oo's asking?' sneered Mr Briggs.

'Someone who takes a rather dim view of that sort of language being addressed to a young lady.'

'Call that tart a young lady?'

'I think, sir,' said the Gastronome, 'you'd better apologize immedi-ately or suffer the consequences.'

'Piss off.'

The Gastronome's mouth twitched. He calmly removed his apron, stepped towards the fireplace, picked up two pokers and tossed one towards Mr Briggs. It landed with a dull clunk at his feet.

'Pick it up,' commanded the Gastronome.

'Norra chance,' said Mr Briggs.

'Would you like the thrashing of your life with or without a means of defence?' asked the Gastronome calmly.

Mr Briggs picked up the poker.

'Giles, can't you stop them?' implored Horatio.

'I appreciate your concern, my friend. But I cannot stand idly by when a lady's honour has been impugned,' said the Gastronome, pointing his weapon towards Mr Briggs. '*En garde*, sir.'

Mr Briggs lunged at the Gastronome, who stepped deftly aside and, as his adversary shot past, whacked him hard on his posterior.

'*Touché*,' said the Gastronome.

'Someone call the police,' croaked Mr Schreck, so pathetically that everyone ignored him.

Mr Briggs picked himself off the floor and, poker outstretched, hurled himself at the Gastronome once more. Again, with a deftness astonishing in one so large, the Gastronome stepped aside, delivering another sharp prod to his enemy's buttocks. This time Mr Briggs did not fall. Instead, he careered straight past the onlookers, until his progress was checked by the marine tank.

It creaked and rocked on its metal frame. Sturdy things, fish tanks. Heavy too. It was bound to hold. It had to hold. Please . . .

With a fizz of ruptured electrical appliances, the cracking of glass and the gushing of fifty gallons of salinated water, the tank crashed on to the floor.

The silence which followed was broken only by the frenetic flappings of a kaleidoscopic display of exotic fish, writhing amid the splinter-strewn pool which seeped slowly across the floor.

Someone coughed nervously. Horatio and his girlfriend tried rescuing the healthier-looking specimens by spooning them into the two unbroken tanks. My father, kneeling amid the gasping fish, shook his head tearfully.

The rest of us stood, crouched or lay where we were, trying not to meet anyone else's eyes. Like revellers at an orgy, caught in mid-act during a police raid.

In fact, to judge by the noise coming from the direction of the kitchen, maybe this was a police raid.

At first it was barely noticeable. But what began as a muffled rattling quickly grew into the unmistakable sound of a wooden door being pummelled very hard.

Still no one moved.

The banging stopped for a second, only to be replaced by the dull, regular thud of glass on wood.

'Rodney!' I hissed.

'Rodney?' echoed Mrs Holmes.

'Fire!' shouted Rodney, from within his vinous cell.

'Fire?' screamed Mrs Holmes, starting towards the kitchen.

'Leave him,' I commanded, seizing her by the arm.

'My little boy's burning alive!'

'It's a ruse,' I said. 'He's better off where he is. Believe me.'

'There is a funny smell,' said someone.

'It's that, you fool!' I said, pointing to the log fire.

'Do you think I don't know the diff . . .'

There was a splintering noise and then a series of crashes of what sounded like – and indeed was – bottle after bottle of costly burgundy and Bordeaux being hurled desperately against the cellar door.

'He's burning alive, I tell you,' shrieked Mrs Holmes.

'He should be so lucky,' I said, accelerating away from her to rescue my wine.

Which, as the blast of heat and noxious smoke warned me the second I yanked open the door to the kitchen, was going to be a rather futile errand.

The flaming pyre perceptible through the greasy blackness in the spot where the cooker had once stood was already burning with irredeemable fury. My eyes stung and shrank in the heat; my throat clogged with acrid, poisonous fumes; my lungs heaved; the hairs on my exposed arms shrivelled and my instincts told me to get out fast.

I probably would have done too had I not been dragged suddenly to the ground. For a second I thought I had been crushed by one of those giant beams that always trap the hero in inferno movies. The hysterical scream of 'Rodney' from the woman lying on top of me told me otherwise. We wriggled and writhed for a few moments, during which I was surprised to notice how much clearer and fresher the air was on the ground than it was when I was standing up. Indeed, I was beginning to feel almost comfortable staying where I was. Rather hot, certainly. But definitely a lot more relaxed. If I just lay there and waited, maybe someone would deal with that nagging worry which, until very recently, had been preying on my brain. What was it now? So difficult to remember when you're a mite dizzy. Something to do with wine, as I recalled. Expensive wine too. I could almost see the range of labels, shimmering before me . . . Montrachet . . . Romanée-Conti . . . Château Latour . . . Oh joy! I had died and gone to heaven. A bit warmer than my scripture teacher had led me to believe. A lot warmer, in fact. Hot as . . . so Jesus was wrong after all . . . Cana was an aberration and the devil really did have all the best vintages . . . So . . . which one should I try first? Perhaps a *soupçon* of

. . . Where the hell had they all gone . . . Where the . . . Ho ho, very funny . . . except it wasn't . . . Some greedy bastard – Cerberus? No, he was a dog . . . Tantalus . . . No, he never got to try any . . . in fact, the Gastronome had a rather amusing Tantalus in his . . . Steady, Giles . . . You're losing it . . . Some bastard's nicking all your wine and what are you doing? What are you doing? What am I doing . . . Something to do with . . .

Wine. That was what they told me I'd been babbling about when they dragged me out . . . After Rodney and Mrs Holmes, which I think gives you a pretty good idea of their misguided sense of priority.

In the ambulance they gave me all the usual guff about 'if you'd been in there just a few seconds longer' and about my 'selfless heroism'. I liked the second bit and would have made more of it if I hadn't been preoccupied by the dull pain in my bandaged hands and . . . Oh my God . . . I tried sitting up, jerked off my oxygen mask and looked anxiously at my father. He was holding the bottle of Domaine Romanée-Conti which I dimly recalled grabbing just before I had been overcome by the smoke.

'Fish Show?' I wheezed.

My father shook his head.

'We can . . . we can try it all again, though, can't we?' I managed to whisper before someone in a Day-Glo jacket put the mask back over my mouth.

'Of course,' said my father in a tone which, even in my confused state, struck me as somewhat insincere.

CHAPTER FIFTEEN

The garden, which had always tended towards anarchy, had now risen in open rebellion against its master. What had once been flowerbeds had long since been choked with weeds. The unmown lawn rioted with dandelions, daisies and thistles. The banks of the stream were swamped with nettles, through which had been scythed a narrow passage leading to a waterside colony of ducks and geese. In the humid, almost subtropical air which smelt of pollen and rank greenery, biting insects whined and buzzed.

Beneath a yew tree near the back of the house stood a large figure which, viewed from afar and with a good deal of imagination, might have been mistaken for a flightless prehistoric bird with a dangling red-and-white crest, a multicoloured body and pallid legs. On closer inspection, you would have recognized it as a fat man wearing a *keffiyeh*, a Hawaiian shirt and a pair of shorts which exposed a pair of pudgy white legs riddled with purple varicose veins.

Nearby, on a tartan rug, sat a youth in a pale blue shirt and fawn cotton trousers. The latter's attempts to strike an insouciant pose were being frustrated by the continual assault of winged insects. But, in deference to the older man's wishes, he was pretending to enjoy himself. Perhaps the wine he was about to taste might alleviate his misery.

'Any ideas?' asked the Gastronome.

I had, as a matter of fact. But, for his sake, I thought I'd better not make it look too easy. I made a show of slopping the wine pensively round my tongue. Looking puzzled. And trying again just to make sure. Definitely a vintage of distinction.

'Palmer '87?'

Smiling, the Gastronome retrieved the bottle from behind the yew tree. It was something from California. A 1987 Opus One.

'Galling, hmm?' he said. 'Buggers have only been at it for, what, a couple of centuries? And already they're outclassing the greatest

Margaux. Still, old habits die hard. If it hadn't been for you, I'm sure I would never have invested in three cases of the stuff.'

I frowned. It wasn't the reckless waste on New World rubbish which bothered me so much as the suggestion that I was partly responsible for it.

'Amazing,' continued the Gastronome, 'to think what I've been missing all these years! Finishing that bally book's been quite an eye opener, I don't mind telling you.'

So, to my chagrin, I had noticed.

I had visited the Gastronome to get away from it all: from Tamsin's reproachful stares; from Andy's unconvincing gestures of friendship; from my colleagues' titters; from the flat which might at any moment be invaded by the fearsome Rob Hunter, the leering Guido Stronzo or any of Eric Talbot's other co-conspirators.

At Jebel Mara lay peace, stability and the reassuring prospect of five-course French dinners, washed down with choice burgundies and Bordeaux. Or so I had anticipated on the train journey down.

Instead, the Gastronome had greeted me with samosas and dals and a fiery phal; with lassi and Cobra lager; with incessant babbling that life had never been so much fun since he had been freed from the tyranny of French cuisine.

On the second day we had lunched on Caribbean and dined on Thai. By the third — Sunday — I had grown weary of my uncle's culinary experiments. And when, instead of the expected roast, he chose to foist on me corn bread, grits, hush puppies and okra gumbo, I decided the time had come to speak my mind.

'Technical term for it all, I believe, is Southern White Trash,' the Gastronome explained, ladling it on to our plates. 'Rather appropriate on a day like this, wouldn't you say?'

'Just what I needed,' I sneered, pushing my plate away. 'A chance to lose some weight.'

'Language!'

'Well, I'm sorry, Uncle. But really. I'd been hoping for something a little more . . . edible, from you of all people.'

'Let me assure you, Giles, you won't taste finer grits this side of the Carolinas.'

'Why should I want to taste grits at all? Or Goan prawns and Jungle curry for that matter?'

The Gastronome regarded me slyly.

'And I suppose you were hankering after something a little more traditional. Roast okapi, perhaps? Or a ragout of flamingo tongues?'

I grimaced.

'Nothing to be ashamed of,' said Gastronome. 'You're old enough now to make up your own mind about what it is you really want. Just so long as you're prepared to accept the consequences when you get it.'

'Get what?'

'No need to play the innocent with me. Remember, I've been there myself. More or less. You'll understand that Hunters sounded rather too active for my taste. And Stronzo – well – I can't abide all that modish nonsense. But I've no complaints about your marvellous osprey egg soufflé. Took me right back to the time in –'

'You've been to Cruel Cuisine?'

'Couldn't miss a chance like that, now, could I? Nor Lucullus, being so close to home.'

'How did you find it?'

'Short hop up the M5. Turn off at Bath –'

'Cruel Cuisine, I meant.'

The Gastronome tapped the side of his nose. 'Contacts.'

'Jesus! They managed it!'

'I'm sorry?'

'Nothing. Well . . .' I was almost tempted by the Gastronome's encouraging raised eyebrow. 'Oh, never mind.'

The sun was setting, the early evening chill had driven off the wasps and my thoughts had turned to the journey home when the Gastronome proposed a farewell drink.

He returned with a proof copy of *The Gastronomy of France* and a Gordon's bottle filled with a milky liquid which definitely wasn't gin.

'Arak,' explained the Gastronome. 'Home-made.'

It stung as it trickled down my throat, but there was a warm aniseed aftertaste.

We drank silently, watching the sky above the orchard change from orange to red, and from vermilion to purple. Only when dusk had settled softly on the garden, draining the leaves and grass of their colour, did the Gastronome speak.

'The song of cicadas. Coal-black bodies gleaming in the fire light. A few stone huts. That's all that's missing – that, and little Ibrahim, of course. We passed many happy evenings like this, Ibo and me. Squatting on the ground, with our araks.'

'What's it made of again?' I interrupted, faintly embarrassed by the Gastronome's descent into purple reverie.

'Dates,' he said. 'Dates like the ones the Gonda women used to gather while the men were out hunting. You can almost see them now. If you look hard enough.'

He was gazing in the direction of the river.

'There. Beneath the palms.'

All I could make out was a dark clump of nettles. And the odd ghostly shape of a duck, rustling through the foliage.

'I was happy then, Giles. I suppose you could say those two weeks in Jebel Mara were my last spell of innocence. The time, if you like, before I tasted the fruit of the Tree of Knowledge.' He looked at me. 'In that respect, I was very much as you are now. Confident. Cocky, even. Damned sure that I knew what was best. That I had all the answers.'

I nodded dutifully.

'I didn't, of course. Any more than you do now. So I'd advise you to keep your counsel and lend an ear, as I tell you the story of what really happened inside that volcano, all those years ago, in the Western Sudan.'

He refilled both our glasses. And began his tale, taking it up at the point when, having finished *A Discourse on Divers Cuisines*, he travelled to the Western Sudan with his faithful companion Ibrahim to find the tribe said to possess the knowledge of the ultimate recipe.

Soon, we were back on the mountainous region of Jebel Mara. A sparse but astonishingly beautiful stretch of ravines, waterfalls, hidden valleys and volcanic craters. In the bowl of one such volcano, he claimed, dwelt a tribe so fearsome that their very name struck terror into the heart of every Sudanese from El Fasher to Khartoum. It was the Gonda who were rumoured to hold the key to my uncle's quest.

There were few takers when the Gastronome and Ibrahim tried recruiting porters for their expedition. No one had ever seen a Gonda before – just the evidence of their nocturnal raids: empty goat and sheep pens and the corpses of those who had tried to guard them. Undaunted, the Gastronome – still weak from the flu he'd caught from his sister – and Ibrahim, with only a revolver between them, set out alone.

After three days following the trails of droppings left by the stolen herds, they reached the summit of the volcano. Here the Gastronome offered Ibrahim one last chance to turn back. But Ibrahim was insistent. He would follow his master to the end.

As they slipped down the crumbling scree, deeper and deeper into the bowels of the volcano, the air, which had been freezing at the top, grew hotter and more humid. Bare rock gave way to scrub. The path broadened. And the Gastronome and Ibrahim became aware that they were being watched.

'At times, we could hear them scuttling behind us. But the moment we looked round, all we saw was scrub and rocks. Ibrahim was terrified, but he would not think of abandoning me. He knew that, with or without him, I meant to continue. A brave, brave boy was Ibrahim.

'And suddenly we saw one. Our first Gonda. Popped out from behind a rock, casual as you like, and just stood there watching us. Then another one appeared. And another. And another. And soon there were hundreds of them, all watching us with their big dark eyes. Keeping their distance. Almost as if they were more frightened than we were. And maybe they were. Doubt they'd ever seen a white man before. And certainly not one standing six foot five in his boots. Nor one packing sixteen stone and a Webley, which I fired into the air, just the once, in case they got any funny ideas.

'I don't recall being as frightened as I should have been. You know how these rumours build up. After all the gossip back in El Fasher I'd been expecting a bunch of seven-foot monsters with two heads and eight arms. They weren't like that at all. Small, stocky mountain people – like the Gurkhas but much, much blacker. As dark as the pumice on the volcano's slopes.'

Followed by two hundred or so warriors, the Gastronome and Ibrahim pressed on. Soon, they reached a scrub fence. Inside were the brush enclosures where the Gonda kept their stolen sheep and goats. And beyond those were the tribesmen's huts, built with volcanic rock and roofed with palm fronds.

'Not a lot different from any other African village, you might think. But my, what a location! Paradise on earth, dear boy. Paradise on earth. So lush. So bountiful. And d'you know why? Because bang in the middle of the village they had a bloody great pond, bordered by these huge date palms. And all around it goats, sheep, even camels – though Lord only knows how they'd got them there – were watering themselves. And on the banks, bare-chested women with tits like aubergines were gathering dates, washing their clothes and singing in whatever language it is the Gonda speak. Gondaese? I don't know.

Anyway that's by the by. The point was, after coming all this way expecting to be hacked to death by hordes of invisible monsters, we'd stumbled on the biggest bloody oasis in Western Sudan. And no one – no one from east of Nyala, let alone Europe – had ever seen it before.

'Anyway. The Gonda seemed friendly enough. But what we needed was an ice-breaker. Something to offer the village chief to show him we had come in peace. And we'd have to think of something quickly because, don't you know, they'd already laid on this welcoming party for us. Common folk and women at the back. Elders at the front, in their grey robes and ibis-feather necklaces. And to one side, another group, equally distinguished – though at first I couldn't for the life of me see why – all of them from eight to eighty, wearing these red robes and snooty expressions. Haughty. That's the word I'm looking for. If they hadn't been half my height, I dare say they'd have been looking down their snub noses at us.

'So there's me and Ibrahim, surrounded by these fellows, wondering how to keep them happy. And the headman – we know it's the headman because he looks about three hundred years old and he's wearing more feathers than anyone else – is standing there, waiting for us to pay homage. So I start fumbling in my pockets. And all I come up with is a handful of Biros. I'm about to put them away again when I notice the headman's eyes light up. So I pass them to him and hope for the best.

'And do you know what he does? He picks at the top of one of the Biros with his fingernails, pulls out the cartridge, pops it straight into his mouth and starts sucking and gnawing at it, like it was some rare delicacy. The villagers are all smiling by now. Except the chappies in the red robes – the Red Men, I'll call them – po-faced bunch, they were. And the chief's mouth is turning blacker by the minute until suddenly he's finished and with as much of a flourish as his withered limbs can muster, he flings his empty cartridge on to the ground and all of a sudden this loud whooping breaks out as the whole village start ululating like billy-oh.

'Well, they must have seen my puzzlement because the next minute, the chief's sent one of his minions scurrying off to his hut. Comes back *tout de suite* with this bloody great pile of Biros. All of them sucked dry. Can't imagine where they got them. And I can't say I really cared. Point was, by happy accident, we'd come up with Big Chief's favourite delicacy. Local version of risotto alla seppia, I suppose. Only without the Arborio.

'So now it's their turn to entertain us. And this they do in some style. They slaughter a couple of lambs in front of us and barbecue them there and then. Seems they've picked up at least a few customs from the Arabs, because guess who gets to eat the eyeballs?

'And so began two of the most blissful weeks of my life. The climate was pleasant. Our lodgings were sparse, but not uncomfortable. The people were hospitable. The arak flowed freely. And the food – well, that was the only real problem. There was plenty of it, of course, but, after a few days, one does tire of eating roast goat and mutton for each and every meal. The Gonda had no concept of seasoning. Just as well I'd brought my own supplies of salt. And they were temperamentally unsuited to cultivating vegetables. So where, I'm beginning to ask myself, did they get this great culinary reputation?

'Well, the more time I spend with them, the more convinced I am that the answer lies with those haughty fellows dressed in red. You see, I've noticed, on one of my early morning constitutionals, that every day, just before dawn, these Red Men make their way to this flat area at the other end of village. But what they get up to, I can't fathom. Because as soon as I try and get anywhere near them, I'm sent packing by these chappies they've put out to guard the area. Which, of course, only gets me more intrigued.

'Problem is, how to find out. Tricky business communicating with these Gonda. Language barrier doesn't help. Like no dialect I'd ever heard. Even Ibrahim's stumped. But with a bit of sign language and the help of one or two of the warriors who spoke halting Arabic, we got by. Got by, that is, with everyone except those Red Men. You know what they're like, these spiritual types.

'Anyway, one evening, my luck's in. I'm taking a swim in the pond – lake, whatever you want to call it – when I notice one of the Red Men watching me. He looks quite embarrassed when I catch him, but I explain as best I can that it's quite all right. Doubt either of us knows what the other's on about, but the upshot is, I land myself an invitation to one of his dawn ceremonies.

'So the next morning, before first light, my new chum leads me to the place where all the Red Men go to practise their mumbo jumbo. They're squatting on their haunches in the middle of this circle marked out with volcanic rock. I'm not allowed inside – I haven't been initiated, you see – but they're prepared to let me sit on the edge and watch.

'Pretty soon, they've begun to drift off into a sort of trance. As dawn breaks, their trance deepens. And by the time the sun's up they're almost lost to the world. At which point – as if they're doing it in their sleep – they set about their work. One by one, they grab a large slate and begin scratching it with sharp pieces of rock. Scratching, scratching away until maybe noon, when they knock off for the day and nip home for a bite to eat.

'Now before they drag me off with them, I've just got time to peek over the edge of the circle and have a look at the work in progress. Pretty crude stuff, it was. Neanderthal art. Ill-drawn animals, hunters, stone huts – the sort of stuff you find on the walls of caves. Quite interesting, I suppose, if anthropology's the bag you're into. But from my point of view, all those hours I'd spent hanging around in the sun, while these fellows practised their drawing, struck me as being pretty much a waste of time.

'Or so I thought at first. But then I thinks to myself, there's got to be more to it than that. These buggers ain't revered by the rest of the village just because they're handy with a pretty picture. So, while we're lunching on more of that blessed goat, I try asking my friendly Red Man what he and his chums were up to. He answers by pointing at the fire where the meat's cooking. I still can't work it out. This time he points into his mouth. Something to do with food. I've gathered that much. But I never was much use at charades. And I'm just beginning to think I'll never get to the bottom of this when, suddenly, there's a lot of shouting, whooping and bleating at the village gate. One of the hunting parties has returned from a raiding mission. They're driving this huge flock of stolen goats ahead of them. And I find myself thinking how familiar the scene looks and wondering why that should be. And then it comes to me in a flash. The scene at the edge of the village is just like the one those Red Men have been drawing on their stones.'

There was – and I suppose I should have guessed it earlier – a message behind his strange tale. It was not one I found palatable. Nor, indeed, plausible.

'You'll have guessed by now what was so special about the Red Men. They were gifted with a remarkable power,' said the Gastron-ome, pausing to run his tongue over his dry lips. 'The power to make their desires come true.'

He must have caught my sceptical expression.

'Do you think I believed in this power any more than you do now? Of course I didn't. Nor was I going to until I'd seen more evidence.

The only logical way of doing so was to try it out for myself. And try it I did. But not before I had undergone the appropriate ritual.

'Now I've seen quite a few initiation ceremonies in my time. So I had a pretty good idea of what lay in store. Perhaps, I'd be forced to smoke some mind-altering drug through a pipe, or end up being buggered by a few of the elders, or hideously scarred with a blunt knife, or strung up by my nipples in the blazing sun. Bit of an anti-climax when I discovered what it really entailed. A quick daub on my temples with volcanic dust. Then a blessing with a lump of polished obsidian. That was it. Painless. Simple. Easy to administer.'

I drained my glass of arak. Then, sensing that some sort of response was in order, I patted the Gastronome on the knee.

'Wonderful story, Uncle. But if you don't mind, I think I'll be heading off.'

'Don't you want to know what happened next?'

'I've already guessed. They gave you these powers. You passed them on to me at my christening. And hey presto, I've suddenly got this incredible ability to magic up anything I want.'

'I'd warn you not to take that flippant tone. You may be in grave danger.'

'Only if I listen to any more of your mumbo jumbo.'

'Giles –'

'Look, I'm sorry. I know exactly what's been going on and I can tell you this – it's got nothing to do with non-existent tribes from the back of beyond.'

'And still you choose to deny it after all you've seen? The restaurants? The case of wine?'

'What case of wine?'

'Why, the Cheval –'

The Gastronome cut himself short. But already he had said too much.

For both our sakes, I thought it best that he did not drive me back to the station. I thanked him for the wine and his hospitality. Then I left him on the lawn and headed off to call a cab.

I will never forget the look of sadness in the Gastronome's eyes as he bid me farewell.

In the study, I lingered in front of the curious collection of photographs depicting the Gastronome in various native costumes. The first time I'd seen them, I'd felt embarrassed but also proud to think that this brave, adventurous traveller was actually related to me. Now, I recognized them for what they were: the sad, desperate posturings of a man who'd stayed just a little too long in the midday sun.

Poor man. He'd done so well to regain his senses after The Dreadful Incident in the Sudan. Writing his *Gastronomy of France* had grounded him in reality. But no sooner had he finished it than he'd gone back to his old ways. The strange food. The bizarre dress. And now his rambling tale of magical powers. The signs were all too plain. This time, I feared, he was lost for good.

But it was only when I rummaged through the contents of his escritoire, in search of a phone book, that I fully appreciated just how far over the brink he had plummeted.

Had he meant me to see those two pieces of paper?

Were they a warning? If they were, perhaps that explained the look he had given me. Maybe he knew that it was the last time he would ever see me.

I called for a taxi to come to Jebel Mara immediately.

I put down the phone and examined the two pieces of paper again.

Both were restaurant receipts. One bore the name Lucullus in Roman letters. The other was an exact copy of the one I had designed only a few days earlier for Cruel Cuisine.

CHAPTER SIXTEEN

Morgues

'This *meat*,' my companion asked. 'You couldn't . . . er . . . give me a rough idea of which animal it comes from?' The waiter did not reply. Nor did his eyes – the only features visible between his surgical mask and cap – register a trace of emotion. He hovered patiently, gloved hand poised above his notebook.

Even if he had spoken – which the staff are forbidden from doing at Morgues – he would never have disclosed the principal ingredient of the dishes we were about to order. That, like the identity of the restaurant's owners, remains a secret he and his colleagues will carry to the grave.

We went for meat soup, meat pie and mincemeat tart. Not a difficult choice. They were the only items on the menu. The waiter glided off with a swish of his surgical gown. 'Friendly sort,' my companion muttered. Though he spoke in a low whisper, his voice sounded deafening amid the sepulchral hush of the vaulted, subterranean chamber. He blushed as our fellow diners turned to stare at him. Morgues is not a place where levity is encouraged.

You will notice this long before you are escorted to your 'table' in this abandoned crypt. Morgues can only be reached via an unmarked doorway set in a dark alleyway near London's Spitalfields. There, you must wait to be inspected by a surveillance camera. Only diners clad in black are permitted to enter.

Once through the door, you are led by a waiter dressed in the standard uniform of surgeon's mask and gown, down a labyrinthine series of corridors lined with reproductions of Goya's *Atrocities of War*. The restaurant proper is concealed behind a heavy black-velvet curtain.

It is cold, forbidding and quiet. The stone walls, inlaid with plaques marking the vaults of long-extinct families, drip with condensation. Such warmth as there is comes from the bodies of customers, shivering in their funereal clothes at marble 'tables' which, on closer inspection, turn out to be old mortuary slabs. Conversation remains confined to a few apprehensive whispers. The only other noise is the swishing of the waiters' gowns, the padding of footsteps across the stone floor and the rumble of trolleys as the restaurant's ghastly fare is wheeled from kitchen to table.

While we waited for our soup to arrive, my companion and I steadied our nerves with a carafe of the purple-red wine which is provided as part of the set-price menu. As I poured, my hands trembled so much that I accidentally knocked over the glass. Its contents trickled into the sluice running round the edge of the mortuary slab, and drained down a pipe on to the floor. My companion said he'd lost his appetite.

Our first courses were hidden inside a plastic body bag, which our waiter unzipped to reveal two skull-shaped bowls brimming with murky crimson glop. It wasn't nearly as disgusting as it looked. Well-seasoned (a hint of paprika, perhaps?) and rich, it reminded me of a properly made bortsch. My companion was less enthusiastic. It tasted, he said, rather like the hole left in your gum when you've had a tooth extracted. There was, I had to agree, something unpleasantly familiar about that salty tang and springy, jellied texture.

Only after several heartening glasses of wine (rough, feral, redolent of mortality and ordure – very likely an old Rioja just past its prime) did I feel ready to tackle the main course. The pie was a disappointment. Though the crust was deliciously crunchy ('That'll be the ground bone,' suggested my companion), the filling was worryingly similar to the soup, only the gravy was thicker and the pieces of meat chunkier. Nor was there much consolation to be had from the side dish of beetroot purée – at least I hoped it was beetroot purée – which

I abandoned soon after my companion started cracking Sweeney Todd jokes.

Morgues has one of two effects on its customers. Either they are struck dumb with awe and terror, or, through nerves or drunkenness, they begin giggling hysterically. On the night I went, the only diner in the latter category was my companion. This did not pass unnoticed by the silent majority, whose stares towards our table were growing increasingly menacing.

I was deeply grateful, then, when our puddings were delivered, causing my companion to desist briefly from his tasteless remarks, preoccupied as he was with his sticky, filling mincemeat tart. But no sooner had he finished it than he began speculating with grisly relish as to where Morgues might have found its 'meat'.

There is little doubt that all the other customers were pondering the same question. Nobody <u>would come</u> to Morgues, after all, were it not for the titillating possibility that maybe, just maybe, the meat really was that rare, forbidden thing it purported to be. But by some curious code of etiquette, they took a dim view of anyone who mentioned this openly.

As I begged, in vain, for him to keep his voice down, my companion wondered aloud why it was that we had seen so few down-and-outs lurking in the neighbourhood. And whether the restaurant had anything to do with the recent spate of grave robberies. Or whether local hospitals were trying to improve their finances by selling off their stock of corpses.

I think it was the word 'corpses' which hammered the last nail into our coffin. Certainly – though I still wonder how this was possible – the restaurant appeared to grow even more silent. Then, striding towards our table with the measured solemnity of a pallbearer, we saw the terrifying figure of the maître d'. He was dressed in black robes with a pointed Torquemada hood. And when he stopped his advance, he was close enough for us to glimpse his eyes, shining evilly in the candlelight, through the holes in his cowl.

He did not speak. What he chose to do instead was

infinitely more effective. With a flick of his wrist, he shot back the cuffs of his long sleeve, allowing us to glimpse – just for a second – the object he was grasping in his right hand. A heavy, bloodied cleaver.

My companion and I paused long enough to toss the price of our dinner, plus an exceptionally generous tip, on to the table before we fled. Today's awkward customers had no desire to become tomorrow's meat pie.

Morgues can be found somewhere in Spitalfields, London E1. For public health and safety reasons, this magazine is unable to disclose the precise address. Dinner for two with service and a bottle of house wine came to £150. Morgues does not cater for vegetarians.

On the Tuesday morning following my weekend at the Gastronome's, my nerve finally failed. Five threatening phone calls and three nights racked with terrible nightmares had persuaded me that even if my plan worked, I would never survive to see it through. My first priority, as I would tell Rodney when we met at our secret rendezvous, was to cancel the Morgues review.

I chose my route carefully. It was essential, I remembered from spy films, that I vary my routine. So I rose an hour earlier than usual, skipped breakfast and, instead of walking to Fulham Broadway, I took a taxi to South Kensington tube station. From there, I travelled on the eastbound Piccadilly line, changed at Holborn and took the Central line to Liverpool Street.

I survived the journey unscathed. Almost, anyway. My leg was slightly bruised, because I'd tried another of those cunning tricks you see in films. To check that no one was tailing me, I pretended to get off the tube at Piccadilly Circus. I lingered on the platform, as if I wasn't sure where I was going. Then, just as the train was about to leave, I leapt back on again. But my timing was slightly awry. The doors closed, trapping my leg. Still, it was a good way of drawing attention to myself. If anything terrible happened, there would now be a carriage-load of amused passengers who remembered my last movements.

I'd chosen to meet Rodney in as public a place as possible: an exposed croissant bar in Liverpool Street Station. From my stool I had a good view of the concourse. I kept myself alert with successive cups of strong coffee and watched for would-be assailants. There were many likely candidates: the suspiciously harmless-looking old lady with the poison-tipped umbrella; the man dressed as a British Rail employee, who betrayed himself by acting helpfully towards a lost passenger; the two students at opposite ends of the building, communicating to each other via radios disguised as Walkmans.

Towards half past eleven, well after the appointed hour, my attention was drawn to an unconvincing homeless person. Alerted by the fact that he was drinking a bottle of wine rather than extra-strength lager, I followed his movements carefully. He was pretending to be drunk, weaving back and forth across the concourse, but moving, inexorably, to where I sat. It was only when a pair of hands closed around my throat that I realized the tramp was a decoy.

The grip tightened.

'Boo!' said Rodney, letting go of my neck.

He soon lost his playful spirit when I told him about the death threats. The first had come late on Sunday night, not long after my return from Devon. I had picked up the phone and a muffled voice had warned me that I'd made a big mistake writing about Cruel Cuisine. 'I know who you are!' I'd yelled back at the anonymous caller. And the line had gone dead.

Over the next two days, there had been further menacing messages – each more specific than its predecessor. The most recent one had given me a long list of demands. I was to persuade my editor to run a full-page apology in the next issue, dissociating *Knob* from the 'evil, fascist abattoir known as Cruel Cuisine'. Furthermore, the magazine was to pay a £100,000 fine to the following charities: Tiger Protection League; Freedom From Fur; TuskWatch; Whale Nation.

'I should just give them what they want,' said Rodney.

'Use your brain. It's got nothing to do with the ASF.'

'Who?'

'Animal Salvation Front. The people who are *supposedly* making these calls. Can't you see? They're just a front for Talbot's conspiracy.'

'Animal Salvation *Front*. Very crafty.'

'Yesterday I told Andy about these calls and do you know what he said?'

'He'd never heard of the ASF, I'll bet.'

'Worse. He pretended they'd been in touch with him too. Said the police were on the case and there wasn't much more he could do. One of the hazards of investigative journalism, he said. And do you know what that means?'

Rodney didn't.

'It means that if anything happens to us, the police are going to think it's been done by animal terrorists. Talbot and his mob will get off scot free!'

Rodney, no doubt prompted by that inclusive 'us', suggested that it was about time we contacted the police.

'And tell them what exactly? They wouldn't even begin to understand the complexities of it all. They'd probably have me locked up in a loony bin.'

'At least you'd be safe there,' said Rodney.

I explained that even if we did inform the police, there was no guarantee that they had not already been nobbled by Talbot.

'Now that really is paranoia.'

'You think so? When even my own uncle's involved?'

I told him about the incriminating restaurant receipts I'd found in the Gastronome's escritoire.

'Treacherous bastard.'

'Possibly. But it could be that, in his strange way, he's trying to help me. Think about it. He's spent the last thirty odd years believing that he gave me some sort of magic ability at my christening. Talbot knows about this. He came with me to the Gastronome's a few times and must have seen that the man was a bit touched. So, years later, Talbot finds some excuse to meet up with the Gastronome and, pretending that he's acting in my best interests, tells him that he's had a brilliant idea. What if Talbot were to make all my fantasies – or, more to the point, my uncle's fantasies – come true?'

'But couldn't he have done all this without your uncle's help?'

'Probably, yes. But you're underestimating Talbot's cunning. First, he needs the Gastronome to encourage me by repeating his silly magic stories – which he still believes in, incidentally. He tried it on me again last weekend. Second, Talbot knows that his revenge will be much sweeter if he can turn my own family against me.'

Rodney stopped me from going on. He needed a few solids to accompany his caffeine and nicotine breakfast. I waited while he worked through a pain au chocolat. Though I hadn't eaten myself, I felt no urge to accompany him. For the last few days, I had lived on little else but coffee and nervous energy.

When he'd finished eating, Rodney gave me an apologetic look.

'I don't mean to sound sceptical,' he said sceptically, 'but don't you think you might be exaggerating – just a little bit?'

I glared back.

'*Et tu*, Rodney?'

'No. No . . .' he said, withering under my stare. 'Don't get me wrong. I'm sure there's a lot of truth in what you've said. It could *all* be true for all I know.'

'You're the only person I can trust. Don't you realize? The *only* person.'

'Believe me, Giles, I'm very grateful for this confidence you have in me . . . but all I wanted to say . . . as a friend . . . is, there's something that bothers me about all this.'

'Yes?'

'It's just that I can't help wondering why Talbot would go to all this trouble. I mean, OK, he probably wasn't too happy when you slagged off his first restaurant. But if this is his revenge, well, it's slightly over the top, wouldn't you say?'

'Talbot *is* over the top,' I spluttered impatiently. 'He's a . . . what do you call those people who like to run everyone else's lives for them?'

'Control freaks?'

'Exactly. He's a control freak! Astonishing, really, that it took me so long to realize it. I mean, it wasn't for lack of evidence. The bullying at prep school, the dinner when you and I met at Oxford, remember that?'

Rodney nodded.

'Now you see what we're up against. A man who always gets his way and always wins! Never stood a prayer did we? He probably saw the Morgues trap coming before I'd even thought up the idea.'

'Do you reckon?'

'Definitely. He'd have seen the way my restaurants were going. It was only a matter of time before I got on to cannibalism.'

'Hence the death threats. He's punishing you for inventing a joint even he wouldn't dare to set up?'

'Quite the opposite. He wants to show me he's not scared at all. By the time my review appears, Rodders, you can bet your life –'

'Steady.'

'– you can be damn sure that Morgues will be up and running. And if we show any indication that we're about to expose him to the police, well . . . ever wondered what it was like inside a meat pie?'

Rodney laughed nervously.

'Quite. So there's only one option left. We cancel that review and throw ourselves at Talbot's mercy.'

'You think he'll be satisfied with that?'

I shrugged. 'Either way, we'll know by this evening. The Death issue goes to press tomorrow morning. So unless I can get that review spiked before then – well, just in case things don't work out, I'm going to give you this.'

I passed Rodney a manila envelope. Inside was a detailed account of Talbot's conspiracy. It had taken all night to type.

'You'd better make a few copies. If anything happens to me, I want to make sure they reach the police, the press and anyone else who can see that the truth gets out.'

'Don't worry,' said Rodney solemnly. 'You can rely on me.'

At Canary Wharf, nursing a second bruised limb after another botched attempt at elusive spycraft, I made for the public telephones in the arcade downstairs. I dialled Tamsin's direct line.

Like the croissant bar at Liverpool Street Station, the Café Zinc was well-suited to my purpose. A minimalist marble-floored café with padded leather stools and mirrored walls inside and zinc tables outside, it was always packed at lunchtime. The Columbian staff knew me by name. I had once complimented them on the quality and quantity of Extra Virgin olive oil they dripped on to my bresaola, rocket and shaved parmesan salad.

I bagged two stools, ordered a couple of cappuccinos and watched the mirror (which reflected the doorway) for Tamsin's arrival.

'This had better be important,' said Tamsin, reaching instantly for a cigarette.

'It's my review,' I said. 'We've got to spike it.'

'Tell me about it,' said Tamsin.

'Is there anything you can do to help?'

'Not unless you find a bloody good reason.'

'I made it up. All of it. It's complete fantasy from start to finish.'

Tamsin sniffed. 'So's most of the next issue. What difference is one review going to make?'

'But don't you think it's irresponsible running a thing like that? Dangerous, even? I mean, what if someone was tempted to copy it?'

'I told you that three months ago.'

'Please. Isn't there *anything* you can do to help?'

'Yep – nothing at all. If Andy goes ahead and runs a fake review, it'll give the rest of us more ammunition.'

'Tamsin, wait . . .' I was about to follow her when I saw something that stopped me, dead, in the doorway. Walking a few steps ahead of Tamsin, with the weaving stroll which denotes a pleasurable lunch, were two men in designer suits. One was Andy. The other, his guest, Eric Talbot.

Before I could chase them, I was called back by the café owners to pay my bill. And by the time I had reached the lifts, my two adversaries had already ascended.

The editor's secretary made no attempt to stop me as I barged through the door of Andy's office.

Andy was lolling back in his chair, trying to light a large, expensive cigar. 'Giles,' he said, cheerfully, between sucks. 'You made it. Take a pew.'

He indicated one of two chairs in front of his desk. The other was occupied by Talbot, who swivelled round to look at me. Talbot too was smoking a cigar. With his right hand he clutched a large, half-filled brandy glass which he tilted, slightly, in a lazy toast. He smiled.

I stood hesitantly just inside the doorway. It would have been easier if they could have done something a bit more confrontational.

'Tried ringing you at home this morning,' said Andy. 'Engaged constantly. Something wrong with your phone?'

Before I could answer, Talbot pitched in. 'Pity,' he said. 'You missed a great lunch.'

'Or what,' agreed Andy. These were evidently not the first stiff brandies they'd had today.

'Anyway,' said Talbot, 'better late than never. You going to join us? Got loads to catch up with.'

He had put on a bit of weight since I'd last seen him, although his expensive-looking suit (worn with a pale blue, open-necked shirt) had clearly been tailored to disguise the fact. There were streaks of grey in his dark hair, which he was now wearing raffishly long. And there were wrinkles around his eyes. I should have been pleased at these signs of age. Instead, they smacked of jet-setting glamour and sophistication. He proffered a hand, which I ignored.

'Actually,' I said, with all the bravery I could muster, 'I think I'll stay where I am.'

Andy and Talbot exchanged puzzled glances.

'Cigar?' suggested Andy. 'Brandy?'

'Nothing,' I said. 'I just want to get it all over with.'

Andy exhaled a thick plume of cigar smoke. 'Get . . . er . . . what over with, matey?'

'Morgues,' I said to both of them. 'I want it spiked.'

Andy snorted derisively.

'Might have guessed.'

Talbot looked askance at Andy.

'The cannibal place I was telling you about. Poor old Giles here's been getting the heebie-jeebies.'

'You know damn well what he's talking about,' I rasped at Talbot.

'Steady,' interrupted Andy. 'I'm not having you upset our lunch guest.' He looked at Talbot solicitously and added, in a stage whisper, 'Those animal rights people. He reckons we should cave in to their demands.'

Talbot feigned a look of concern.

'You are looking a bit rough, Giles. Sure you won't have a brandy?'

'Please!' I said. 'Will you stop playing games!'

'Think he'd better,' said Andy to Talbot. He poured out a large measure of brandy and pushed it towards me.

My knees were starting to buckle. Taking the poisoned chalice was preferable to a humiliating collapse. Lurching from my position in the doorway, I grabbed the glass and propped myself against Andy's desk.

'And not another word till you've had a seat and got your act together,' Andy commanded.

'There you go,' said Talbot, pushing the swivel chair towards me.

I reached for its arm, steadied myself and, having pulled the chair further away from Talbot, I sat down.

'Now listen to me,' said Andy. 'I tried explaining to you yesterday. These threats and stuff. It all goes with the territory. I can't go spiking my lead feature just because my star writer's got cold feet.'

Lead feature?

'New development,' Andy explained. 'We've had to bury Rupert's "Seven Days in Hell" feature. Great pix. Powerful intro. Problem is, that's as far as he got. Just four words. "The horror! The horror!"'

I clawed desperately at my face and turned to Talbot.

'Please,' I begged. 'Can't *you* call it off?'

'What are you asking him for?' said Andy.

'Please,' I said, slipping off my chair and kneeling at Talbot's feet.

I grasped at his trouser leg. '*Please!* I swear I'll never cause you any more trouble. Just stop *doing* this to me.'

'Jesus!' said Andy. 'Another of my team's gone AWOL!'

'Shh,' Talbot ordered Andy. He patted my head. 'There, there, Giles,' he said. 'It's going to be all right. Everything's going to be all right.'

'You mean that?' I gasped, looking up at him. My eyes had swollen with tearful gratitude. 'You'll stop it? All of it?'

'All of it,' said Talbot, smiling beneficently. 'You've been through enough. I can see that.'

'Thank you,' I sobbed. 'Thank you so much, Talbot.'

'Eric,' said Talbot. 'Please. Call me Eric.'

CHAPTER SEVENTEEN

In Normandy, I supped on étrilles, agneau présalé and pressed duck; in Bordeaux, on a creamy mouclade of Atlantic mussels, wild boar with chestnuts and Pichon-Longueville; near Dijon, I glutted on po-chouse and Montrachet; amid the peaks of the Auvergne, I sampled a ragout of partridge with lentils coloured deep green and turquoise by the rich volcanic soil. And after a fortnight's intensive dining in every corner of France from Champagne to the Languedoc, I felt a great deal better. Unfortunately, my bank balance did not.

I had tried to live frugally – staying in modest auberges, not always plumping for foie gras or the *menu gourmand*, never buying wine priced at more than five hundred francs a bottle, sometimes even forgoing the local three-star Michelin for a lowly two- or one-star establish-ment. Under such a parsimonious regime, I thought, I could hold out for at least another week. The proprietor of a waterside restaurant in Sète decided otherwise. Shortly after I had polished off a platter of his excellent Bouzigues oysters, some plump moules farcies, an unctu-ous sèche en rouille and a modest bottle of Picpoul de Pinet, he presented me with my credit card – snipped in half.

My father, who had to cable me the fare for my flight home, was not sympathetic. Nor, from what I can remember of her tirade as I lurched across the arrivals lounge, was my mother. 'Idle . . . gluttony . . . as bad as your uncle . . .' I heard her saying, before her voice grew inaudibly distant and the room swirled into blackness.

'. . . or am I going to have to feed you myself?' continued Mother. Or was it Mrs Schreck? Yes. Much more likely. It was one of those recurring Belton House nightmares. I could tell from the smell of rancid pig, fried bread and overcooked scrambled egg, a forkful of which was now hovering near my nose.

'Come on, Giles' – (Giles? Mrs Schreck had never been so intimate) – 'you'll never get better if you don't eat something.'

I allowed the fork to enter my mouth.

'Better?'

I nodded. Now I had focused properly, I could see it was Mother. 'And about time too. I was beginning to despair of ever getting my hair done. Eat up. We'll be leaving in an hour.'

She left before I could inquire what, exactly, had happened since I'd last seen her in the airport terminal. It must have been pretty extraordinary because, according to the date on the *Daily Mail* by my bed, I had skipped a whole day.

I glanced idly at the headline. 'What Have They Done to My Grandpa?' it said, above a picture of a little girl looking into an open grave. Feeling far too ill to cope with such a mawkish story, I put the paper down. But as I did so, one word, buried in the last column, caught my eye.

I read and reread the story. Then I turned to my father's copy of the *Sun*. 'The Return of Burke and Hare?' said the headline. Beneath, in small print, next to an asterisk, was written '(That's two famous grave-robbers, folks)'.

Both papers had reached similar conclusions. Surely it was more than coincidental, they suggested, that the spate of grave robberies followed the reported opening of a clandestine restaurant in East London.

'Ready?' said Mother. 'Good. Now I'd like you to meet me at the garden gate. Don't dawdle! We're already late.'

I carried my suitcase into the corridor.

'And keep your head down,' added Mother, as I passed one of the windows looking out on to the drive. 'I don't want them to know you're here.'

I looked askance at her. And peeked out of the corner of the window. It was raining heavily. Gathered by the front gate were four or five bedraggled men in raincoats and anoraks, some of them carrying cameras. One of them looked up and shouted to his colleagues.

Mother headed for the Volvo. I ran across the lawn and waited by the back gate. As soon as I heard the screech of brakes, I darted into the car. We sped off, closely followed by two other vehicles.

'I think,' said Mother, 'you owe me the courtesy of an explanation.'

'Would you believe me if I said it was your brother's fault?'

Mother floored the accelerator.

Our pursuers did their best to keep up. But they were no match for Mother's local knowledge. One of them skidded off the road in the wet mud. We lost the other long before we reached Oxford. Mother dropped me off on the High Street end of the Cornmarket, gave me a a couple of banknotes and urged me never to darken her door at least until I had resolved my difficulties. And preferably not even then.

I took shelter from the rain in a café opposite Christ Church and pondered my predicament. My head ached; my stomach groaned; I was cold and wet; and I barely had enough money for my fare back to London. But these were the least of my problems.

Andy was bound to be furious at my prolonged absence. My next review was well overdue. And if I refused to deliver the sort of copy that he – or rather his master Eric Talbot – wanted, he would surely have no qualms about sacking me. Or worse. For what use was I, now that I had pushed my invented restaurants to their logical extreme? And with the press in full pursuit of the grave-robbery story, would Talbot trust me not to reveal the identity of Morgues' owner? Or would he take measures to ensure that I never spoke again?

I eked out my coffee until long after the rain had stopped, watching the porter turning away visitors from the Tom Quad entrance. 'Best job in the world,' Rodney had once claimed. 'You get paid a fat wodge to stand around and do nothing but insult foreigners.' And undergraduates, he might have added. The porters had taken against Rodney and me ever since the night we'd celebrated an unusually bibulous dinner at the Elizabeth by throwing a few bicycles into Mercury. Rodney had been rusticated. I'd been banned for life from the college.

Strange. A vintage silver Rolls Royce had just pulled up opposite me; the chauffeur had opened the doors to let out two young men – one of whom was the spitting image of Rodney Holmes. It couldn't have been, of course. His companion – very tall, thin, dressed in a green Loden – oozed money and distinction. Rodney never moved in such elevated circles. Yet whoever it was had got his drunken gait down to a tee. Now he was turning in my direction. It *was* Rodney Holmes.

'Visitors through the Meadows Building,' announced the porter.
'I'm a member of the House,' I replied crisply.
'Here for the Gaudy?'
I nodded.
He directed me into the porter's lodge.
The man behind the desk frowned when I asked where Rodney

was staying. With a shudder, I recognized him as the porter who had apprehended me during the bicycle incident.

'You've just missed him,' he said, squinting as he tried to place my face. 'Passed by not two minutes ago with Mr . . .'

I didn't catch the name. Something Eastern European ending in 'off'.

'Though quite what a clever young man like him sees in that Mr Holmes, I couldn't begin to guess. Makes himself a fortune in publishing. He can pick and choose his friends from the highest of the high. And who does he spend his time with? Rodney bleeding Holmes.'

'Takes all sorts.'

'Know him well, do you?'

'Not very.'

'Only it was a young man just like you who –'

'You were going to tell me the room number.'

Rodney had never introduced me to the rich recluse with whom he had shared his rooms in Peck Quad during his first year. He hadn't even mentioned his name. Having seen the man's Rolls Royce I could understand why. By maintaining the exclusivity of their relationship, Rodney could imagine himself grander than he actually was. And no doubt he was reluctant to allow anyone else to share in his friend's largesse.

I paused outside their room, listening to their conversation. It appeared that I had arrived at just the right moment. The recluse was proposing lunch at Le Manoir aux Quat' Saisons. Rodney seemed to think this was a splendid idea. So did I and I was just about to knock on their door when I noticed something rather unsettling.

There were two cards stuck to the door. One said 'Mr Rodney Holmes'. The other was printed with the name of his room mate.

Maximilian Fischow.

In that instant, I understood how Rodney had come to finance his share of our business venture. And why it was he had been so adamant about the choice of name.

I also knew, as I heard them both coming towards the door, that it would not be in my best interests to hang around a second longer.

I ran. Someone shouted after me. But I kept running as if my life depended on it. For now I realized that I had got it all wrong. Because of my jealousy, because I had been so keen to lay the blame at Talbot's door, I had misinterpreted all the evidence.

At first it came to me in fragments. As I pounded across gravel and grass towards the Canterbury Gate, my head filled with snatches of remembered conversation. 'Very hands-on', 'Makes himself a fortune in publishing', 'Recluse. Never been photographed'.

I glanced back. Rodney was struggling to keep up. Fischow was dialling his henchmen on a mobile phone.

I hurried on, lungs heaving, past Oriel College. No time to check for traffic on the High Street. The sound of screeching brakes and angry horns. And I was safely over, weaving my way through the throngs of pedestrians in Turl Street.

Now it all made sense. All those clues I had overlooked.

There was the *Knob* launch party, when we'd been speculating as to the identity of our mysterious proprietor. Rodney had feigned ignorance though he must have known. It was his friend Fischow who had invited him.

Once I realized that Fischow was 'the Geezer', everything else fell into place. It wasn't Tamsin who had persuaded Andy to keep me on in those fraught early days, but his boss. Fischow, as a huge admirer of *A Discourse on Divers Cuisines*, would no doubt have been delighted to do his bit for the author's nephew. But I would pay a price for his generosity. I would become his plaything.

Perhaps, like some spoilt child, he had grown bored with his toy. Perhaps, Rodney had egged him on. Whatever the reason, Fischow had decided that my invented restaurants were far too entertaining to remain in the realms of fantasy. He must make them come true. One by one. Never mind how bizarre they were, how difficult to engineer, or how dangerous.

Fischow, clearly, was a driven man. He was also a very sick one. If he was prepared to dig up corpses to supply the kitchens at Morgues, he was scarcely likely to prove unduly squeamish when it came to ridding himself of the one person who might divulge his secrets.

'Ever wondered what it's like on the inside of a meat pie?' I'd joked to Rodney. No wonder his laughter had sounded hollow.

The silver Rolls Royce was cruising west along Broad Street as I reached the top of the Turl. I waited until it had disappeared and, unable to run any longer, hobbled in the opposite direction past Blackwell's bookshop. I was going the wrong way for the train or bus stations. But those, in all likelihood, were where Fischow's minions would be concentrating their search.

If I could make it as far as the North Oxford ring road, maybe I could hitch a lift back to London. There I could surely find someone who would help. Tamsin. Andy. Anyone. The important thing was to escape the city centre as quickly as possible. And hope against hope that whoever picked me up wasn't working for Fischow.

At this rate, it was going to take me a long time. Whenever I saw a car approaching – quite a frequent occurrence – I had to dart for the cover of the nearest driveway. It took me almost an hour just to reach the point where the Woodstock and Banbury roads intersect. Maybe it would make more sense to get a taxi to father's Garden Centre.

I found a phone box and dialled his number, glancing around me to make sure I hadn't been spotted. Then – joy of joy – I noticed a Volvo coming towards me. I rushed out of the phone box.

'Mother,' I yelled, waving frantically. 'MOTHER!'

If Mother had noticed me, she wasn't going to do anything about it. The Volvo sailed swiftly on – unlike the vehicle following, two cars behind. It came to a sudden halt just a few feet from where I was standing.

I sprinted off. I heard a car door slam and the thud of feet on Tarmac. My pursuer was so close I could almost feel his breath burning the back of my neck. I accelerated, terror conquering exhaustion. At any second, I expected to feel my enemy's adamantine grip. And I knew I would be unable to maintain the pace for much longer.

Now the man's driver had joined the chase. He drove past me and pulled up, a few hundred yards ahead. I was trapped, unless, somehow, I could get away from the road. The garden gate to my left was the only chance. No time to open it. I would have to try vaulting it.

And suddenly, heaven knows how, I was over. Through a rose bed, clawed by thorns, and on across a lawn. Over a wooden fence. On to a muddy track. Which way now? Doesn't matter. Just keep going!

But how could I? My lungs were on the verge of imploding. My legs were like jelly. The mud was so heavy and slippery it was like one of those nightmares where you're running through marshmallows and your assailant is drawing ever closer. I could hear his squelching footfalls and heaving breath. Come on, Giles! Come on! You can't let him get you. You can't –

I skidded headlong into the mud. No point in trying to get up. My pursuer was too close. Here he comes now. Last few feet. Almost on top of me and –

'You all right?' said a middle-aged man in track suit and trainers. He grasped my arm and helped me to my feet.

'Mmm. No damage done, by the looks of it.'

'*They* –'

'Can't hang about, I'm afraid,' he said, tapping his watch. 'Heading for a lap record.'

The jogger ran on. It had started to rain again. My ankle was slightly twisted. But at least there was no sign of my pursuers.

It was too wet to stay outdoors. Shivering and drenched, I took refuge in a place where no one would think to look, least of all Rodney, who was allergic to any cultural activity which did not involve food or drink.

I was not a big museum-goer myself. But the Pitt-Rivers was different. In my student days, I had sought solace there whenever I grew sick of the relentless socializing. Being vaguely academic, it was a good place to avoid fellow undergraduates. It was cool and gloomy enough to subdue the worst of hangovers. And because of its forbiddingly fusty, old-fashioned air, it tended not to attract too many parties of screaming schoolchildren.

Apart from its collection of human heads which had been shrunk by some cannibalistic tribe or other, I had never really paid much attention to the exhibits. Dried butterflies and ethnological artefacts, mostly. The sort of thing I could see any weekend in the Gastronome's sitting room.

That was probably why, despite my recent travails, I now felt curiously secure. The dim yellow light, the smell of must and furniture polish, the strange ethnic handiwork crammed higgledy-piggledy into glass cases – it all reminded me of those happy times in Devon before life grew sour and complicated. When, instead of imminent death, my worst conceivable fear was that the burgundy might be corked, or that my uncle might bark at me for having uttered some culinary solecism.

Or was it something more compelling than nostalgia that led me to linger amid those dusty aisles? Logic told me that the sooner I made my escape from Oxford the better. Instinct urged me to stay just a little longer. So I did. I began concocting silly excuses as to why I shouldn't leave: it would help clear my thoughts; I needed to recover my strength; it was about time I learned to distinguish between a peacock and a red admiral.

And so it was, just before the curator announced that the museum was about to close, that I reached the last case in the gallery. The one containing the item which confirmed, once and for all, that my uncle's tales were true and that the great conspiracy was merely a figment of my paranoid imagination.

The exhibit was so unspectacular that I might easily have overlooked it. Just a large piece of rough, rust-coloured cotton cloth, which the notes identified as a cloak belonging to an extinct African tribe.

Little was known about this people save that they had dwelt in the mountains of the Western Sudan, where they had been discovered in the mid-1960s by one Xerxes Dante. They had perished shortly afterwards during an influenza epidemic. All that remained was this ragged cloak which, claimed the notes, was believed to have magical properties.

The tribe's name was Gonda.

CHAPTER EIGHTEEN

My next-door neighbour, leaving for work, gave me a sympathetic grin. He stepped over my suitcases and said, 'Changed your mind, then?'

'Excuse me?'

'Must have got it wrong,' he said. 'But I was sure they said you'd left for good.'

'Who did?'

'The removal people. They . . .'

I was already sprinting to my front door. I did not need a key to open it. The latch had been forced.

'A very professional job,' observed the constable who visited me that evening, when I finally had a chance to report the crime. He promised, in a monotone, that the matter would receive his station's fullest attention. Before he left, he re-examined the inventory of missing goods.

'Just the wine, you say?'

'Yes, Officer,' I said bitterly. '*Just* the wine.'

By then, I had grown heartily sick of sarcastic men in blue uniforms. That morning, I had run into the first of them guarding the entrance to Canary Wharf Tower.

'Do you have any identification, sir?' he asked, while a colleague rifled through my briefcase.

'What is this? Some kind of police state?' I snapped.

'If you wouldn't mind, sir. I'm afraid we can't let you in without some form of identification.'

'Oh, for God's sake,' I said, fumbling in my pockets. 'Will this do?' I thrust him my credit card.

'That'll do nicely, sir,' said the policeman, poker-faced. He examined my card. 'Mr G. Fripp. Not *Giles* Fripp, by any chance.'

'And what of it?'

'I understand that a couple of my colleagues are waiting to interview you.'

It was only nine o'clock and the office was still half-empty. Those few of my colleagues I encountered on my way to find Andy gave me resentful looks as they brushed past. It was a relief to find a friendly face outside Andy's door. Or it should have been, except that Tamsin met my smile with a scowl

'Welcome back,' she said grimly.

'That bad?' I said. 'Do we have time for a chat before –'

'Uh-uh,' interrupted Tamsin. She indicated her office. 'They've been here since eight. I'll see you when they've finished.'

I swallowed hard, tapped on the door and entered.

Sitting behind Tamsin's desk were two policemen. They rose and introduced themselves as Detective Constable White and Detective Sergeant Figgis.

DS Figgis switched on a tape-recorder.

'Interview commenced at 0903 hours, Monday, 15 September,' announced DS Figgis. After checking that he had my name and address down correctly, he said, 'Now, Mr Fripp. Before we proceed, I am required by law to inform you that anything you say may be taken down and used in evidence. Is that clear?'

I nodded.

'Is that a yes or a no?' asked DC White, a sallow, baby-faced specimen. He pointed towards the tape-recorder.

'Yes,' I hissed. I was unimpressed by what was obviously an attempt to demonstrate his punctiliousness to his superior.

'Very good,' said DS Figgis, who was playing the double act's 'Mr Nice'. 'I'll explain what this is all about. DC White and myself are currently investigating a case which you may have seen described, in unduly sensational terms, in the tabloid press during the last week.'

'I've been away,' I said.

DC White jotted this down.

'So you have, sir,' my inquisitor continued. 'In France, I believe.'

I nodded.

'In that case, sir, you might have missed the story about the spate of, ahem, grave robberies in the London area?'

'You're accusing me of robbing graves?'

'No, sir. You are not being accused of anything at this precise moment in time. However, in the course of our investigation, it has come to our attention that on 4 September, the day on which the first incident was reported, this article was published in *Knob* magazine.'

DC White passed me a copy of the Death issue. Its cover was

divided into eight squares, each with a lurid picture of ruins, soldiers, tanks and corpses. I turned, with leaden heart, to the restaurant review page. 'Morgues', it was headlined. 'By Giles Fripp.'

'Now, sir. Would you mind confirming to me that you are the author of this piece?'

'I am.'

'And can you recall the date on which you visited Morgues?'

'No.'

'It may jog your memory if I tell you that, during an interview with Mr Andrew Bell, we were provided with a receipt from the aforementioned restaurant. You submitted it as part of an expenses claim, I believe. The receipt is dated 14 August. Is that the day on which you visited this establishment?'

'No,' I said. 'It was just the date I wrote down on my fake receipt.'

DS Figgis glanced at his colleague and then looked back at me.

'I'm sorry, sir,' he said. 'I don't quite understand.'

'Well, as I tried explaining to Andy . . . Mr Bell . . . the restaurant was a hoax. It doesn't exist.'

'You get that, Bob? He says that the restaurant doesn't exist.'

'I got it,' said DC White wearily.

Their expressions were far from friendly.

'I should warn you, Mr Fripp, that withholding evidence is a criminal offence. In the light of that, would you care to confirm or deny your assertion?'

'You can ask me a hundred times,' I said, 'and I won't change my story. Morgues was . . . is . . . a complete figment of my imagination.'

DS Figgis rolled his eyes and lit a cigarette. DC White drummed his fingers on the desk. They patently did not believe me but, as was suggested by their rather feeble attempts to catch me out thereafter, they both realized that their present line of inquiry was fruitless.

Apparently, I had been behaving rather oddly before my departure. Did I have anything to say about that?

'Wouldn't you behave rather oddly if you knew that a restaurant you'd invented was about to appear in print?'

DC White asked me sarcastically whether it was common practice for journalists to fabricate their stories.

'Not as common as it is in your profession,' I was about to say, before I decided that a curt 'No' might be more tactful.

At 9.45, having warned me of the penalties for withholding evidence, and having ascertained that I would not be leaving my address in the near future, they thanked me for my 'co-operation' and wound up the interview.

Tamsin was waiting next door.

'Sorry about that,' I said in the most nonchalant tone I could manage. 'You can have your office back now.'

'It's not my office,' replied Tamsin. She said it so unhappily that I thought she was going to tell me she had been demoted. Then I noticed that Andy's fridge, espresso machine and drinks cabinet were missing. And his old desk was occupied by the infamous spike. I smiled.

'But . . . Tamsin. This is brilliant news!'

'Is it?' She fished a cigarette from one of several packets on her desk. Her ashtray was already half full.

'Yes! It's what you always wanted, isn't it?'

With a sigh, Tamsin lit up her cigarette.

'Number one,' she said, 'I'm getting daily death threats from your friends the Animal Salvation Front.'

'I shouldn't worry,' I said. 'They're all talk and no action.'

'Try telling that to the cleaner who found the firebomb in the men's loos,' said Tamsin.

'Oh.'

'Number two,' she said, 'I've got a couple of costly lawsuits on my hands. One from a Mr Rob Hunter' – she fixed me with a nasty stare – 'and another from Rupert's parents. They're suing us for damages to their son's mental health.'

'Poor Rupert.'

'Number three,' she said, 'I've got three months to build up sales and staff morale before the publisher pulls the plug on the whole venture.'

'The Death issue wasn't a success, then?'

'It *died*.'

'And Andy?'

'Head-hunted.'

'Who on earth . . . ?'

'*Country Life*,' said Tamsin.

She stubbed out her cigarette viciously and added, 'So to answer your original question, no, this isn't what I've always wanted.'

'Even so,' I said. 'If anyone can bring it off, it's you. And anything I can do to help . . .'

Tamsin snorted.

'Don't you worry,' I said. 'I shan't be turning out any more of those stupid reviews.'

'No,' said Tamsin, 'you won't.'

'I mean' — I was gabbling desperately now — 'we both know the only reason I wrote all that rubbish was to please Andy. And . . . and . . . as you always told me —'

'Giles,' said Tamsin, her voice little more than a whisper, 'we're not going to be needing your reviews any more.'

'Quite right. You're absolutely right. Complete waste of time. What you want . . . and I don't mean to sound presumptuous . . . but what you need are proper full-length features. Serious stuff about . . .'

'. . . changes,' Tamsin was saying. 'A softer, less combative approach. Considered pieces on the more traditional forms of cuisine. French provincial. Italian farmhouse . . .'

'Exactly,' I said. 'Just what I was saying. Like the pieces I used to . . .'

'. . . replace you,' said Tamsin.

'I'm sorry?'

Tamsin winced. 'I said I'm really sorry. But I'm going to have to replace you.'

There was a long, long silence. I bit my lip. And, when finally I plucked up the courage to meet her eyes, they were hard, black and pitiless.

'But —'

'I know what you're going to say, Giles . . . And . . . it probably seems terribly unfair . . .'

I nodded.

'. . . but you've got to look at it from the magazine's point of view. You're too closely associated with its old image. The image we're doing our best to bury . . . Personally, I —'

'Personally? You don't know the meaning of the word.'

'Giles, please. Don't make it harder. Whatever you may think of me, I'd still like to consider you my friend and' — my eyes had strayed to the framed picture on her desk: a photograph of Eric Talbot — 'I've done what I can to get you a decent redundancy package.'

'How considerate.'

'And . . . there was one other thing . . .'

'Yes?'

'I hate to lay this on you. But your replacement — Susannah Hobbs

– she's still working out her term at *Zed* . . . and I – I suppose, we could do it in house . . . but . . . well . . . you probably need the money and . . .'

It was the first time I'd ever seen Tamsin lost for words.

'Could you see your way to doing us one last review?'

CHAPTER NINETEEN

'Well?' whispered the Gastronome, his eyes scintillating in the candlelight.

I shifted uncomfortably on the high wooden bench and squinted through the gloom. Beneath the vaulted stone ceiling, which dripped with condensation, a dozen or so groups of diners sat, hunched over cold marble 'tables' like ours. All wore black; few of them spoke and when they did, it was in low, solemn tones. Had it not been for the soft, piped funereal music and the swish of the masked waiters' surgical gowns as they glided from table to table, the room would have been almost silent.

Despite the chill, I felt a trickle of sweat crawling slowly down my spine. My hands were shaking.

I swallowed hard.

'Good,' said the Gastronome quietly.

Behind me, there was a rustling of stiff cloth. I looked over my shoulder and saw a man in a pale green gown. In one slippery gloved hand, he clasped a notepad. In the other, his pen was poised to take our order. All I could see of his face were his eyes. They were dark and expressionless.

'You order,' I croaked to the Gastronome.

I stretched, trying to look relaxed, and shuddered as my left hand brushed against the clammy wall next to our table. Hanging from the moist stone was a fading woodcut, captioned '*Tenochtitlán (Mexico City) 1521*'. It depicted a group of conquistadors, one on horseback. All were looking towards the summit of an Aztec pyramid, save one who was holding a human skull and weeping. At their feet were more skulls. Hundreds. Perhaps thousands of them. Laid out in neat rows on racks.

'Precious eagle-cactus fruit,' said the Gastronome, following my gaze.

I frowned.

'It's what the priests called the hearts of their sacrificial victims. Best job you could have in Montezuma's day. Being a priest, I mean. You got the first bite of the cherry.'

'They ate human hearts?'

'Funnily enough, it was about the only bit they didn't eat. Fed them to Quauhtleuanitl, their sun god, to keep him sweet. While the hearts were still beating, of course.'

'Urgh!'

'Well, you couldn't offer your sun god stale meat, now, could you? Quite a stickler, was old Quauhtleuanitl. Which is why they had a strict pecking order with the priests at the top. They'd drag the victims – prisoners usually, including the sixty-odd Spaniards you see, those fellows mourning up there – to the top of their pyramids, stick a few feathers on their heads, make them dance around – they liked their entertainment, did the Aztecs – then they'd tear out the hearts with stone daggers –'

'Stop!'

'Hang on. I'm just getting to the good bit. They'd rip out the hearts, and while they were spurting blood all over the place, the priests would stick their straws into the aorta and have a good drink. Then –'

'I think I'm going to be sick.'

'You did ask,' said the Gastronome matter-of-factly.

The waiter returned with two skull-shaped bowls brimming with a deep red unidentifiable liquid. And two straws.

It tasted sickly. Like pork fillet liquidized with tomato ketchup. My straw kept getting blocked with meaty fibre, making disgusting slurping noises which the hush of the restaurant seemed to amplify. There was something almost comforting in this. It was as if, during a particularly fraught scene in a Shakespearean tragedy, someone in the audience had loudly broken wind.

Encouraged, I ventured an observation which, before, I had been too nervous to raise.

'That picture,' I said, staring at the Aztec cannibal scene, 'I never mentioned it in my review.'

The Gastronome glowered at me. 'Nor, as I recall, did you remark upon these straws. Nor the fact that I am wearing a purple bow-tie. Nor that we were searched at the entrance and blindfolded before being led to our tables . . .'

'Well, now you mention it . . .'

'Nor that we came to dine here at a quarter past eight on a balmy Monday evening? Nor that our waiter's eyes were coloured hazel? Nor –'

'Point taken,' I said.

'Is it, though?' hissed the Gastronome, his eyes narrowing. 'Until you learn to accept responsibility for your own actions, I fear there is nothing I can do to help you. Do you understand that?'

I nodded.

'That is why I brought you here,' he said. 'Because I knew that unless you were presented with the strongest proof of your powers, you would spend the rest of your life trying to deny them. Just as I did after those terrible events on the slopes of Jebel Mara.'

The Gastronome gulped down his red wine, surveying me over the rim of the glass. Apparently satisfied with my submissive air, he continued more gently.

'Then, perhaps you are ready to hear what really happened on that dreadful day in 1964. You will recall how I had just been initiated into the circle of the Red Men, those select members of the Gonda tribe who possessed – so it seemed – the ability to conjure up whatever they wished by the simple act of drawing the objects of their desire on slabs of stone.'

He continued with his story in a low, hypnotic voice. Soon, I had all but forgotten the discomfort of our surroundings and the bowl of sanguineous slop in front of me.

'And so it was that on the first dawn after my initiation, I eagerly accompanied the Red Men into their stone circle, and imitated them as best I could. I squatted down, practised some of the meditation techniques I'd picked up in India and pretty soon I was gone to the world. That was the easy bit. The real problems came with the drawing part. Just you try scratching a recognizable animal shape on a piece of slate one day, and you'll see how difficult it is. Talk about separating the sheep from the goats! You certainly couldn't with mine.

'I was becoming so frustrated I was about to give up altogether. And that was when my chum suggested that, rather than doing it with a sharp stone and a slate, I tried using tools with which I was more familiar. Pen and paper.

'First, I drew a blob with two legs, a long neck and a beak. Then, something with four legs, which could have been anything from a jackal to a horse. Then, I tried sticking a couple of horns on it, which made it look worse. And so it went on. Useless, I was. Absolutely useless.'

'So what were you trying to draw?'

'Beef. Poultry. Shellfish. Anything to get away from that infernal goat and mutton they'd been serving up all week. But my drawings were so damned awful I knew it wasn't going to work. Or if it did, I was going to end up with something I never wanted like roast jackal. Ever tried roast jackal?'

I shook my head.

'Once tasted, never forgotten. The thought of eating it again was so dire I was all ready to throw in the towel. And, I dare say, I'd have walked out of the circle straight away except that my chum – the fellow who'd organized my initiation – might have thought it a bit off. For his sake I decided to give it one more try. And this time, I wasn't going to muck around with any more silly drawings. I was going to do things *my* way.'

The Gastronome was interrupted by the waiter who, with a raised eyebrow, was inquiring whether we had finished with our starters. My uncle indicated that this was the case.

'Now,' he continued, 'perhaps I should explain at this point that I'd suddenly had a couple of pretty useful ideas. The first was this. These Gonda fellas were, to all intents and purposes, illiterate. No written language, you understand. Just pictures. So I thinks to myself, I thinks, what if, instead of trying to draw the blessed things I want, I just jotted them down instead?'

'In ordinary handwriting?'

'Just so. Or at least the handwriting itself was pretty ordinary. But the subject matter most definitely wasn't.'

The Gastronome gazed at me intently.

'You see, my boy, that was the other idea that had struck me. I remembered that I'd damned near lost sight of my original quest. What in blue blazes was I doing, I asked myself, trying to conjure up beef, chicken and what have you when I'd just travelled thousands of miles, at great personal risk, to try the ultimate dish?' He tutted, irked at the memory of his stupidity. 'So, I sits there for a while, in that stone circle, wondering if there is an ultimate dish and what it might be.'

The waiter returned with our main courses. The Gastronome absent-mindedly dug his fork beneath the pie crust and retrieved a meaty morsel. He popped it in his mouth.

'Mm,' he enthused. 'Quite, quite delicious . . . And, you know, it didn't take me long to decide exactly what I was after. Dare say, I'd known it all along. So I began writing it down' – he looked at me slyly – 'And this time it felt different. Perhaps it was the effect of sitting out in the sun so long. Or maybe it was just that I was feeling so bloody desperate for some decent food. But the longer I sat there, scrawling away, the more vivid it seemed to become. I could almost see it. Smell it. Taste it. By the time I'd finished, I was salivating like a rabid hound. And the instant the ceremony was over, I leapt from the stone circle, fully convinced that in a few moments I would be supping on the dish I had just described. So I ran to my hut, as fast as my legs could carry me, burst through the entrance and . . .'

He teased out the moment by taking another forkful of pie and rolling it thoughtfully round his mouth.

'And all I found,' he said, spraying me with flecks of half-chewed meat, 'was Ibrahim, taking his midday nap.'

He washed his food down with a draught of wine.

'Giles,' he said, 'there are no words to describe my desolation. Though, I dare say, you'll have experienced something similar before your case of wine arrived. Am I right?'

'Well . . . er . . .'

'Course I am. I can just imagine you. Pacing round your kitchen, telling yourself what a blithering idiot you've been for thinking, even for a moment, that it was ever going to turn up on your doorstep. Well, that's exactly what I went through over the next day or so. Perhaps all that jiggery pokery really did work for the natives, I thought. But it certainly wasn't going to work for me.

'A couple of days later, I'd made up my mind to cut my losses and run. So, after the inevitable farewell feast and the dishing out of gifts – one of which was that cloak you spotted in the Pitt-Rivers – Ibrahim and I set off. We made good headway. By early afternoon, we had passed over the crater rim. Shortly before nightfall, we had slipped down the scree, with enough light left to find a good campsite. And that evening, we quaffed a gourd full of arak which the tribesmen had given us and laughed long into the night at their mysterious ways. Young Ibrahim could hardly wait to tell his friends how he had survived an encounter with the dreaded Gonda.

'I am glad the night passed so gaily, for it was the last we spent together. The next day, you see, it happened. Suppose the arak was partly to blame because, somewhere down the line, we'd taken a wrong turning. We were hopelessly lost.

'And it was while we were trying to pick up the trail again that we came unstuck. We were passing through a narrow cleft in the rocks. Ibrahim was leading, casting anxious glances over his shoulder to see that I was all right. By the time we heard the rumbling it was too late. There's precious little you can do when you're caught directly beneath an avalanche.

'It only lasted a few seconds. The air was filled with choking dust. Couldn't see anything at all, but all around, you could hear these bloody great rocks crashing down. Bump. Bump. Bump.

'All you could do was pray none of the buggers would hit you. Never was much of a church-goer. Which is probably why God saw fit to let me cop one in the leg. It didn't really hurt. It just suddenly went all numb and useless, buckled under me and left me sprawling on the ground.

'Well, I prayed extra hard then. Another number like that on my bonce and I'd be finished. I'd just reached "Hallowed be thy name", when it ended. As quickly as it had begun.

'It took a while for the dust to settle. And when I looked up, the path was unrecognizable. Piled high with rocks – some as big as houses. Heaven only knows how I'd survived. But I thought to myself, if Him Upstairs has let me off the hook, he's bound to have spared little Ibrahim too.

'Any minute now, I thought, he'll come scampering up to me – a cheeky grin on his face – and, I don't know, lug my fat old body all the way down the mountain. Of course, he never did. I called his name a few times. And when there was no answer, I dragged myself from underneath my rock and crawled to where I'd last seen him.'

The Gastronome trembled, unable to continue.

'You found him?' I prompted.

'I found him,' croaked the Gastronome.

'Dead?' I said.

The Gastronome shook his head slowly.

'Would that it had been so,' he whispered, adding hastily, nervously, 'But no . . . no! He did not have much longer to live. I'm sure of it. Sure of it! There was . . . blood trickling from his head and from the side of his mouth. And both his legs were completely crushed and . . . and . . . when I reached him, I saw it in his eyes . . . the fear, the pain . . .'

He drained two more glasses of wine.

'The sun had risen to its full height. We had strayed far off the paths used by the Gonda raiding parties. And all our provisions had been lost in the avalanche. All, that is, save the contents of my rucksack. The Primus stove and the small sachets of condiments I carried for emergencies. A flask of arak. And another of water. But a fat lot of use any of those were going to be. At most, I estimated, we had enough to keep us going for two days. And so, sheltering Ibrahim as best I could from the heat of the sun, I lay down next to him, cradling his head in my arms, and prepared to die.

'For hour upon burning hour, the sun blazed down upon us. And all the while, I gazed into Ibrahim's eyes, whispering to him that it was all going to be fine, while hoping inwardly that the poor boy would hurry up and die. If you had witnessed his agonies, you would have wished the same.

'But it was not to be. By nightfall, there was still the faintest pulse in his frail wrist. And when I moved to pick up the water flask and force a few precious drops between his blue lips, his eyes followed me. He could not speak. But had he been able to, I am sure to this day that he would have given voice to the thought that was preying on my mind – that I should put him out of his misery.

'That I did not, I can only put down to cowardice. I suppose I imagined that the chill of the night would do the job for me. It did not. He was a brave, loyal servant, was Ibrahim. And, d'you know, it's only a suspicion, mind you, but what I reckon is that he wasn't going to pop his clogs until his beloved master had given him permission. Certainly, when dawn broke, poor Ibo was still alive. And suffering greatly as a result. And perhaps he'd go on suffering, unless I did something about it.

'It was that realization which finally gave me the courage to do what I should have done much, much earlier. I kissed him softly on the lips. And then, having laid a handkerchief over his baleful eyes, I picked up the biggest rock I could find and brought it down as hard as I could on his head. Just one crack. That was all it took. Ibrahim was gone. And I had every intention of going with him. So before I could change my mind, I raised the bloodied rock one more time and brought it down . . . bang!' – he slapped the table with his fist – 'against the side of my head.

'Many's the time since when I've wished that I could have struck that second blow just a little harder. As it was, I awoke, God knows how long later, with a blinding headache, a raging thirst and – you may find this a mite tasteless but I'm only telling you the way it was – a terrible rumbling in my stomach.

'And, of course, the first thing that I see when I wake up is the body of little Ibrahim. Stiff; turning blue by now; but, forgive me, ever so slightly appetizing. Naturally, I put the thought out of my head at once.

'Problem is, Giles, I'd given myself a fair old wallop on the bonce. My mind, I realize now, was starting to go. It must have been because I was starting to hallucinate. One minute I would see a liveried waiter coming to take my order. The next it would be Ibrahim, prancing about, right as rain, repeating the same thing to me over and over again.

'And do you know what he was saying? "Eat me!" he was saying. "Eat me. Eat me. Eat me." Quite off putting, I can tell you.

'It wasn't always like that, though. For the most part I remained lucid enough to appreciate that Ibrahim really was dead. Even so, I couldn't help wondering whether he was somehow trying to communicate with me from beyond the grave. He loved me, after all.

'By the time the moon had risen, I had grown delirious. I started to rave. "Bugger the day I was born an Englishman," I cried. I had a point too. Your Frog, your Hun, your Dago or your Chinaman wouldn't have thought twice about gobbling up little Ibrahim.

'And that was when it struck me. Had I really eaten my way through the umpteen-course dinner that we know as life only to call it quits at the pudding stage? Denying myself, as it were, the House Speciality?'

He gazed unfocusingly into his wine glass, as if wondering whether he should bring his story to its inevitable conclusion. Then he shook his head. Took a long swig, and studied me curiously.

'Giles,' he continued, 'they found me. The next morning. A party of twelve, all heavily armed, led by the district commissioner. Told me they'd long given up hope of finding me alive. And I could see by their expressions that they rather wished they'd been proved right.

'No one mentioned it. They put my leg in a splint and carried me on a stretcher down the mountain and back to El Fasher. Some of them congratulated me on having stayed the course. But I knew they didn't mean it. I had done something that no Englishman should ever have done. The evidence had been all too clear.'

He swallowed. But it was evident, by now, that he had overcome most of his squeamishness, because he pressed on quickly.

'I had succumbed. I can't pretend it was easy, doing what I did with only a pocket knife. The meat – I had to treat it just as meat –

required savage hacking before it came off the bone. Rigor mortis, I suppose.

'It was a messy, drawn-out business. My hands were numb, my blade was blunt. Still, one thing I didn't lack that night was time. A lesser man might have tucked in there and then. But not me. I wanted to prepare my last meal properly.

'I chopped up the muscle into bite-sized morsels and trimmed the sinew. Wasn't any fat, unfortunately. Skinny lad, was Ibrahim. So I couldn't fry the meat or even seal it first. Nor could I roast it because there was no wood around. I'd have to make do with stew.

'Seasoned it with a bit of rock salt I always carried with me. Bunged it in the jerry can. Flamed it with a good dash of arak. Added a drop of water and then left it to simmer for as long as the gas in my stove lasted.

'Three hours, I waited. Three hours of the most dire temptation – and the stiffest self-control. Lord knows how many times I was about to scoop a mouthful out of that bubbling pot only to check myself at the last second. I was ravenous. The aroma was unbearably appetizing. But I knew that the longer I waited, the better.

'At the very instant the flame flickered out, I dug my spoon into the pot, not caring whether or not I burned myself. I popped the biggest chunk into my mouth and just let it rest there for a few scorching seconds, allowing the juices to trickle slowly round my tongue.

'Now you'll no doubt tell me I was in no fit state to appreciate what I was eating. You might say that in my desperation, anything that passed my lips that moment would have seemed appetizing. Even, who knows, a salad.

'But I swear to you that nothing I have eaten before or since that day has ever tasted so good as those little morsels of arak-flamed Arab boy, stewed to tender perfection, 10,000 feet above sea level in a rocky cleft beneath a volcanic peak in the mountainous region of Sudan known as Jebel Mara.'

He paused and grinned wickedly. Then he looked into his empty bowl and said, 'At least not until today.'

CHAPTER TWENTY

'Fuck!' said Rodney gleefully. 'You're a cannibal!'

'Don't be ridiculous.'

'Of course you are. You ate the soup, didn't you?'

'Yes –'

'It's all right. Your secret's safe with me.'

'Rodney! I am *not* a cannibal.'

'You can deny it all you like, but the facts speak for themselves. That soup was made with human flesh.'

'No, it wasn't.'

'Your uncle said it was. And he should know.'

'He was joking,' I said.

'Give me a break, will you?'

'He was!' I said. 'He told me when I'd come back from the loo. He said the fact I'd been sick proved I believed his story.'

'Oh, right. Your uncle was *lying* to make you *believe* him.'

'Yes!'

Rodney shook his head and thought about this for a while.

'I suppose there's always the Trades Description Act,' he suggested.

'Sorry?'

'If we can't do the bastards for serving up dead bodies, at least we can get them for misleading their customers.'

I looked at him blankly.

Rodney tutted. 'They've got to you, haven't they? After your uncle told you that stupid story they threatened you or . . . or bribed you to keep quiet?'

'No,' I said. 'We just sat talking for another hour or so. Had the pudding. And some coffee. And then the Gastronome dropped me back here.'

'Brilliant!' said Rodney. 'They don't suspect anything.'

'Rodders,' I said, 'there is no conspiracy.'

He gave me a look which implied that, this time, I really had lost my marbles.

'You're not seriously telling me you were taken in by all that rot about weirdo African tribes and cannibalism and . . . ?'

'Why not?'

'Because . . . because . . . there are hundreds of reasons why not. The wine, the receipts . . .'

Rodney chuntered on, unintelligibly. There were no words strong enough, it seemed, to articulate the depths of my stupidity.

'Suppose for a moment,' I said, 'that I did have these powers –'

Rodney huffed.

'Just let me finish, will you? Say I had this ability whereby everything I wrote came true –'

'Which you quite obviously don't –'

'Then it hardly requires a huge logical leap to infer that my ability extends to restaurant receipts.'

'Oh dear,' said Rodney, gesturing that I must have a screw loose.

'So,' I continued, 'even though the notepaper I was sent by Rob Hunter and the receipts I found in my uncle's writing desk were exact copies of the ones I designed in the printer's shop, it doesn't necessarily mean they weren't the genuine article.'

'Did you get all this from your uncle?'

'The gist of it, yes.'

'The same treacherous uncle who tried . . . no . . . *succeeded* in making you believe that your powers worked when he sent you that case of wine?'

'The wine arrived, didn't it? Just like I said it would in my review.'

'Of course, it bloody arrived,' groaned Rodney. 'But your review didn't say it was going to come from one of your relatives.'

'The point is,' I said, 'that someone sent it. I never specified who.'

'I see,' said Rodney, who patently didn't. 'So I suppose you're now going to tell me it's completely irrelevant who's behind all your restaurants, because the only thing that matters is that you wrote about them and they came true.'

'You're catching on.'

'Giles, I wasn't being serious. You can't just wriggle out of it like that. Those restaurants didn't just appear out of thin air!'

'I'm sure they didn't.'

'So tell me, if Talbot and Andy and your uncle weren't responsible, who was?'

'To be perfectly frank, I don't care.'

'YOU DON'T CARE?'

'Not especially, no. It's enough for me to accept that, for whatever reason, life decided to imitate art.'

'Oh, so your reviews are art now?'

'Art. Uncannily prescient predictions. Call them whatever you want.'

'And that's it? That solves everything?'

'Maybe not. But until you can come up with a better explanation –'

'We've already got one! The conspiracy!'

'No, Rodney,' I said. 'I know this is going to be difficult for you to accept. Maybe even harder to swallow than the idea that I really do have these magic powers . . . but I've decided that I had it all wrong about Eric.'

'You're talking about the bastard who's just stolen your girlfriend.'

'Tamsin was never my girlfriend. Anyway, she says they're just good friends.'

'If you believe that, you'll believe anything.'

'I do believe it,' I said softly. 'And if I'm wrong, well, don't you think that's preferable to spending the rest of my life being bitter and resentful?'

'You, my friend, are living in fantasy land.'

I smiled. 'So what's new?'

And there it might have ended: Rodney exasperated by my self-deluding cowardice; me content to let him simmer. But at the back of my mind there still lingered a vague unease about the way my conversation with the Gastronome had ended. I repeated the gist of it to Rodney.

'D'you know,' said my uncle, picking at his mincemeat tart, 'when I think about what we've both gone through, I can't help calling to mind that adage about there being no such thing as a free lunch.'

I asked him what he meant.

'So obvious, it's scarcely worth explaining, really,' he mused. 'It's just that . . . when I was up there on that mountain, tucking into little Ibo, it did occur to me what a lucky fellow I was. Terrible thing to say, I know. But can you imagine how many chaps like me there've been over the years, itching to get a crack at The Dish That Dare Not Speak Its Name. And how many of 'em succeeded, do you reckon?'

'Not many.'

'Brillat-Savarin, say? Or Curnonsky? Babinski? Or dear old Harry Luke? Great men, all. But did they once get to taste the forbidden fruit?' He shook his head. 'Everything but, I should say. Everything but. So where does that put me in the Gastronomic Hall of Fame?'

'I wouldn't like to say.'

'Hmm. And neither would I. But what I do know is this: I wish I'd never been in a position where I could ask myself such a question. Expect you feel the same way, what?'

'Well, since I've never tried' – I looked down at my untouched tart – 'you know what . . . or, at least, I hope I haven't.'

'I'm not on about the blessed Dish That Dare Not Speak Its Name, you fool. I mean your restaurants.'

'What about them?'

'It's what you always wanted, wasn't it? I got my dish. You got your restaurants.'

'Er . . .'

'Never mind the specifics. It's the principle of the thing. In your own way, you got to be the greatest restaurateur this country's ever known.'

'I did?'

'YES!' barked the Gastronome, in a voice that brooked no opposition. 'And where did it lead you? Up the same bally creek as me, that's where.'

I nodded.

'And that,' said the Gastronome, 'is what I meant when I said there's no such thing as a free lunch. We both of us got exactly what we wanted without the slightest bit of effort. But did it bring us any satisfaction? Of course it didn't. And do you know why? Because these things were never meant to be.'

The Gastronome beckoned the waiter and asked him to fetch us our coffee.

'I sometimes wonder whether it wasn't divine providence that saw to the end of the Gonda. Perhaps it was their punishment for disclosing a secret which should never have been revealed. Just think what the consequences might have been had other outsiders inherited powers like ours.'

'Well, you never know,' I said. 'They might have had better luck than we did.'

'You still believe that?' said the Gastronome gruffly. 'Have you still not understood that these powers, divorced from the simple, unambitious race for whom they were intended, can only lead to disaster?'

'Well –'

'Trust me, boy. Happiness can never come from instant gratification. I discovered that at Jebel Mara. And you, I hope, have learned the same lesson.'

He looked at me so severely that I dared not do anything but nod sagely.

'And if ever again you are tempted to dabble with your powers, just remember this,' he said. 'Nothing worth having was ever achieved except through hard work. So Brillat-Savarin knew when he toiled over *La Physiologie du goût*. And so I was to learn when I wrote *The Gastronomy of France*. Twenty-eight years, it took me to finish that book. Twenty-eight years! But I'll tell you something, Giles. The work I put into it gave me more satisfaction than ever I'd have had if, PAF!' – the Gastronome clicked his fingers – 'I'd just gone and magicked the bugger up in a day.'

I knew which option I would have preferred. But I kept my thoughts to myself.

'Forget your powers,' said the Gastronome finally. 'We are normal human beings, you and I. Ordinary, flawed, mortal human beings. Accept that and you will begin to learn where true happiness lies.'

As I repeated the Gastronome's concluding words, Rodney made a nauseated gurgling noise.

'He actually said that?' Rodney asked.

'And what of it?' I said.

'Well, it all sounds so disgustingly sincere and worthy that . . . maybe he was telling the truth all along.'

'Generous of you,' I said.

'Not at all,' said Rodney. He drank the remains of his coffee. 'No,' he mused. 'The more I think about it, the more I'm in agreement with him. You've always had a pretty inflated idea of your own importance. But now it's official. You're as ordinary as the rest of us poor mortals.'

'I don't think that was quite what he was saying,' I said.

'No?' said Rodney. 'Well, I'm buggered if I'm going to waste any more drinking time arguing the toss. What say we two flawed, mortal humans got something inside us stronger than this bloody coffee?'

It was just gone 2 p.m. It felt quite odd to think that, until I could find another job, this was how I was destined to spend my week. Rising as late as possible. Killing off yesterday's hangover with a stiff dose of caffeine. Then off down the pub to cultivate another. Had I really fallen to Rodney's level?

'Well, I can't offer you anything here,' I said, 'for obvious reasons.'

'You sure they cleaned you out completely?'

'Positive,' I said.

With unwonted vigour, Rodney sprang from his chair and made for the kitchen.

'I tried everywhere,' I shouted.

Rodney answered with a series of banging noises as he opened and shut every cupboard. Then, ignoring my suggestion that we make straight for the off-licence, he continued his search in the bathroom, the storage space under the stairs and my bedroom.

He returned, dusty but triumphant, his arms clasped behind his back.

'Ta-da!' he announced, whipping the bottle from behind his back and thrusting it within a few inches of my face.

'Do you think this is the right occasion?'

'Oh, for goodness' sake.'

I took the Sacred Bottle from his grasp – gently so as not to agitate the sediment – and brushed away the dust. Strange that the grandest of all Burgundian wines should have chosen for itself such a modest label. It had neither a flashy coat of arms nor a seal, nor a picture of the estate. Its name was printed on a plain white background in equally plain capital letters – all written in black, save for the discreet green legend *Appellation Romanée-Conti Contrôlée*. In the bottom left-hand corner was the year: '*Année 1978*' – one of the best, according to all the guides.

Each time I'd examined it before, I'd wondered under what circumstances I might get round to drinking it. My wedding to Tamsin maybe? Our first child? New Year's Eve 1999? Whatever the occasion, it would have to be truly momentous.

'If you're still worried about opening it . . .' said Rodney.

'Worried?' I said. 'Not at all.' I reached for the corkscrew. It could have been any old plonk for all I cared.

'Only, I was going to say,' said Rodney, 'that if you *were* worrying, you needn't . . . Do you realize what day it is?'

'Tuesday,' I said.

'The date, I meant.'

'September the fif . . . Good Lord!'

Today was the anniversary of Fish Show.

I sliced quickly beneath the rim of the bottle and pulled off the soft metal disc. The cork was encrusted with green mould which I wiped off with a tea-towel. I dug the tip of the corkscrew with nerveless precision into the middle of the cork and twisted. I pulled calmly. There was a soft pop. The bottle was open.

I half-filled our two glasses (no time to waste with decanting). Rodney grabbed his immediately.

'Jesus!' he said, sniffing the bouquet. 'This is absolutely in*credible*!'

I smelt the aroma too. And what I smelt bore little resemblance to the awestruck adjectives pouring from Rodney's lips.

'Spices, old leather, cinnamon . . .'

'Rodney –'

'. . . blackberry, clove, toast, smoked meat. . .'

'Rodney. I think it may be –'

'I can't wait any more,' said Rodney, taking a good slurp.

'In fact,' I said, after a cautious sip, 'it's definitely . . .'

'A revelation! I'm getting a lot of black fruit here. Bags and bags of black fruit and minerals and spices and –'

'. . . corked.'

Rodney gave me the sort of look a small child might give his parent, just after being told that Santa Claus does not exist.

'You're not used to this sort of sophistication, that's all,' he said. 'It's . . . It's . . .'

But my second sip served only to reinforce my initial impression.

'I'm sorry, Rodders,' I said. 'These things happen.'

He tasted it again, his face a mask of desperate concentration. He looked up, scowling. 'You've gone and ruined it for me now. You've put ideas into my head.'

'It's not me,' I said. 'It's the wine. It tastes corked because it *is* corked.'

Rodney put down his glass and swore.

'You know what this means,' he said, after an interval. 'We're going to have to get down to that offie right now. Buy as much booze as we can carry. And get so wrecked that –'

'You can if you want,' I said. 'But count me out.'

'Giles, we've just suffered the greatest disaster of our lives since Fish Show! We need help! Badly.'

'No, Rodney,' I murmured. 'There's something I've got to do.'

'There's plenty of time for that. Loads and loads of time. You're unemployed, for God's sake!'

'Not quite,' I said. 'I've one more piece to write.'

'Yes, but you don't have to do it now.'

'I think I do,' I said. 'While it's still fresh in my mind.'

'While what's still fresh in your mind?'

'What it is that I really want.'

'Giles,' said Rodney, fast losing patience, 'you've got what you wanted. Like your uncle said. You –'

'The Gastronome was wrong,' I said.

'This is your last chance, Giles,' said Rodney.

'I know.'

Fish Show

Having learned in this column of Britain's rudest, most dangerous, decadent, reactionary and tasteless restaurants, regular readers may have wondered whether I could ever find anywhere quite so bizarre again. I am happy to report that I have found such a place. Less so, to tell you that this is the last review I shall be writing for this magazine.

This month's recommendation is based on such an extraordinary concept that some of you, I fear, will scarcely credit its existence: the restaurant which attracts its custom not through tawdry gimmicks, preposterous decor or unusual cuisine, but through the highly controversial methods of friendly service, a welcoming ambience and imaginative, well-prepared cooking.

In a bold departure from current trends, the restaurant has been designed so as to afford diners the greatest possible comfort. The decor, in blues and golds, with soft, woollen carpets, fine seascapes and gilt mirrors, is opulent but not intimidatingly grand. The linen-draped oak tables – large enough to accommodate the generous silver, crystal and fine china *mise-en-place* – are spaced far enough apart for customers to converse without being overheard by their neighbours. The chairs are solid but well-padded. And the dining area, while imbued with a deceptive air of spaciousness, is small enough to retain the intimacy of a private dinner among friends.

This warmth is reflected in the members of staff. These are not mere waiters who will attend your needs. They are fashion models, actors, ballet dancers, jesters, professors of body language, of philosophy, of oenology, of gastronomy — all rolled into one. For them, waiting is not a tiresome way of scraping together a few pennies before moving on to something better. It is a career. An art. The most noble profession known to man.

And it shows. The complexities of the menu are explained in a way contrived to prevent you from feeling ignorant. The various dishes are expounded with enthusiasm and wit. Never will you hear the words 'It's all good, otherwise we wouldn't be serving it.' These waiters can digress for ever on the origins of each dish, the precise way in which it has been prepared and tell you which one is on particularly fine form. They will have watched the supplies come in. They will know whether that morning's cut of bluefin looks more succulent than the amberjack, or whether it would be wiser to opt for the tuna. And in the end, they will present you with a choice: should you plump for the best or the best?

You will have gathered by now that the restaurant I have in mind specializes in seafood. Yet this is no dreary ghetto, churning out endless stolid servings of sole meunière, lobster thermidor and scallops mornay. Yes, you will certainly be free to order such traditional items, faithfully and unfussily prepared, from the ever-changing menu. But there will never be a lack of dishes designed to titillate the palate of the more adventurous diner.

Perhaps you will be tempted by that rich speciality of Spain's Costa Dorada, the inky seafood paella swollen with fleshy white chunks of squid and gambas; or a platter of spicy, rust-red Cajun shrimps; or a silver-brown bowl of Indonesian gado-gado; or fresh grilled sardines such as you might find in Portugal; or pale pink Swedish gravadlax; or Japanese abalone sushi.

Alternatively, you will always be able to rely on a solid

core of French provincial dishes: succulent swimming crabs, shipped in daily from the Normandy coast; cuttle-fish pulverized to mouth-melting tenderness, served with a rouille as intensely flavoured as ever you could hope to encounter in a Sétois bistro; likewise the bouillabaisse, so authentic that it would put to shame those cheap parodies foisted on tourists by Marseillais charlatans.

You could visit this restaurant a hundred times and never experience the same dish twice. Partly, it is because the chef de cuisine believes that variety and experimentation are the key to operating a happy, enthusiastic kitchen. Partly, because the menu is always governed by the available ingredients. Be it *Halibut Hippo-glossus*, landed off Aberdeen, Grimsby haddock, Newlyn grey mullet or Bourgeois and Parrot fish flown in direct from the Indian Ocean, nothing is served unless it is fresh and in season.

The wine list has been chosen with similar attention to detail. For the traditionalist, there is an extensive selection of sensibly priced white burgundies, Bordeaux and Loires. For the budget-conscious, there are two inexpensive house whites (a buttery Pays d'Oc Chardon-nay and a sprightly English Sauvignon Blanc). And for the New World wine enthusiast, there is everything from Williams-Sellyem's exceedingly rare Allen Vineyard Chardonnay to that symphony of lychees and green fruit, the celebrated Cloudy Bay Sauvignon Blanc.

Whatever you order – even if you are the sort who likes to wash down his grilled trout with a Pinot Noir, or her turbot with a Californian Zinfandel – you need not be afraid of incurring the sommelier's wrath. He is there to advise, charm and inspire but never to condemn.

By the time you reach the pudding course – perhaps an unimaginably light feuilleté pastry steeped in chocolate sauce, an ambrosial crème brûlée, or a tangy mango sorbet – you may well find yourself blinking in disbelief. After the cheeses – melting camembert, pungent roquefort and runny goat's cheese which explodes on the tongue – you will be pinching yourself to see whether it is not a dream. And as you sip your coffee, trying in vain to resist the temptation to squeeze down those delectable chocolate morsels which have accompanied it, you will be swearing to yourself that — despite the evidence of your eyes and sated stomach — there could never be a restaurant as wonderful as this.

But of course you'd be wrong. The restaurant's name is Fish Show. Modesty forbids me from naming the proprietor.